Li

His gaze was glittering not with something Carly was afraid to identify because it made her knees weak, and she couldn't breathe from the intensity and pace of her heart pounding in her chest.

He wanted to kiss her.

He didn't *want* to want to kiss her—she could read that in his expression, as well—but she knew he did. And right then? Cop or not—mistake that it would be—she wanted him to kiss her, too.

The parking lot was deserted, seductive in its darkness, the shadows enveloping them in a net of safety that protected them from prying eyes.

If he kissed her now, no one would ever know....

Dear Reader,

Thanks for picking up the first book in my North Star, Montana, miniseries. These new stories are set in the same fictional town as my very first release, *Montana Secrets*. Each of my books stands alone; however, if you're interested in reading about some of the people and places mentioned herein, be sure to check out *Montana Secrets* and *Montana Skies* for an earlier peek at how this new series came about.

The first time Carly Taggert appeared in *Montana Skies* she was an awkward teenager trying to figure out boys, backstabbing friends and ways to be popular. She was also trying to come to terms with the fact her mother had simply walked out and abandoned her and her sheriff father. Fast forward nearly fifteen years, and Carly has a new goal—to figure out if she has what it takes to be a mother herself. How do you know if you're mother material? How do you know when you're ready?

I hope you enjoy Carly and Liam's story. Look for more North Star, Montana, stories in October and November, as well as in early 2012. Also, I love to chat with my readers, so if you're interested in more information about me or my books, you can find me online at www.kaystockham.com, as well as on Facebook and Twitter.

God bless,

Kay Stockham

The Sheriff's Daughter

Kay Stockham

TORONTO NEW YORK LONDON
AMSTERDAM PARIS SYDNEY HAMBURG
STOCKHOLM ATHENS TOKYO MILAN MADRID
PRAGUE WARSAW BUDAPEST AUCKLAND

Recycling programs
for this product may
not exist in your area.

ISBN-13: 978-0-373-71728-6

THE SHERIFF'S DAUGHTER

Copyright © 2011 by Dorma Kay Stockham

For questions and comments about the quality of this book please contact us at Customer_eCare@Harlequin.ca.

® and TM are trademarks of the publisher. Trademarks indicated with ® are registered in the United States Patent and Trademark Office, the Canadian Trade Marks Office and in other countries.

www.Harlequin.com

Printed in U.S.A.

ABOUT THE AUTHOR

Kay Stockham has always wanted to be a writer, ever since she copied the pictures out of a Charlie Brown book and rewrote the story because she didn't like the plot. Formerly a secretary/office manager for a large commercial real estate development company, she's now a full-time writer and stay-at-home mom who firmly believes being a mom/wife/homemaker is the hardest job of all. Happily married for more than fifteen years and the somewhat frazzled mother of two, she has sold ten books to Harlequin Superromance. Her first release, *Montana Secrets*, hit the Waldenbooks bestseller list and was chosen as a Holt Medallion finalist for Best First Book. Kay has garnered praise from reviewers for her emotional, heart-wrenching stories and looks forward to a long career writing a genre she loves.

Books by Kay Stockham

HARLEQUIN SUPERROMANCE

*The Tulanes of Tennessee

This book is dedicated to:

Tonya Kappes for answering so many questions about the inner workings of Children's Services. Any mistake is entirely my own.

To editor Johanna Raisanen for telling me she hoped Carly and Skylar would one day have their own stories, and to senior editor Wanda Ottewell for helping me bring their stories to life.

And, as always, to my family and readers.

Much love and thanks to you all.

CHAPTER ONE

DEPUTY LIAM MCKENNA hit the flashing lights the moment he saw the woman limping down the dark Montana road. It was just past midnight on Friday night, and although the small town of North Star, Montana, was fairly peaceful, he'd arrested more than a few adventurous prostitutes who saw fit to travel from Helena on the warm summer weekends to be closer to the ranch hands looking for company. Not to mention stumbling upon a few druggies and drunks over the years, as well. Question was—which one was she?

The woman turned at the blink of red and blue, automatically lifting her hand to shield her eyes from the bright beams of his headlights. In an instant, he took in snug jeans and a shiny black halter top, wild red hair that had fallen out of its neat twist.

"Ah, crap." He'd know that hair anywhere. And he could only imagine what Sheriff Taggert would say when he heard about this.

What was the sheriff's daughter doing way out here at this time of night?

The fact that Caroline "Carly" Taggert wasn't hysterical or bleeding helped calm the kick of adrenaline surging through him. But it did nothing to quell the mix of fear and anger that put thoughts in his head he didn't want to consider.

She was alone, walking, with no car in sight. And since he knew for a fact her shiny, red Rav 4 was parked in the driveway outside her house because he'd noted it as he'd driven by twenty minutes earlier, that meant someone had left her out here.

Liam stopped the cruiser and got out. "Carly?"

She winced as though hoping she wouldn't be recognized, her full lips pulling away from her teeth in a telling grimace before she managed a weak smile. "Yeah, hi. Pretty night, isn't it?" She turned her face away from the lights and made a show of looking up at the sky. "I mean, look at those stars."

He didn't take his gaze off her. "Are you all right?"

Liam approached, searching for clues and signs of what had taken place. She smelled like a brewery.

Carly flashed him a look from beneath her lashes, as though he'd asked the stupidest question on the face of the earth. Maybe he had. But *all right* didn't leave a woman abandoned on a dark road or smelling the way she did.

"I'm fine. But I, uh, don't suppose there's any way you won't mention this to my dad?"

Her father had spent a full hour that very morning ordering his men—Liam especially, since Jonas had chosen Liam to head things up while he and Mrs. Taggert were on a cruise—to keep an eye on Carly and make sure she stayed out of trouble. The answer to her question? He wasn't sure yet. "What happened? Why are you out here by yourself?" When she didn't immediately respond, he followed those questions with, "Why are you limping?"

She shifted her weight and shrugged. "You'd be limping, too, if you were wearing four-inch heels."

Her toes peeked out of the front of her bright red shoes and Liam noted how her jeans didn't quite cover the spike in back. Sexy or not, he'd never understand why women did that to themselves. God knew she didn't need the height. At least five-seven in her stockinged feet, Carly met him at eye level in those stilts. "Those aren't exactly walking shoes."

She didn't seem drunk, even if she had obviously gone out for a date—or a party—and something had gone wrong.

Liam angled himself in front of her since she refused to face him completely and that's when he noticed her halter top was misshapen, as if it had been yanked and stretched on one side. So much so the material gaped instead of lying flat against her skin where it roped around her neck and tied.

"Stop that right now, Deputy. I can see what you're thinking but you're wrong. I'm *fine*."

But she wasn't. What did she expect him to do? Take her home and not say a word? For the next two weeks, her safety was his number-one priority. "Have you been drinking?"

"No." She rolled her eyes. "My date was, though, and after he dumped half a bottle on me, I left. Want me to take a Breathalyzer test?"

Up close and able to see into her eyes, he knew it wasn't necessary. Her gray eyes were clear and heated with aggravation, her cheeks hot with embarrassment. "No. Let's go."

She looked as though she wanted to argue but the pain of her footwear spared him the hassle. Liam reached out and grasped her elbow in a gentle grip, her freckled arm cool beneath his hand. "Do you need a doctor?"

"No, I twisted my ankle a little ways back, but once I get off my feet it'll be fine. And you can stop staring at me like that. Nothing happened and there is absolutely no reason to tell my father. It's not like I'm sixteen or something. Blisters and a sprained ankle do not warrant a report to the sheriff."

"You're sure that's it?" He glanced at her blouse and hated himself, because the sight of her cleavage was an instant turn-on.

He'd always had a soft spot for Caroline, first because she'd been nice to him from the day he'd met her in high school, then because she was so gullible and he couldn't help but watch out for her. He'd also always known she was out of his league. She'd grown up the town sweetheart, while he was the badass kid from the wrong side of the fence.

But for the past year, whenever Carly had stepped foot inside the station he'd noticed her more and more. For some reason he found himself staring at her mass of curly hair, smiling whenever she smiled. And the way she crinkled her nose?

Man, he had it bad—not that he could or would do anything about it. Even he knew not to mess with his boss's daughter. The fact the sheriff carried a gun for a living merely hammered home the stupidity of his thoughts.

But whoever had messed with her tonight…the guy would answer to him. The sheriff could wait his turn. "You're sure?"

She paused again, her gaze smoky and sensual-looking, accented by her makeup and the full moon.

"Positive." She tilted her head to one side and sized him up. "Wait a minute... Did Dad give you orders pertaining to me?"

Liam saw the spark in her eyes. Not a good sign. "Your father left a lot of instructions before he left."

"Oh, no. No, you know *exactly* what I mean. Did he tell you to *babysit* me?"

She didn't give him time to respond.

"Oh, for the love of— Are you *serious?* He didn't trust that I could handle myself for two *weeks?*"

It wasn't only the sheriff.

Liam chose not to mention the betting taking place at the station. The firehouse. Even the diner.

Carly was as smart and intelligent as anyone could be but her big heart overcame her common sense more often than not and she had a propensity for getting herself into scrapes. Just look where she stood. "Let's get you home."

"I have no doubt Dad ordered you all to call him if I break a nail, but don't you dare. It took Rissa *years* to talk Dad into taking this cruise. You wouldn't really ruin their vacation because I sprained my ankle?"

Liam opened the passenger door of the police cruiser and held her arm while she dropped into the seat. He saw her wince as she lifted her injured ankle inside.

Swearing softly, he checked their surroundings for any sign of whoever had left her there before he turned on the brighter work lights inside the car and squatted, his back against the open door for support. "Let me see."

Not giving her a choice, he gripped her calf and gently removed the ridiculous shoe, surveying the damage.

"Definitely swollen." He ran his thumb over the bone and pressed gently. "That hurt?"

"Just a little. It'll be okay."

She leaned toward him and the position left him with a prime view down her top. Despite the shadows cast by the lights, he saw black lace and seductive cleavage, more than she'd had in high school. He'd looked then, too, fool that he was.

Focusing on something guaranteed to get his mind off her as a woman and on the present. He fastened his gaze on the stain he could now see mucking up the front of her blouse. The stain…and the ripped seams. "What happened to your shirt?" When her lips formed a thin, firm line, he added, "You either tell me, or you tell the sheriff when I call the ship."

The other thing he'd learned about Carly after sharing science labs and classes with her in high school was that she had a tendency to be a regular chatterbox when she was nervous—or on the hot seat. He'd been more interested in getting by and getting out, whereas Carly had been all about her grades. On test days, she'd driven him insane with all her fretting. And the one time she'd wound up sitting beside him in the principal's office?

He smiled at the memory. Taking the blame for her screwup in setting the classroom on fire had made sense. It wasn't as though he hadn't done other things like it and not been caught.

Carly leaned back in the seat and clutched the shoe he'd handed her. She'd painted her nails some dark, mysterious color that had a gleam of purple, and out of nowhere came the mental image of her stroking her nails down *him*.

Swearing silently at his lack of control, Liam shoved

the temptation away. "Well? What's it going to be, Caroline?"

"I had a date."

As if he hadn't already figured that out? Liam narrowed his gaze. He wanted a name. Details. So he could take the guy down for ripping her shirt and leaving her here this way.

What if he hadn't been the one to find her? What if some pervert had come along and snatched her? It happened. On a long stretch of road like this one, anything could have happened and the thought made his hands shake like a boy's.

"It went badly. He spilled his beer on me. I left. End of story."

"Why do you date losers?"

"Ever hear the saying about kissing a few frogs? You can't tell who's who just by looking at them."

He didn't want to think about what she'd done with the guys she'd dated. "All I'm saying is that there are nice guys in this town. Why don't you ever pick one of them?"

"What do you think I'm trying to do? People roll their eyes if you say your biological clock is ticking, but you know what? *Tick-tock*," she stated, her temper getting the best of her. She slammed her head against the padded seat. "Dating sucks."

"Only because you're picking the wrong guys," he repeated.

"So who should I pick? A deputy? One of the firefighters? Are those the guys you mean?"

He thought of her with one of the men he had to work with and see every day on the job and shook his head. Bad idea.

"No way," she continued, closing her eyes. "I lived with a cop for over twenty years. No way would I give myself a life sentence, always wondering if he will come home at the end of the day."

Couldn't get much clearer than that. Not that he was thinking of himself. "Who was the guy who left you here?"

Time to get back to the problem at hand.

"Ooh, nice try, but I'm not about to share that information."

She crossed her arms over her chest, the move emphasizing the cleavage he was trying so hard to not see. "Caroline, who was it?"

She rolled her eyes. "It's Carly, remember?"

He ignored the reminder that she preferred the name she and her stepsister had cooked up in an effort to change what Caroline considered her "boring" image. Any more exciting and he'd not make it through the next fourteen days.

"Can we just *go?*"

"Not until you tell me who left you out here."

A rough huff left her chest. "Then I guess we'll be here all night."

He couldn't allow himself to consider the possibility and waited patiently, barely breathing, because with every inhalation he got a combination of her perfume—and the guy's beer.

"I won't tell you," she insisted, beginning to fidget and squirm. "I mean, *why* would I tell you? Do you *know* how hard it is for me to date in this town with everyone watching my every move? All my life I've been the sheriff's daughter. I've had to deal with guys who are afraid of ticking off my dad, or else *wanting* to. Dad might have said for you to watch out for me, but I refuse to tell you, when I know you'll go after the guy like some Old-West posse."

He didn't acknowledge the statement, unwilling to lie and say it wouldn't happen, when they both knew it would.

"Look, I took care of the problem myself. He isn't out drinking and driving, so all you have to do is drive me home, okay?"

No, it wasn't okay. His brain cycled through what she'd said a second time, focusing on the hint of quiet satisfaction that shadowed the disgust in her tone. "How did you take care of it?"

She hugged her arms around her front and squeezed. And damned if he didn't notice. Again.

Liam rubbed a hand over his mouth. Pavlov's dog had better manners.

Carly groaned. "You are *impossible*. What is it with cops? You all have alpha complexes that are borderline cavemanish. I don't know how Rissa puts up with my dad sometimes."

He wasn't about to be outmaneuvered. "How did you take care of it? Am I going to find a body somewhere?"

She glared at him before she blinked twice and gripped her shoe tighter, as though she wanted to conk him over the head with it. "I wasn't allowed to date until Dad taught us self-defense. He insisted Skylar and I be able to protect ourselves. Knowing that, how do you *think* I took care of things? If I had to guess, I'd say right now the guy is using his cooler of ice on his crotch."

CHAPTER TWO

CARLY WAS AWARE of Liam's look of surprise. Not that she cared. Like her father, Liam McKenna had a tendency to take life a little too seriously and wore a perpetual scowl. The guy needed to smile a little.

This was so embarrassing. Of all the people to find her like this, of all her father's men, why did it have to be Liam? The other men...she could have fooled them into thinking she'd broken down or something. But not Liam. He was always watching her. Not in a creepy way but always...there.

"I see."

I see? "If you laugh at me, so help me—"

"I'm not laughing. The self-defense thing isn't public knowledge?"

Beneath the interior lights, Liam's chocolate-brown gaze pierced her with an intensity she couldn't look away from, the bronze flecks in his eyes more of a golden-topaz and freakishly intense, like a hawk waiting to strike—or a cop waiting for the right time to make his move. She'd learned to be leery because every cop she knew seemed to have some sixth sense about deception. "Skylar and I didn't want the news broadcasted so we swore Dad to secrecy in exchange for agreeing to learn. I mean, how would you feel knowing I can take you on?"

Liam froze for a split second, his gaze shifting down as though he checked out her boobs. But that had to be a mistake, right? Because the one *good* thing about Liam was that he never looked at her that way. They were the casual sort of friends.

Liam wasn't her type. Handsome or not, he held too many of the same cop qualities as her dad and that wasn't her idea of a good time or date material. She'd meant what she said. She was looking to settle down with the right man, not one so ready to sacrifice himself at the first sign of trouble.

Liam shoved himself upright. "Let's get you home."

Just like that Liam shut the cruiser's passenger door and Carly sighed, relieved he'd dropped the matter of her date's identity for now. Getting Liam off that pursuit entirely wouldn't be easy, but no way was it worth ruining her father and Rissa's cruise to Alaska—or her two weeks of total freedom out from beneath her father's dictates. Her father hadn't had a decent vacation in years, and talking him into the trip was no easy feat. It had taken Rissa and Carly months to convince him.

And now that he was... She was twenty-seven years old, for pity's sake. She did not need Liam acting as her keeper.

The object of her thoughts climbed inside the cruiser and settled beside her. The breeze carried Liam's cologne across the expanse.

Frowning, she watched as Liam hit the switch and the lights began to dim.

"I can take you back to get your jacket from the guy."

The sudden suggestion made her smirk. "Nice try, but I didn't wear one." She should have, considering her sleeveless top, but she'd planned on being dropped off at her door, not forced to walk home.

Liam shook his head, visibly disgruntled that his attempt to identify her date had been shot down. He went about turning off the flashing lights, securing his seat belt and putting the car into motion.

Carly stared discreetly, focusing on the bridge of Liam's nose. Her father's nose had a lump, too, courtesy of a drunken brawl he'd tried to break up.

Her father called it his rookie mistake, having quickly learned to let the brawlers duke it out and run out of steam before stepping in.

North Star wasn't the hub of crime but she wondered where Liam's lump had come from. She knew better than to ask, though, since Liam would likely require her to answer his question to get a response.

Carly tugged at the material encircling her neck and frowned when she felt the sagging, broken stitches. She'd paid thirty-five dollars for this top, plus shipping. And if Liam or her father found out Roger Billings was responsible for the shredded stitches, she'd never hear the end of it.

Biting back a growl of upset and anger with herself for accepting the date in the first place, she stared out the window at the moonlit fields beyond the road.

She'd felt sorry for Roger, that's why she'd said yes. Newly divorced and missing his kids since they'd moved to Kentucky, Roger had seemed down and lonely, and she knew that feeling. Back to the frog thing again. What could she say? She identified.

But once Roger had stopped the car and turned into an octopus, her pity had gone out the window along with one of Roger's hair plugs.

"Carl Butcher."

Liam's voice broke the silence and she shook her head to rid herself of her morbid thoughts. Everyone made mistakes, including her, and finding Mr. Right in a town the size of North Star wasn't easy. "Pardon?"

Liam spared her a searching glance, his expression as tight as his hands on the steering wheel.

"Your date. Was it Carl Butcher?"

"No." Carl Butcher was a nice enough guy, but she'd never been able to stand the way he sucked spit through his teeth to clean them. Gross much?

"Guy Richards?"

"*No.* Stop asking."

"I will when you tell me. Darren Collins."

She turned toward her window and didn't bother responding. She wasn't going to play Twenty Questions. Liam could name every guy in town if he wanted to. Luckily her house was but a few miles away. Had she worn sneakers, she could have made better progress and eluded Liam entirely.

She made a mental note to carry a bigger purse next time, and a pair of socks. Maybe a can of mace, too. "So, how are your brothers? Zane? I saw him in town the other day at the feed store."

"They're fine." Liam all but growled the words.

He'd never been that patient. In high school she used to babble about nothing, just to get his focus on her rather than the way the other kids treated him. Not once had Liam caught on to what she was doing. Guys like him liked being needed, she thought, unable to quell the small smirk that pulled at her lips.

"Mac Nelson?"

Considering Liam was a man of few words, tossing out all those names had to be using up his quota of words for the week, maybe the whole month. "Mac's getting married tomorrow to Sara George."

And she was invited to the wedding. The fact that she had gone *out* with Mac a time or two depressed her. Mac was actually one of the nice guys in town and one who possessed all her required qualities in a man, but one—*spark*. Him tying the knot was disheartening. If she and Mac had sparked as anything but friends, maybe it would have been the two of them meeting at the altar with her wearing the white dress.

Liam continued to offer names as he thought of them. She ignored him and stared at the shadows of the passing scenery. Finally they arrived at her house, but when she grabbed her purse and shoe in one hand and the door handle in the other, he got out, as well. "What are you doing?"

"Walking you to the door and making sure the guy didn't cart his ice pack here to wait for you."

Oh. She hadn't thought of that. Surely she wouldn't be seeing Roger again anytime soon. Did he really want another hair plug removed the hard way?

Carly glanced around at her quiet neighborhood, scouring the bushes and yards for Roger's bulky form.

You sure know how to pick 'em, don't you? Did you really think Roger *could be Mr. Right?*

Sometimes she let desperation get the better of her, she'd admit. Roger was definitely a frog—one of the warty, toady ones. She'd known Roger *wasn't* Mr. Right but a girl could only sit around and wait so long. She had dreams she wanted to fulfill, a life she wanted to lead. Going on one date with Roger was her way of pretending she was getting closer to her goal. "No signs of him. Thanks for the ride home," she said with a gentle slam of the cruiser's door.

Head down, she made a one-shoe-on-one-off dash to the porch and prayed for a clean escape.

Liam caught up with her on the steps.

"I'll help you."

She didn't bother arguing anymore, willing to do almost anything to call it a night and pull the covers over her head so she didn't have bags under her eyes when she was forced to hug Mac and his happily glowing bride tomorrow.

She entered her small house but blocked the door when Liam tried to step through. Enough already. This ship had sunk before leaving port.

"I'm going to find out who left you out there."

The smirk was back but this time she didn't bother trying to hide it. "I'm sure you will."

But it would take Liam until morning, if not longer, and maybe by then his temper would have cooled and he'd see no harm was done—except to Roger.

She removed her remaining shoe, welcoming the cool floor against her aching feet even as she noticed how Liam's broad shoulders filled the frame. It really was too bad he was a cop. She'd liked him much better in high school when he'd been a rebel without a cause.

That thought prompted others. Such as why the big change? How did one go from being a punk to a deputy? *Why?*

"You'd make things a lot easier by telling me."

"Yeah, but where's the fun in that?" she asked as she began to swing the door closed. "Good night, Liam. Oh, and don't have the boys circling the block all night. You'll freak out my neighbors."

CHAPTER THREE

THE NEXT EVENING, Liam watched Carly from the shadows of the theater. An unexpected twist in an afternoon arrest had left him swearing a blue streak—and eyeing Carly in a totally new light.

Could twice in twenty-four hours really be a coincidence? Was the good-girl routine all a sham? God knows it wouldn't be the first time he'd caught a so-called Daddy's girl taking a trip on the wild side but—*Caroline?*

The movie played on but he was completely uninterested in the latest suspense flick on the big screen and entirely focused on her. What was she doing out on that road last night?

Carly sat alone, but every now and then she glanced around in self-conscious awareness. Yeah, he didn't imagine she came to the movies by herself very often. And to have two dates with two different guys in the same weekend? Who was she seeing tomorrow?

Scowling, he blinked when the screen flashed to a bright summer day. He shifted his gaze to Carly, the light allowing him to see her more clearly. Her lower body was in shadows but she'd dressed in another sleeveless top like the one she'd worn last night. The lack of material drew attention to her toned arms and the delicate curve of her neck.

Carly glanced at her watch for the fiftieth time, then turned and looked toward the entrance at the rear of the cinema. Liam was slumped in his seat but he knew the moment she spotted him. She stiffened and no doubt turned as red as the burgundy carpet beneath their feet before she whipped forward to face the screen like a kid caught cheating on a test.

So, who was she? A party girl or innocent?

Liam rose and stepped into the aisle of the newly remodeled theater. The building was a relic of the past, the pet project of a California producer who'd brought his kid to the Second Chance Ranch for vacation and had liked the area so much he'd decided to invest his money in it.

The carpeted floor and too-loud speakers disguised his presence until he plopped into the empty seat beside her. Nothing could hide her groan, however.

"Go *away,* Liam. I'm meeting someone."

"You mean, you *were* meeting someone."

Carly turned to glare at him, her lips shiny and looking way too kissable.

"What did you do?"

Liam didn't think it possible to hiss the word *do* but she'd managed it. He fisted some of his popcorn and tossed it in his mouth. He was not there to contemplate the kissableness of the sheriff's daughter. "I didn't *do* anything. Your date, on the other hand, tried to drive off without paying for his gasoline—or the box of condoms, the cherry freeze and packaged brownies he'd helped himself to at the Pit Stop. Then again," he murmured for her ears only, "he really shouldn't have had a bag of weed in his car, either."

Carly blinked at him in unfeigned, openmouthed horror. "Are you *serious?*"

"Why would I lie?" Her appalled state gave him the answer he needed and he released the breath he wasn't aware he held. "You'll be happy to know you were his one phone call. Must have gone to voice mail, but he isn't visiting his sick mama like he said."

She closed her eyes and slumped in her seat. "But... he's an *accountant.*"

"Yeah, well, apparently he had the munchies." He watched her, waiting, and cursed himself because even though his gut said she was on the up-and-up, he had to be sure. "You two have plans for that weed?"

Carly sat stock-still for a moment, her expression revealing her dawning comprehension and the trouble she could be in if her father found out, before she grabbed her purse and scooted to the edge of her seat. "No, I did *not.* I had no idea he did stuff like that or I wouldn't have agreed to go out with him. I met him this afternoon at the wedding. He's Mac's cousin and one of the groomsmen."

"Yeah, well, now he's trying to make bail."

She got to her feet. "I have to go."

Liam didn't budge. "Why?"

"Down in front!" Someone called from behind them.

Carly immediately sat, but glowered at him. "Move your legs so I can get out."

"Why?" he repeated. "We paid good money for the tickets and it's supposed to have a surprise ending. Might as well stay."

Carly released a put-out huff and settled into her seat. "You accused me of smoking pot. Why would I want to sit through a movie with you?"

"I had to know if you were into that type of thing," he said, careful to keep his voice low. "Exactly like the sheriff would've done."

She said something he couldn't hear and he leaned closer toward her. She smelled like a fresh rain in the mountains, a mixture of wildflowers and earth, and the bittersweet tang of her Coke. "What was that?"

"I said I've never done drugs, thank you. I like my brain cells just fine." Her eyes held his, her lashes so long a shadow fell on her cheek from the lit screen.

Liam waited a few seconds to let her cool down before he offered her his popcorn. "I believe you."

She had her arms crossed over her front, a cute pout on her face. Carly wore her hair mostly pulled back in that messy way women managed to achieve with pieces falling around her shoulders in finger-twitching waves he wanted to touch, just once. Maybe it was the lure of the forbidden but it was all too easy to imagine his hands buried in the length.

Seconds passed and Caroline finally released a deep breath, nudging his arm. "Give me the popcorn. I need to binge."

Liam handed it over without comment.

The movie continued over the next hour and Liam sat there, watching Carly with his peripheral vision. She seemed totally absorbed and unaware of the fact she'd devoured his sad excuse for a dinner. He watched her more than he did the screen, trying hard not to notice the way she licked the salt from her lips or how she dropped one of the kernels and it fell right into the V of her breasts.

It had taken everything in him not to groan when she peeked at him then quickly dipped her fingers into the material to dig it out. He didn't want to think about what her skin would taste like now. Or how much he'd like to find out.

The movie heroine gained his attention when she tossed a vase toward the wall in frustration. She was a forensic scientist working to solve a murder but she'd become a target in the process, the hero the detective trying to save her life.

It was easy to picture Carly in the white smock and heels the character wore. Wearing her glasses instead of her contacts and her hair in a twist, Carly would make the perfect studious professor or science geek, one who'd whip off the coat, toss the glasses aside and turn into a vamp in a matter of seconds like some had in '80s music videos or—man—like the actress in front of them.

His breath froze in his chest as the characters began to rip at each other's clothes and go at it. Moans and heavy breathing filled the air and even though the screen eventually faded to black, a lot of skin was revealed beforehand and Liam could almost guarantee every guy in the darkened theater was finishing the scene in his head.

He certainly was.

The back of his neck felt hot, his lower body made it known once again that he hadn't hooked up with anyone in a while and— Ah, man, why had he imagined Carly wearing that smock?

CARLY BARELY DARED to breathe by the time the lights came on in the theater. For a suspense/action movie, there sure had been a lot of sex. On-the-run-from-the-bad-guy sex. Hiding-out-in-the-motel sex. We-caught-the-killer celebration sex. And all the while Carly sat beside Liam, furious that he'd accused her of smoking pot and strangely, suddenly, more than a little aware of how handsome he really was. Not in a Hollywood-stud kind of way but darker and more…brooding?

You don't like brooding, remember? You like fun, easygoing, responsible types.

She couldn't deny it. The last thing she'd wanted to do was stay and watch the movie with Liam but the time had allowed her to calm down and realize Liam's reaction and questions were perfectly reasonable. She had no right to be too upset.

Her father certainly would have demanded answers had he been the one to arrest her date. And considering she and Liam hadn't exchanged much more than social pleasantries when their paths crossed at the station or around town since high school, how would he know what kind of life she led?

But it was mortifying. And the condoms? Thank goodness Liam hadn't commented on *that*.

"You going to sit there all night?"

The question pulled her from her daze and she realized Liam had not only stood, but also moved into the aisle and thereby cleared her way to the exit.

She grabbed her purse and tried to bolt by him, only to have him fall into step immediately behind her.

"You in a hurry?" she heard Liam ask after she nearly mowed down a little kid holding a box of Twizzlers.

Was he kidding? Of course she was in a hurry. Muttering so only he would hear, she said, "I was stood up because you arrested my date. The only thing I want to do is go home."

Focused as she was on Liam, she bumped into a guy from behind. "Sorry."

Liam took her arm and gently steered her away from the crowd waiting to enter the seating areas for the next show.

Face blazing with heat, she pulled away and realized that she and Liam were attracting attention.

Maybe because you're bouncing around like a pinball machine?

She ducked her head and barged through a crowd of people coming through the door.

Outside, Carly kept going, leaving the front of the theater and hanging a left on the corner, speed walking as though the cops were after her—which he was.

But with every step she took, she was aware of Liam. Once she cleared the mob of mingling people, Liam grasped her elbow in what she considered a cop's tug-'em-along hold and pulled her to a stop.

Carly reluctantly complied, but only because he wasn't letting go. And since he was enough like her father to not give up until he had his say... *"What?"*

Okay, so maybe she could have phrased that a little nicer. But she knew a lecture was coming and she hadn't done anything wrong, so Liam got what he got.

"You hungry? Want a burger or something?"

Whoa. Where had that come from?

Taken aback, she stared at him in surprise. The diner was around the corner and a great place to eat on a Saturday night but it also meant facing a boatload of small-town gossip if they were seen there together after being seen *here* together. Plus, she had the feeling Liam asked because he had an ulterior motive—like keeping track of her. Was she right? "Uh..."

One of his black eyebrows rose. "You have other plans for the night?"

Did a date with her hot tub and a pint of Chunky Monkey count?

Liam was good-looking, some might even think he was hunky—okay, so he *was* hunky—but he was a cop and that's where she drew the line. No exceptions. She couldn't change who her father was or what he did, but by sheer avoidance she could make very sure dating or marrying a cop wasn't in her future. Liam included. Or should she say *especially?*

Jumping the gun, aren't you? He said nothing about a date—or marriage.

Didn't matter, though. If people saw them together, there would be talk. And even though it was only a *burger or something* and Liam asked as a way of interrogating her, she wasn't about to go down that rabbit hole. She'd worn her ruby slippers last night and had the blisters to prove it.

"No, you go ahead. I'm going home. It's been a long day."

Liam's expression hardened, as though he hadn't expected her to say yes but yet he wasn't happy she'd said no. Another thing she didn't need—a conflicted man.

"I'll walk you to your car, then. I have some questions for you about your date tonight."

And there it is. You might not know how to pick a date but you rock when it comes to reading cops.

She could only imagine what questions Liam had left, and if he asked her about the box of condoms she'd die, right there in the parking lot.

Really, who brought a *whole box* on a first date? Scott was an *accountant!*

Yet another example of your lousy dating skills.

Carly put her feet into motion and felt Liam's presence hot on her heels.

"You should always park where others can see you. At least under a light."

"I parked under a light."

"It's blown out."

"I didn't know that when I parked under it." Men. Did they really think women didn't know these things?

"Carly, you know your father asked us to keep an eye on you while he's gone."

Yes, but she'd chosen to ignore her father's comment about siccing his deputies on her. "Yeah, about that. How about you say you did, but you really leave me alone? Liam, I'm a big girl. I don't need babysitters and watchdogs dressed in uniforms."

"I'm not convinced of that. You've had two close calls in two days. How is that possible when you said you couldn't date in this town?"

"I didn't say I couldn't date." And how nice of him to take it that way. "I *said* it was hard to date, given my father's the sheriff. And, technically, the second incident never happened because you arrested Scott before he even got here, and the first I took care of myself. You were simply my ride home. Keep your facts straight, Deputy."

Liam glowered at her and ran a hand over his head. It didn't take a genius to see he was frustrated by her lack of cooperation. Yeah, well, she was, too. Frustrated, that is. Dating was hard enough without throwing a gun and badge into the mix.

First dates sucked, and hers? They sucked more than the norm. Maybe in larger cities women her age weren't considered old, but in small rural towns she was getting up there. She wasn't delusional in thinking her time was running out. Fact was most people her age had paired off in high school or soon after.

What was it about her? Was she too picky? Too vocal? Not pretty enough? All the doubts were enough to drive a woman to OD on chocolate.

She hated going home and having no one to talk to. Hated sleeping alone. Those on-screen love scenes were the best sex she'd had in years—especially since she hadn't *had* sex in years. There had been offers and one near-engagement but when her fiancé mentioned bringing his mother on their honeymoon, Carly had handed back the ring then and there.

She unlocked her car and threw her purse inside before she turned to find Liam not a foot away.

"Carly…"

The breeze blew her hair across her mouth. She used both hands to push it back but what she didn't capture escaped and covered her face again. Before she could take care of it a second time, Liam's hand was there, his fingertips raspy-rough against her temple.

And just like that everything changed, slid away. All the embarrassment from tonight and her life, all the anger. It disappeared in an instant.

Liam was one of her father's men, someone who could very well be the next sheriff of North Star. But even that soul-sucking, run-far-far-away awareness was replaced by the blatant in-her-face knowledge that Liam was a sexy, frisk-me-officer-and-take-it-*real*-slow man down to his bones. And no amount of denial, self-lectures or restraint could change that.

When he should have let go, when he should have

moved away and let her take care of her own flyaway hair, he didn't. Liam stared at her, his gaze glittering hot with something she was afraid to identify because it made her knees weak and she couldn't breathe from the intensity and pace of her heart pounding away in her chest.

He wanted to kiss her.

He didn't *want* to want to kiss her—she could read that in his expression, as well—but she knew he did. And right, then. Cop or not—mistake that it would be— she wanted him to kiss her, too.

The parking lot was deserted, seductive in its darkness, the shadows enveloping them in a net of safety that shielded them from prying eyes. If he kissed her now, no one would ever know….

Carly wet her lips, trying to find clarity and distance because she knew this wasn't what she wanted, knew *he* wasn't what she wanted. But as she opened her mouth to remind them both what a disaster it would be, Liam swore softly and closed the distance between them.

His mouth settled over hers with mind-numbing possession and it was way better than the on-screen kisses she'd envied. Way better than— Wow.

Liam released a husky groan the second his tongue swept into her mouth to touch hers. Fire exploded in her veins, a hot rush of feeling and sensation that obliterated the chiding voice in her head, screaming at her to run.

She felt his fingers slide into her hair and tighten, the palm of his hand against her shoulder and neck, pressing her closer.

She didn't need the encouragement. She went willingly, eager to explore this kiss that shouldn't be happening, drawn into the heat of him, the musky taste of him. The long, hard, OMG *feel* of him.

Tall, dark and he could *kiss*.

But as quickly as it had begun, it was over. Liam released her so fast she wobbled on her rubbery legs and didn't stop until her hips bumped against her car. If not for the vehicle, she probably would have fallen on her butt, and wouldn't that have topped off her night like a cherry on top of runny whipped cream?

What *was* she thinking? What had just happened?

"I'm sorry. That was a mistake. It won't happen again." Liam held his hand up—the one so recently tangled in her hair—as though he made a pledge.

Wide-eyed, she watched him stalk away, his angry strides eating up the distance to his cruiser, which was parked at the curb by the theater.

Talk about a dash of cold water. The silver-and-blue emblem on the side of the car gleamed beneath the streetlights, bringing an instant flash of regret.

Carly poured herself into her car. On autopilot, she locked the doors and fastened her seat belt, gripping the wheel like a life preserver.

Liam had kissed her. Tongue-in-mouth, nipples-hard, make-me-ache kissed her—and he called it a mistake.

Which hurt way more than it should based on the past two days and her past two dates. Yes, it was a mistake because they were friends, but she was well on her way to getting a complex. And when she saw Liam again?

"Oh. Oh, not good. This is going to be *awk-ward*."

Because even now, if she closed her eyes and let herself, she could easily imagine Liam's mouth doing wickedly naughty things friends didn't *do* to each other.

It was a kiss, nothing in the scheme of things these days, but still... It had been a *hot* kiss. An *amazing* kiss.

After all those days in chemistry and biology class when she'd been a hormonal teenage girl and she'd stared at that tiny scar on Liam's upper lip, she finally had the answer to what it would feel like to kiss it— *him*.

Too bad it was ten years too late.

CHAPTER FOUR

L IAM'S HEAD POUNDED as he entered Franks's Grocery in response to a shoplifting call made by one of Delmer's employees.

Sunday mornings were typically slow. The ranch hands and cowpokes tearing it up on Friday and Saturday nights were either sobering up, in jail or sleeping in. Sunday afternoon, they'd come to or be released, pile into their trucks and head to the ranches, which meant Liam and the other deputies were on the lookout for DUIs, speeding and the like.

Knowing the way to the front office, Liam knocked on the door and let himself inside. "Hey, Delmer. I got a call about a shoplifter?"

"Liam." Delmer Frank dipped his head in a nod of acknowledgment. "Didn't know the girls had called it in. Sorry you made the trip but I'm not pressing charges today."

Delmer was dressed in his Sunday church clothes, a lariat around the neck of his crisp white shirt. He sat behind the office desk, a frown of concern marring his typically jovial face. Charlie Mason, an old drifter who'd made North Star his summer hangout, was on the other side.

The old man had become a familiar sight, never causing any trouble to speak of and keeping to himself. Zane had hired Charlie out at the Circle M the past five summers, gave him a bunk and food, enough pay to see Charlie through the winter when he headed south.

But there was always something about Charlie that Liam found unsettling. To discover Charlie a thief didn't really shock Liam, not when there were reasons to be leery of men who never put down roots. Drifters weren't exactly known for their honesty.

Charlie lifted his head, giving Liam a quick, shamefaced glance. Charlie's graying brown hair hung in greasy, unwashed strings along the collar of his coat. The man's face was ringed with deeply creviced wrinkles and sagging skin, a month's worth of whiskers on his cheeks. Dark purple bruises stained both eye sockets and one corner of his mouth, while the deep cut on his cheek looked infected.

Sometime over the winter, the man had hit hard times. He'd aged, lost a considerable amount of weight. Twenty or thirty pounds on a man already lean from the nomadic life he led.

"Who did that to you?" Liam asked.

Charlie had been eating out of a plastic deli container so fast he'd dripped gravy onto his chin and beard. He loosed his fist and dropped the plastic fork, his hand shaking slightly as he picked up his napkin to wipe away the mess. He eyed the food like an animal—or man—starved, which from the looks of things he was.

Desperation, so potent the little hairs on the back of Liam's neck stood on end, reeked from the man.

"Couple punks in New Mexico. They were paintin' one of the boxcars and saw me. Decided to have some fun."

"How long ago was this?"

"'Bout a month."

And he still carried the bruises. Liam could only imagine the beating Charlie had received to still be healing.

"Liam," Delmer said softly, "you're busy. No need to hang around. But since you're here, why don't you go to the deli and pick up the order? I forgot to cancel it this week and it's packaged up. It's on me."

Liam had forgotten about lunch. Sheriff Taggert provided lunch for all the deputies every Sunday afternoon at shift change as a way to keep track of the goings-on around town. The men probably didn't expect Liam to take on the task but he wanted to do his best when it came to filling in for the sheriff.

"You sure about that?" Liam asked, indicating Charlie with a subtle shift of his hand.

"Positive. I already called Zane," Delmer said. "He's sending someone to pick up Charlie and drive him out to the ranch."

Liam frowned at Delmer's statement. Zane would be out of his mind to hire Charlie after this. And given the way Charlie favored one side as though he had some broken ribs to go with the bruises, it was obvious he wasn't fit to work.

Zane could hire plenty of ranch hands who wouldn't steal from him, so why take a chance by hiring a thief?

"Zane knew you'd have your hands full at the station. He said he'd take care of Charlie."

Take care of him how, though? That was the question. Knowing nothing would change Zane's mind at this stage, Liam nodded. He didn't have time to argue with his adoptive father now. Best to wait until he could talk to Zane face-to-face. "Thanks for the offer of lunch but I'll pay for the order. No need for you to pick up the tab."

Liam exchanged a look with Delmer that made it clear he was to call Liam if Charlie caused any more trouble.

Delmer and Charlie were about the same age, so Delmer was probably putting himself in Charlie's hole-ridden shoes. Maybe that was Zane's connection, as well. Maybe he'd agreed to take Charlie on because he felt sorry for the man. God knows Liam and his brothers could attest to Zane having a big heart. But Charlie's actions definitely called for more scrutiny. The Circle M made an effort to hire only quality workers.

Liam let himself out of the office and pulled his cell phone from his pocket. Zane might be willing to overlook the obvious but Liam wanted to alert Brad to the circumstances. His older adopted brother would keep an eye on Charlie and Zane both.

Almost to the deli, Liam didn't see the cart or its driver until he'd stepped in its path.

"Oh, I'm so—" Carly's eyes widened as she recognized him. "Seriously? *Three* days in a row?"

Pain throbbed up his shin from where the cart had hit him. "Assaulting an officer is a serious charge." Dammit, why wasn't Brad picking up? He flipped the cell phone closed with a snap, his head pounding harder. Carly, Zane, Charlie. He didn't need the added complications of his personal life creating more havoc when he was more or less the acting sheriff.

"I didn't hit you on purpose."

The way she said it made it seem otherwise. "Now, why do I doubt that?"

"It's true. If I'd known it was you, I would've hit you

harder," she countered with a lift of her chin. "I specifically asked you to not have the guys circle my block all night."

She'd noticed? He'd stressed the need for discretion. "Bob was doing his job."

"You told him?"

"Didn't have to. Your date told everyone how getting arrested screwed up his plans with you. Bob was concerned about you."

So was he. Not only about her recent behavior and rash of bad dates but— What was she thinking, kissing him back last night? Why had she *let* him kiss her? "What are you doing here so early?"

Carly tucked a tendril of hair behind her ear. "I'm filling in for Dad at the station. You know, lunch. He didn't tell you?"

Settling the Sunday-lunch issue must have been the one thing the sheriff had forgotten to mention, given his long list of pre-vacation must-dos. But first things first.

"Look," Liam said, glancing around to make sure they wouldn't be overheard, "I'd appreciate it if you'd forget all about what I did last night. I'm sorry. Pretend it never happened, okay?"

She looked insulted, angry, more than a little amused and a whole lot ornery. "You mean, you don't want me telling my father your tongue was in my mouth?" she asked with pseudo-innocence.

He should have known she'd make this difficult.

The *last* thing he wanted was for Jonas to find out. Liam liked his job and he didn't want Carly's father thinking he couldn't handle things—even the simple job of babysitting her.

That kiss was a mistake on so many levels he couldn't count them and he'd been kicking his own ass all night for pulling a stunt like that. He didn't know why he'd kissed her. It had seemed like the thing to do at the time, given the pretty night and...the pretty girl.

"Fine. Whatever. Like I would anyway. You know, I should've known you'd take his putting you in charge a little too seriously. You did that in science lab, too. You like playing hero, don't you?"

He wasn't going to go there. And if he hadn't taken charge in science lab, she would have blown herself up more than once. At least the fire she'd caused was an accident. "None of the men want to face your dad if something happens to you, Caroline. That's why we're taking his orders seriously. You've got to admit you've given us reason to think you could use some looking after."

Her jaw dropped before she narrowed her deadly, gun-metal-gray gaze on him. "Does this mean you're dogging every other single woman in town? Driving by her house? Walking her to her car?" Her hands settled on her hips. "Wait a minute, what *are* you doing here? Did you follow me?"

"I was responding to a call." He pretended interest in the produce nearby instead of the snug fit of her tomato-red T-shirt. The material was lightly puckered across her breasts and emphasized her assets.

The sight sent his blood pressure soaring because the material also didn't quite meet the waistband of her pants, which were gathered above her hips with nothing more than a string.

He had a serious problem on his hands. He had to get a handle on his fascination with her, stop viewing

Carly as attractive and see her as nothing more than a citizen, a regular civilian. The *daughter* of a man he respected. If Jonas knew the thoughts running through Liam's head… "You're fixing lunch? But Delmer said—" Liam caught himself in time and shut his mouth. Making lunch meant she could be watched and maybe he could convince one of the older deputies to talk to her about her dates.

"Yeah, Dad insisted. I was trying to decide what to make. Bob likes my barbecue but it's too late to fix it."

"Hungry men will eat whatever's put in front of them." He wanted to smack himself in the head the moment the words registered in his brain. What an idiot.

That was *it*. He was hungry. That was why he was noticing so much about her. It wasn't so much Carly but that he was the perfect example of a hungry man. Obviously he'd been too long without female companionship if he was eyeing Jonas Taggert's little girl as anything but a responsibility.

Kissing her? He hadn't kissed a woman in a couple months at least. He wasn't focusing specifically on Carly, he was simply noticing her as a woman. It made perfect sense.

She had filled out in all the right places and even with the trendy black, no-nonsense glasses on the tip of her nose she turned heads. No wonder he was distracted. But a casual hookup with a pretty woman would take care of his problem and keep his mind *off* the woman in front of him.

A cell phone blared out Fred Flintstone's *Yaba-daba-do!* and, given his line of thinking, Liam welcomed the silly interruption. He shifted his weight to one foot and crossed his arms over his chest to wait her out, his confidence returning now that he had the situation figured out.

But then Carly dug into the pocket of her pants, pulling the waistband lower until Liam spotted the barest hint of lace belonging to very feminine panties.

The sight hit him with the force of his brother Brad's right hook, and Liam wiped a hand over his mouth and tried not to swallow his tongue.

Getting his mind off Carly wasn't going to be easy, especially now that he'd gotten a glimpse of her underwear.

"Oh, my...I—I..."

Mentally lecturing himself on keeping his thoughts and hands to himself, Liam tuned in to Carly's conversation and the fact that whatever was being said on the other end of the line wasn't necessarily good news.

Carly closed her eyes, wrapped her free arm around her stomach and hugged herself, causing his gaze to drop before he caught himself and forced it to her face.

"No. I mean, yes, yes, absolutely. No, really. It's just a surprise, that's all. I'm a little flustered because I'm in the grocery store. Yeah, but it's fine. Yes, I'm sure. I just—I didn't think it would happen so soon." Carly listened for a moment, nodding. "I understand. Better get used to it, huh?" she asked with a soft laugh. "Yes, I'll be there. Most definitely. Thank you for calling. Goodbye."

She pressed a button on her cell to end the call, the huff of air leaving her chest accompanied by glassy-eyed surprise. She blinked at him, then looked away, swallowing, blinking some more, as though she couldn't believe whatever it was.

"What's wrong?" Liam ran his hand down her arm

from shoulder to elbow, and at the touch of her skin he couldn't help himself. He stepped close—close enough to smell her hair. "Sweetheart, what's wrong? Who was that? Did something happen with your parents?"

"What? Oh, no. No, they're fine." She released a strangled laugh. "I'm fine. I'm… Oh, Liam. I'm going to be a *mother*."

The air whooshed from his lungs faster than a cannon blast. A mother?

Images bombarded him. The sight of her limping along the road, how her blouse had obviously been yanked and stretched. The loser he'd arrested last night. Which one was the father?

Another choked laugh emerged from her throat as though she struggled to contain her emotions.

His arms tightened and the world around them slipped away. It wasn't noon yet and thankfully the back of the grocery where the deli was located still lacked the post-church rush, otherwise the rumor that he was feeling her up by the grapefruits would be all over town.

And what about the news of her pregnancy? How would she handle it? How would the sheriff? Did her parents know? "It'll be okay."

Hell if he knew how, though. Jonas would go through the roof.

"I can't believe it. I didn't think it would happen so soon."

So soon? She was *trying* to get pregnant? "You did this deliberately?"

She lifted her head and flashed him a starry smile that cleared the confusion from her face. "Of course! I've always wanted a family."

He tried to wrap his mind around her words. She was

definitely the picket-fence type. Always had been. No doubt she'd dreamed of a home and a couple of kids, a husband who worked nine to five and played some kind of organized sports on the weekends. But she'd never struck Liam as the type to get things out of order and there was no ring on her finger.

"I just can't believe it, you know? I mean, it's so much to take in. There's so much to *do*."

Yeah. He imagined so. "Who's the lucky guy?"

He was careful to keep the anger from his tone, hidden. Because whoever the guy was, Liam would kill him for knocking her up if he had no intention of marrying her.

Maybe Carly had planned to get pregnant but in Liam's mind every man had a responsibility to take care of the possibility of parenthood, regardless of what a woman said. And given her history of losers, it wouldn't surprise him if the father hightailed it out of town at the first mention of the news. What was she thinking?

Her eyes flared wide. "The lucky— You think I'm—" She laughed, the sound more like her normal self. "I'm not pregnant."

Confusion swamped him.

"You thought I was *pregnant?*"

Someone turned the corner and he released her like a hot potato, careful to keep his voice down. "You said you were going to be a mother," he muttered, uncomfortable at the amusement he could see in her eyes. What the hell was going on?

"I am, but not like *that*." The huff of her husky, mocking laughter filled his ears.

He felt like a fool. A confused fool. "I'm glad you think this is amusing. Will your father think it is?"

Her full lips pulled back in a wide grin. "Oh, stop. It's just so funny you'd think that I'm— Well, anyway, that was Children's Services. I've been approved to be a *foster* mother. I'm getting my first child today. Can you believe it?"

Children's Services? He stared into her gray eyes and felt the hot-cool rush of anger. She was going to be a *foster* parent?

"You don't look pleased."

Hell, no, he wasn't pleased. "Does your family know about this?"

The query had her shifting, her prettily painted toes digging into her flip-flops. "No, not exactly. I mean, the background check was done, and Dad wasn't thrilled with me *wanting* to do this and we had words but..." She rolled her eyes and grimaced. "No, he doesn't know I went on with the process. But if you talk to him, you're not going to tell him. You *can't!* Liam, promise me you won't say anything. I'll tell them as soon as they get home from their trip."

And in the meantime? She was going to get a kid *today.* Did she have any clue what she'd gotten herself into?

"Liam?"

No. No way could she know. She didn't have a freaking clue the problems that came with those kids. But he did. He'd been one of them and he could tell her every dirty, low-down trick there was.

"I can tell you don't approve. Dad didn't approve, either." Right in front of him, he saw her guard go up. It hammered home the fact of how very different they really were. He couldn't imagine bringing a child into this world, couldn't imagine raising one—and here Carly was taking in kids that weren't even her own?

"Stop looking at me like that. I make a good living and I can provide for them. I'm of sound mind and body—"

"The mind is debatable."

She inhaled on a gasp and glared at him. "I can provide a caring, loving home. Why shouldn't I be a foster mother?"

"Because you're single, beautiful and have no idea what you've taken on. Call C.S. back and tell them you can't do it. Tell them you've changed your mind."

"But I haven't." Her hands flattened on her slim hips and damn if he didn't get that flash of lacy underwear again. What if her "kid" had a history of sexual misconduct? What if the kid was just male and horny? How would she handle *that*?

"Whatever. Be that way, I don't care. But I'm not going to be able to make lunch this afternoon after all."

"You said you promised your father," he said, needing time to come up with a plan, a way of getting her to rethink her decision. "You promised. Tell C.S. you'll take the next kid." Liam gave himself a mental pat on the back. That request was reasonable, not too dictatorial. Maybe by then her father would be back from his cruise and could handle things, taking the responsibility from Liam.

Instead of meeting him halfway, Carly's chin lifted to a stubborn angle. "I can't cook now. I have to go home and clean, and open the car seat and get it installed and…"

Her words trailed off and he could see Carly making

a mental list. She abandoned her empty cart and took off down the toiletries aisle.

Unable to help himself, Liam followed her—and opened his mouth even though he ordered himself to keep his trap shut. "You won't be able to handle this, Caroline. Those kids— You won't be able to handle them, the realities of their lives. You'll get sucked in."

She paused by the jumbo packs of toilet paper and turned to glare at him. "That's your argument? That I might *care*? Why shouldn't I help a child in need? Give back to my community? You and Dad do it every day you put on that badge. No, you do more because you put your very lives on the line. All I'm doing is—"

"Making a huge mistake. This isn't something to take on lightly."

"Who said I am? Do you think I was approved overnight? I put a lot of thought into this decision, and you know what else? I would've thought, of all people, *you* would understand. Where would *you* be right now if Zane hadn't adopted you and your brothers?"

Probably in prison. God knows that was where he'd been headed behaving the way he had. "Zane was an older man more than capable of handling out-of-control kids by knocking our heads together if needed. And listen to you—you've jumped from getting your first foster kid to *adoption*. You haven't even seen this kid and you're in over your head. Caroline, don't do this. Think about your future." He lowered his voice when an older woman dressed in a flowery pantsuit glanced their way with interest. "You like to date, right? You want a husband? That's the goal, isn't it? You want kids, a house, PTA meetings?"

A second or two passed before she assented with a slight nod.

"How are you going to get that when there are an awful lot of guys who have a problem dating a woman with kids of her own? What are they going to think when you tell them you're taking this on when you don't have to?"

"Do you think because these kids have been removed from their homes, they're less important than biological children? That they've been tainted by their pasts?"

He knew it for a fact. Every kid in the system had a history of some kind, him included.

"Stop making assumptions about *my* life." She closed the distance between them and poked a finger into his chest. "And if the guy can't handle it? Then he isn't the guy for me," she stated confidently. "It's as simple as that, Liam. As to you and your opinion, you're free to have one—even if it's wrong. Just do me a favor and keep it to yourself."

"Your parents aren't going to like this."

He didn't think it possible but she stiffened even more, drawing herself up to her full height. "Leave them out of this. If you call them on their *anniversary cruise* to tell them about this, if you ruin their trip, I'll never forgive you." Her voice lowered. "And I might very well be put in jail for assaulting a police officer—*you*."

Liam glared at her when she whirled and stalked away, wishing he could find the words to change her mind and so angry he could spit nails.

A long string of curses filled his head, followed by an even longer string of memories he'd thought long buried.

CHAPTER FIVE

THAT AFTERNOON, LIAM was out on patrol near the ranch when he decided to talk to Zane and check on Charlie while he was at it.

He pulled up to the house and saw the windows of his old bedroom open, the curtains flapping in the spring breeze. "You've gotta be kidding me."

Inside the house, he found Zane in the kitchen. "You put him in my old room?"

Several of the hands Zane had hired drove in from their homes and families nearby instead of staying on the ranch. The bunkhouse had available beds. Charlie would have been fine in one of them. "Didn't Delmer tell you what Charlie did?"

"I did. And he did," Zane said slowly, answering both questions while pouring himself a cup of coffee. "How'd lunch go?"

Lunch? "You brought a thief into the house and you want to talk about lunch? The whole town's going crazy," Liam muttered to himself. "Lunch was fine. Now can we talk about why I drove out here to check on you?"

Zane raised a thick white eyebrow high. "Boy, the day you have to check on me like some old man is the day I hang up my boots."

"Why did you put him in the house? Delmer didn't

press charges but if he had, Charlie would be sitting in a jail cell right now."

"One mistake doesn't define a man," Zane said, adding cream to his mug. "I've been thinking of hiring an assistant foreman. Brad's got his hands full and could use the help. Figured with Charlie's injuries we could put some of the responsibilities and chores off on him."

It was all Liam could do not to gape. What the hell was going on?

Above his head, he heard the squeak and rattle of the old bathroom door, the sound of water surging through the pipes lining the kitchen wall near where he stood.

"Hope you don't mind but I also gave him some of your old shirts and jeans you left behind. He seemed grateful. You, on the other hand," Zane said, wagging a finger at him, "seem bent all out of sorts."

Liam was. Because since his conversation in the grocery aisle with Carly all he could think about was growing up in the boys' home and foster care, being put in the system and bounced around from the time he was five years old. What behavior he hadn't learned from his abusive mother, he'd learned at the hands of other boys.

"Charlie was hungry, Liam. The kind of hungry that makes a person do things they wouldn't otherwise consider doing. You ever been that hungry?"

Liam swore and shoved a chair closer to the table with the toe of his shoe. He'd been that hungry more than once.

Growing up the son of a single mother who liked to party more than she liked to spend her money on things like food or heat or clothing, he'd hated who he was. Where he'd come from. Another mouth born out of wedlock. A reminder of the past his mother tried so hard to forget.

Yeah, he knew hunger. He remembered choking down cereal so stale and old he'd closed his eyes so he couldn't see if there was anything else in it. He remembered wearing clothes that smelled so bad no one would sit with him on the bus to school. And whenever it seemed as though things were taking a turn for the better, something bad would always happen.

"Liam, his gear's gone. He only has the bag of toiletries Delmer gave him. Whoever those punks were, they robbed Charlie of everything but the clothes on his back. You gonna deny him a decent place to sleep on top of all he's been through?"

Zane shook his snow-white head in disapproval. Only fifty-six, Zane's blond hair had started turning white a few years ago. From the time Liam had known him, Zane kept his hair buzzed military short, his equally white mustache thick and drooping down nearly to his chin. Zane cut the very image of an old cowboy with his calloused hands and barrel chest, his pale blue eyes lined with wrinkles from all the years of squinting beneath the rim of his hat.

"Leave Charlie to me, son. I'll take it from here. You go on to work and focus on being sheriff while the sheriff's gone."

Zane seemed awfully eager to be rid of him. "Something happening I should know about?"

A wry smile pulled one side of Zane's mustache out of alignment, making him look as though he had an albino fishing worm squirming on his upper lip.

"You were born to be a cop, you know that? No, nothing's happening, just two old fools and their pride. Charlie didn't *want* to take your room, Liam. I had a hard time getting him to agree and I don't want him coming down here and seeing your shorts in a knot about it because he'll take his sorry butt out to the bunkhouse."

"And that would be a bad thing why?"

Zane slurped his coffee. "Because I'd bet my championship buckle he's got a half-dozen broken ribs. Might be spring but the nights are cold yet. You want him out in that? It's a wonder he doesn't have pneumonia now. Son... Charlie wants to think he's still a young buck able to go and do as he pleases but I think his regrets in life have finally hit home. Sometimes it's hard for a man to admit he's getting old and made mistakes. And having a young'un like you coming to *check on us* bent out of shape over some of Delmer's produce and me giving Charlie a room makes it worse."

"What about that assistant-foreman bit? How's Brad going to feel about that?"

If Liam was a born cop, his older brother was a born rancher, content to spend his days on a horse or a four-wheeler riding fence, checking on livestock and running the ranch like the multimillion-dollar business they'd all built it up to be.

"He'll be fine. There's plenty of work to go around." Zane's gaze narrowed on Liam. "What's up your craw today? Something going on in town with your new assignment?"

The question reminded Liam of Carly and her announcement of being a foster mother. Had the kid arrived yet? Or had she wised up and told C.S. that she'd changed her mind?

He shoved his hat on his head, knowing the odds of that happening, given her mood. He wanted to ask

Zane how often he'd regretted adopting him, Brad and Chance but he was too leery of the answer. Zane might not own up to regretting adopting him, but Liam regretted hurting Zane the way he had. "Nothing I can't handle. But it would make it a lot easier on me if I didn't have to worry about Charlie robbing you blind."

"I don't look at Charlie and see a thief, son."

Liam shook his head in frustration and headed out the door. Zane had always been an easy mark. Gullible, accepting, easily deceived.

But Liam couldn't say that to Zane, not without revealing *how* he knew it to be true.

CARLY WIPED HER sweaty palms on her jeans and opened the door, smiling nervously at the older black woman on the other side. "Hello, again."

She held the door wide so Abigail Jones could step through. With her salt-and-pepper hair and wide smile, one immediately got the impression of a loving grandmother, which Abigail was.

What Carly knew casual observers didn't see was the passionate caseworker on call round the clock to help children who couldn't help themselves. "Here, let me get that," Carly said, taking the plastic bag from Abigail's hand.

"Thanks. So, are you ready to meet this little chick? Her name is Sierra Tripp, and she's eight months old."

The baby was strapped into a car seat, the kind with a handle, which was presently looped over Abigail's arm. The baby wore only a diaper and what used to be a white Onesies, now filthy and stained. Her limbs were dirty, as well, her hair stuck together in nasty clumps.

Carly felt her lungs seize, the smell and sight of the baby one she wouldn't forget for a long time.

"Eight months?"

Abigail nodded. "She's on the tiny side. A lack of food can do that to a child. This is her first time in the system." Abigail set her purse on the table by the door. "Let's hope it's the last."

Big blue eyes stared at Carly, eyes that were wide and scared and heartbreakingly fragile. Sierra's little bow of a mouth quivered and puckered up.

Abigail made shushing sounds as she set the car seat on the floor, then dug around in the plastic bag. "I brought a couple bottles, a can of formula—you'll need to get more tomorrow—and two jars of baby food."

If she had been smart, she would have picked some up this morning in the grocery instead of abandoning her cart and leaving Liam behind. "I will tomorrow."

Tomorrow. Work. She'd have to take off work, not an easy thing to do when you were the sole administrative assistant to eight single-person offices.

She'd planned on hiring someone part-time to fill in when she finally received her approval, but she hadn't planned on getting approved and her first child in the same minute.

"Good. Now, you've got enough food to get you through the night and tomorrow morning. Mix it in with mashed green beans or whatever you have on hand to get by. You purchased a car seat?"

"Yes. It's in my car, ready to go."

"Perfect. Don't forget to pick up diapers while you're out. She's a tiny thing so I'd say a size two would work. Now, let's see… Your check is in the envelope and should cover the most immediate needs. Her medical-

card information is listed there along with the number
for the doctor to call when you take her in. You've got
my numbers if there's an emergency, the hotline number if you change your mind—"

"I won't."

"Or," Abigail continued, "if you get sick or something comes up and you simply can't care for her. Someone will immediately come to get her. I'll be in contact
to check on you, since I know she's your first. We're
trying to track down her daddy. We hope he'll take cus-
tody as soon as possible."

Sierra began to cry in earnest and Abigail raised both
eyebrows as though urging Carly to do something about
it.

Carly squatted and pressed the buttons to release
the handle. She unbuckled the baby and got her out,
then immediately fell into the bounce-swing-rock move
she'd learned working summers at the Second Chance
as one of their child-care employees. "We'll be fine,"
she said. If only she felt as confident as she sounded—
or didn't have Liam's expression and comments flitter-
ing through her head, taunting her.

She could do this. She'd worked at the Second
Chance every summer from the time she was fourteen
until she'd graduated college, some winters, too.

But not 24/7. And not by herself.

She's a baby. You can do this.

"I know you will." Abigail checked her watch. "I
seriously doubt Sierra's on any kind of a schedule, but
the child has to be hungry and sleepy. And she needs a
bath."

A bath. She was a total stranger to Sierra and yet

she was supposed to strip the baby down, shove her in water and bathe her?

Did you think they bathed themselves?

Abigail shot Carly a tired look. "The family's case-worker said nothing was clean and the roaches were so bad you couldn't take a step without killing a baker's dozen. Check her closely when you wash her, just in case."

Her arms tightened protectively around the little girl. In her training class, she'd heard stories of children with insects in their ears. She didn't want to think about that but knew she had to be thorough and note anything she saw for Sierra's doctor's appointment.

Poor thing. Sierra *smelled.* And not even in a normal milk-soiled baby way, but in a mold and rotten food and urine and dirt way.

"Your mentor will call tomorrow, but the number is on the sheet if you need her before then. And, Carly, remember—they're all difficult at first. It's not you, it's where they've come from. Even bad parents are missed when they're the only thing the kids have known. It takes time to adjust."

Carly nodded, bracing herself for what was to come when Abigail walked out the door and Carly was offi-cially on her own with Sierra. "I understand."

Abigail patted Carly's arm, then ran her palm gently over Sierra's little back. "Good. My advice? Give her a bath and let her play in the water and the bubbles for a little bit before you feed her. Between the two, she'll relax and be sleepy."

"Okay. That sounds like a plan."

Abigail smiled, her head tilted to one side. "You'll do fine. Carly, I have no worries about you. All new foster moms are nervous at first." She grabbed the car seat and headed toward the door. "I'll be in touch."

Carly shut the heavy door behind the caseworker, bouncing and cooing and trying to calm the fussy baby.

What must it be like to be Sierra? So tiny and small and scared. Taken from her mother by one caseworker, handed over to Abigail, now given to Carly, all in the space of hours. All strangers. "Shh, it's okay. We're going to be okay. Come on, sweetie, don't cry. No, don't cry, it's okay. You wanna take a bath? Play? Yeah, we'll do that. We'll take a nice bath."

Sierra blinked at Carly from beneath her long eyelashes—then she took a breath and *screamed*.

CHAPTER SIX

LIAM MADE IT until eight-thirty that night before he gave in to the compulsion to check on Carly with the excuse that he'd not only tracked down her Friday-night date but also the news that, after a one-on-one chat, Roger Billings wouldn't be bothering her again.

Finding out it was Roger hadn't been all that difficult, merely time consuming. In the end, it had taken a two-hour stop at the diner for coffee and a slice of Porter's apple pie to hear all the local gossip—including how Roger had been in the diner Friday afternoon, bragging about his upcoming date with the sheriff's daughter.

Once that bit of news had been voiced, Porter, the owner, had made his concern about Roger's reputation known and mentioned as much to Liam. Seeing as how Porter knew the sheriff was out of town, the older man figured the boys at the station would be keeping an eye on Carly and felt it best to fill Liam in.

In instances such as this, Liam appreciated small-town life where coffee and pie equated a wealth of information. Like so many of the townspeople who had watched Carly grow up during the sheriff's long-standing career, Porter had a special fondness for her. Which is why Liam had readily promised he'd look into the matter.

Which he had.

On the drive to town from the Circle M, Liam had stopped by Roger Billings's place and had taken pleasure in seeing Roger turn pale as a ghost when he opened his door to find Liam on the other side, cruiser parked in the driveway behind him, lights on.

That was the thing about bullies. They were all mouth until someone called them on it. Then they practically wet themselves trying to come up with alibis and excuses.

Ever since Roger's divorce, the man partied harder than a frat boy, desperate to prove he wasn't the boring old fart his very young and now very *ex*-wife said he was.

But the question remained—why had Carly agreed to go on a date with him in the first place? She was a smart woman. Beautiful. Why date a loser like Roger?

He might be a loser, but she's never given you a second glance.

Nearly growling, Liam thought of her comment about dating a deputy or firefighter—someone who put his life at risk whenever he put on the uniform. That thought led to others, brought memories of their kiss outside the Sooner Theater, and Liam's hands tightened on the steering wheel, his mood as dark as the thundercloud overhead when he pulled into Carly's driveway.

He got out of the cruiser, his anger spiking even more when he noted he could see into Carly's house. He knew she owned curtains. She needed to use them so anyone wandering by couldn't see in and know she was alone—at least as alone as she could be bouncing a baby in her arms.

Carly was on the other side of the picture window.

She walked back and forth, swinging the baby gently. But no matter what Carly did he could hear the baby's screaming cries, and even from a distance he could see the tension and fatigue and worry on Carly's face.

He knocked twice, watched as she faced the window and realized he could see her every move. Her shoulders slumped, then squared, and she wouldn't make eye contact before moving out of sight. Finally the door opened.

She fixed a fake smile to her full lips, but failed to hide her frazzled state. The kid had a good set of lungs and Carly's face revealed the stress she felt over the drama.

"Is there a problem, Deputy?"

The shrill, angry cries coming from the squirming baby never wavered and the baby reared back, slamming its head against Carly's sternum and drawing a wince.

"Are you all right?"

Carly glanced out the door to the houses behind him. "Fine. Did someone call you because of the noise?"

"No."

She looked relieved. "What are you doing here?"

Liam studied the baby's tear-and-snot-covered face. "I was wondering if you'd changed your mind."

Carly began bouncing the baby again like a human gymboree. "Goodbye, Liam. As you can see, I'm a little busy. *Too* busy for one of your lectures, which sound frighteningly familiar to my father's."

She stepped back to shut the door but he put out a hand to prevent it. "Is there someone you can call for help?"

"Yes."

"And?"

Carly simply stared at him. "And what? You expect me to call?"

"Yes." Why did she act hurt by the suggestion?

"No," she stated firmly. "I'm *not* going to call. She's scared, she's in a strange place, she just has to get used to me."

Damn, he didn't like stubborn women, and the one across from him was the ultimate. Why couldn't she see that she was in over her head?

"I know what you're thinking."

He removed his hat long enough to run his fingers through his hair, then replaced it. "No, trust me, you don't." She didn't have a friggin' clue. His orders were to keep her out of trouble and she presently bounced it in her arms. "How long is it staying?"

"*She*—and I don't know. The caseworker will call me when or if other arrangements are made. But don't worry about it," she said, her tone holding a definite edge. "According to you, if I have Sierra with me, I won't be dating, and that means you and the boys won't have to circle my block every hour."

Liam struggled for patience, for the words to make her understand that he wasn't trying to be an ass toward the kid or what she was doing, because he understood the importance and need for foster parents, but Carly... "Your father isn't going to like this." He held the door when she tried to shut it again. "It's been what? Eight hours since she got here? Six? Have you eaten? Sat down?"

"It doesn't matter. She's *scared*, Liam. Wouldn't you be scared?"

An image flashed through his head, the look on his

mother's face the first time C.S. took him and his half brother away, the sick way he'd felt when the caseworker dragged him to the car and locked him inside while the police drove his mother to jail. "Carly, these kids… You're trying to do a good thing."

Her gaze turned suspicious. "But?"

He searched for the right words. "You're too soft-hearted for this."

"Why do you say that?"

"You cried when we had to dissect the baby pig."

"I'd just watched *Babe*," she said defensively. "Liam, what am I supposed to do? Not help because they have bad lives and I might actually have to deal with a taste of it? What kind of person does that make me if that's all it takes for me to bury my head in the sand?"

Liam looked into the kid's eyes and swore silently. He knew exactly what Carly was saying. But how fair was it to pull a kid out of hell, give him a taste of heaven, then send him back to hell again? He'd seen both sides, lived it.

He didn't want to sound like a bully. He didn't want to belittle Carly's skills and abilities or put her down, because she was one of the smartest, kindest, savviest women he'd ever met. But those qualities were her biggest downfall, too.

He'd watched her over the years since high school. She might not have said more than a few words to him but he'd listened to Jonas talk about her, the things she did and said.

Those qualities wouldn't help her here but they'd definitely hurt her in the end when she found herself attached to the kid. And what about the kid?

When he thought of how long it had taken him to

learn not to count on anything out of his control...
When he'd learned the foster parents he had one day
might not be the ones he had the next, that some were
kind and some weren't... What lessons would this kid
learn at a too-early age?

He didn't want to know.

Carly lifted her chin, her hair a mussed, wild mass
around her shoulders, her shirt covered in stains, and
looked at him as though she could see all the way to
that place inside him he never let anyone see.

Liam shifted, breaking eye contact and stepping
away from the doorway. He hadn't agreed to this.
Watching over Caroline didn't include this. He could
send Bob over to check on her, and increase the patrols
around her house. He didn't have to be *in* it.

"Look, maybe Sierra will go back to her mother one
day. But while she's here with me, she'll know she was
safe. She'll know that *somebody* cared enough to take
her in, feed her, play with her, *hold* her when she cries,
and that not all homes are bad or scary. That's a good
thing, Liam."

It was a great thing. What every kid deserved. Carly
had a point and it was admirable. It was heroic and
sweet. But what about when one of those kids turned
on her? What about when they stole from her, fought
her attempts at discipline with brute force because that's
all they knew? When they made her the victim? They
wouldn't all be helpless babies.

Carly hefted the girl higher in her arms. "Right now,
Sierra has nowhere to go and no one to care for her
but me." The false smile she'd greeted him with transformed to one of determination, her eyes gray steel.
"I know what I can do to help her," she said. "What I

don't know is why you're taking this so personally. Is it really because you're afraid my father will be upset you didn't stop me or is it because of something else?"

He couldn't answer the question, because he refused to delve deeper into his past or the reason he'd been available for Zane to adopt. She wanted to do this? Fine. He was washing his hands of it.

Liam repositioned the hat on his head yet again and moved to the steps. "It's your decision. I'm simply doing my best to follow your father's orders to keep you safe."

"I'll be fine."

He paused on the third step, remembering the other thing he'd come to her house to tell her. "Roger Billings has been warned to stay the hell away from you. If you so much as see the back of his bald head as he runs away from you, I want to know about it."

Rolling her eyes, Carly retreated over the threshold, holding his gaze as she slammed the door.

CHAPTER SEVEN

ON MONDAY MORNING after she'd called her clients and let them know an emergency had come up and she wouldn't be in the office, Carly yawned as she pushed Sierra, safely fastened in a cart, through the entrance of the store.

She hurried past the throng of older men gathered on benches with their coffee cups in their hands, and headed to the rear because she didn't know how long it would be before Sierra began crying again.

The baby girl had cried herself to sleep last night. Woke up several times during the night and cried for an hour or so before falling back to sleep, and, since waking, had whimpered off and on most of the morning. Once her screaming jags began, who knew when they would end, and Carly needed to replenish Sierra's supplies before she really had something to cry about.

Carly found the formula and baby food, but didn't get to spend nearly enough time looking at the clothes. Choosing outfits for Sierra was hard but only because there were so many adorable things available. But the reality was she just needed the basics because Sierra could be leaving soon and the next child might not be able to wear or use them.

Frowning, Carly paused by the cutest pair of cow-girl boots in Sierra's size, but forced herself to continue on. She couldn't let herself forget the temporariness of Sierra's presence in her life.

Had they found her father yet? Would Sierra be with him at the end of the day?

Carly didn't know. And that was why, despite the oh, so precious little blue eyes giving her a shy, inquisitive stare, she recognized what Liam was trying so hard to warn her against—getting attached. She could care for Sierra, help her, protect her and even love her, but she couldn't love Sierra too much. Carly was setting herself up for heartache if she did.

But why was Liam so against her being a foster mother if her eyes were open to the realities of it? What had happened to him to make him feel the way he did?

Why do you care?

She didn't. Okay, she did but not because she *cared*... much. Well, fine, she did care but only as a friend. The truth was there was a lot about Liam she didn't know and she wasn't sure she liked it.

She didn't understand how he could be so unfeeling when, if not for Zane, Liam would have spent his childhood in the youth home for boys located between North Star and Helena.

Zane had adopted Liam and his brothers. Given them so very much. Foster parenting and youth facility homes were totally different things but how could Liam view being a foster parent as bad? Wasn't it better than a dormitory-style room with paid supervision?

Despite the upset churning inside her, Carly yawned again, found the diaper aisle and made another selection. So many decisions. Little things, really, but important all the same.

"Oh, what a little dear," an older woman said as she walked by. "She's adorable. How old?"

"Uh…eight months," Carly replied, wondering how Sierra would react to the attention.

Sure enough in response to the stranger, Sierra blinked, stuck her lower lip out and began to whine, the sound chock-full of fear and heartbreaking insecurity. As though she was afraid the woman would take her away again.

Carly murmured an excuse and pushed the cart farther down the aisle, but it didn't help. Sierra lurched sideways in the seat to watch for the woman. And when Sierra didn't see her anymore the child began to notice all the faces staring at her because she was crying—then cried louder in response.

Knowing this was only the beginning, Carly sped toward the checkout line.

She could do this. She had to. Not only for her sake but also for Sierra's.

THAT EVENING, LIAM heard the baby crying as he approached the house, the sight of Carly's overgrown grass a reminder that, even though it had only been a matter of hours, things had changed.

People were creatures of habit and in small towns those habits were more noticeable. Delmer went to church every Sunday unless he was ill or one of his managers needed the day off. The sheriff cooked lunch at the station to sit down with his men and get the scoop of what was going on not only in their lives, but also on their patrol. And Carly mowed her grass and worked in her yard every Sunday afternoon as though it was her personal homage to the big guy in the sky.

But not this week.

No, this week she'd become a single mother instead.

Liam knocked on the door, harder than he'd intended. "Carly? It's Liam."

At least she'd lowered her blinds.

The baby's cries intensified even before the door opened.

Carly looked like hell.

"Liam, you don't have to keep checking on me."

He pushed his way inside and walked into her kitchen, dropping the bag of food from the diner on the table crowded with department-store bags. "Put her in her chair, sit down and eat. She can cry in the high chair as easily as she can cry with you holding her."

One glance said Carly wanted to argue but her stomach growled loud enough to be heard in between the kid's howls.

Carly pulled the high chair close to the table and plopped the kid inside, strapping her in. Once that was done, she piled the tray with a handful of toys.

That got his attention. He'd been in her home only once when the sheriff had asked if any of the guys were willing to help move Carly into this place. One thing was for sure, though. At no point had it ever looked like a house with a kid in it. "Where did all the stuff come from?"

Carly looked around and shrugged. "I bought it. It's just a few basics."

The *basics* looked expensive. Once she finally wised up and turned the kid in did she really want to stare at all the baby crap everywhere?

Along with the high chair there was a plaything set up on the living-room floor, a laundry basket with formula, toys, clothes, a portable crib still in the box and a couple large stacks of diapers.

Getting angry all over again, he looked at the kid at the center of the drama. Since he was keeping his distance, the baby had quieted down some but she still whined and hiccuped, her nose running like a broken water main. She never took her eyes off him, either, which freaked him out more than he cared to admit.

Kids learned to watch their step early on when the immediate response was a bad one. A slap, a yell, a push. Didn't matter the age. She was old enough to have learned to be leery, and from the look of her, she had.

He inhaled and sighed. As much as he didn't like Carly getting involved with fostering on his watch, a part of him reluctantly admired what she was doing. "Something wrong with your lawn mower?"

"No, why?" Carly asked around a mouthful of turkey-club sandwich.

She had mustard on the corner of her mouth, which made him think of licking it off, which made him remember the kiss, which pissed him off even more.

Sheriff's daughter.

Foster mother.

Husband-hunter.

He knew it was bad that he had to keep reminding himself Carly was all those things.

"Where is it?"

"In the shed. The key is on the hook by the door. Do you need to borrow it?"

"No."

"I don't understand. Is something wrong?"

Yeah, something was wrong. Everything was wrong. It was day three of Jonas's vacation and his daughter had shadows beneath her eyes from caring for a kid, there was a thief in his bedroom at the ranch and no one was listening to his warnings, which frustrated him to no end. He needed to burn off some steam and, while there was plenty of work at the ranch to be done, he knew he was needed here more. "Your lawn. That's what's wrong."

"Oh. I, uh, didn't get to it this week."

She blinked a few times and stared at the baby. Liam could see her trying to figure out the logistics of mowing the grass while not leaving the kid alone.

"It's not that long. It'll have to wait until she… sleeps."

Which meant instead of sleeping herself, Carly planned to catch up on all the things falling behind? There were dirty dishes in the sink, laundry in the hall sorted into piles and two trash bags by the back door. "I'll take care of it."

"No." She shook her head firmly. "I can't ask you to do that. I'll mow it as soon as I can. I know how picky Mr. Cooper next door is. The last time my grass grew too long, he cut *mow me* in my front yard."

Yeah, he'd heard that story. And fielded complaint calls at the station because Cooper was retired and bored and had nothing to do but complain about people living their lives while he sat on his porch and watched it happen.

Carly went back to eating, eyes closed as though Porter's sandwich was the best she had ever tasted. And that look, the fact she'd put some kid she didn't even know over feeding and caring for herself, took him down like a linebacker.

Without a word, he grabbed the trash bags and the shed keys and headed out the door.

AN HOUR LATER, LIAM let himself into the house via Carly's back door. The grass was cut, the weeds whacked and blown off the street and drive, the trash moved to the curb for pick-up in the morning.

"Thank you."

Liam turned at the sound of Carly's soft voice. She sat in a chair in the living room, the baby asleep, sprawled facedown across her chest. Drool leaked out of the kid's mouth and made a dark spot on Carly's shirt.

But the sight of her that way, her arms wrapped so tenderly around the baby, sent feelings he couldn't identify crashing through him.

Carly was drowsy-eyed. It looked as though she might have been dozing herself, but now that the baby was quiet and content Carly looked...content herself. Like everything he would never have.

Her words seeped into his mind and he finally got around to responding. "Jonas would've done it if he was in town."

It was a reminder for her and himself. He was here for one purpose and one purpose only. And with Carly looking every bit like the mother she obviously wanted to be, keeping his distance emotionally wasn't going to be a problem.

"I know you don't understand, Liam. I know there probably aren't a lot of single women out there who would take this on. But this is something I *need* to do. It's not a matter of volunteering for a cause or... I'm not only doing this for Sierra and the other kids but for me, too."

Drawn, Liam moved toward her, careful not to bump into anything or make any noise that would wake the baby and get the kid going again. He waited, hoping to understand Carly a little better even as he told himself to leave. The chores were done. He was free to go.

"You and me...we never really talked about anything important in school," she murmured. "I mean, really important. Rissa's my stepmother, not my mom. Did you know that?"

"No."

"Rissa's great, the absolute best. She's always treated me like her own daughter. But there's a part of me that's always wondered why..."

Her words trailed off and a push of her bare foot put the rocker in motion.

"I've always wondered *why* my mom took off. She left my dad and me when I was little. How do you up and leave a kid like that?"

He wasn't sure what to say. He felt bad that Carly and Jonas had been treated that way. They were both decent people. But bad things happened to everybody, and being on the receiving end of something like that didn't mean doing what she was doing. If anything, it meant being more protective and guarded, not opening yourself up to hurt. "My mom left me, too."

Even as he said the words, he couldn't believe he'd uttered them. His past wasn't something he discussed. Ever. And now that he had, Carly looked inquisitive, as though she were going to ask questions, so he beat her to the punch. "Where did she go? Your mom?"

"New York, L.A. She fancied herself an actress and model and even got some work. Every now and again she'd send my grandmother copies of ads she'd been in."

"She didn't send them to you?"

"No. For a while I got what I thought were birthday cards from her but...I think they were really my grandma's efforts to make it seem like my mother hadn't abandoned us. What about you? Where did your mom go?"

"Jail, for a while. After that, I don't know."

"And your father?"

"Some guy she met in a bar."

"Oh."

Seconds ticked by, but he made no effort to elaborate further.

"I know you don't understand why this is so important to me," she repeated softly, "but this is my way of... testing myself."

Testing herself for what? "What do you mean?"

"These kids need love and they have issues with abandonment and trust. Things I understand. Thanks to my dad, I never had the life they've had but I know that feeling, that fear of waking up one morning and my mother being gone, not because she died but because she didn't *want* us anymore."

He couldn't imagine anyone not wanting Carly. But he also knew that feeling. And he did not want to identify with her or the kid. He couldn't afford to feel more than the slightest twinge of sympathy or responsibility for them because to feel more would be to feel too much.

And even though telling her about his past might help her see the danger she was potentially putting herself in, he couldn't force the words to come, couldn't reveal any more details of the life he'd led before winding up with Zane.

"Maybe I'm not cut out to be a mother. Maybe I'm like *my* mother," she whispered softly. "I have to know one way or the other. I have find out before it's too late and I have a child of my own. Maybe it *is* twisted logic but…I know Sierra and the others are temporary. I *know* I won't have them forever. If I can't handle them the short time they're with me, how on earth could I handle raising a baby of my own for eighteen years? A lifetime? I have to know if I have what it takes."

Her words struck a chord in Liam he couldn't deny. How many times had he asked himself the same question over the years? Considering himself worthy of being Zane's son wasn't easy, especially considering the things Liam had done.

"Zane's treated you well, Liam. I know you enough to be certain you wouldn't still be hanging around if he hadn't. Didn't it make an impact when you met him? When he adopted you and your brothers?"

"They're not my brothers." Unable to stay still, he paced to the other side of the room, uncomfortable in his own skin, much less beneath her inquisitive gaze. "That rumor got started because we're dark-haired and were as wild as all get-out. But we're not really related. We're not family. We just didn't want anybody in our business so we didn't bother correcting the gossip."

"Of course you're family. Maybe you weren't then, but after all these years? What are you if not family?"

He didn't answer the question, couldn't. Things were getting too touchy-feely and complicated for him. If he were smart, he would have tossed the keys to her shed onto the ring and left. He wasn't responsible for heart-to-hearts. "I have to go."

"Why? Because I asked why you're getting so up-tight about your family?"

"They're *not* my family. You want the story behind my adoption? Fine. Zane caught us joyriding on one of his tractors. We'd done a crap-load of damage to it and his property and he knew we'd probably get a slap on the wrist if he tried pressing charges. So instead, Zane asked the home to order the three of us to work off the damages at the ranch."

"And you've been there ever since. It's been how many years?"

Thirteen. Thirteen years. Maybe they were family in a sense but he considered himself the best of all cops because he *didn't* have the family ties the other deputies had. He got up in the morning and did his job and if the day came when he didn't make it home at night, he knew Zane and the others would go on without him. That was a good thing.

Liam glanced at Carly, saw her watching him with an expectant look on her face and decided to give her the truth, not softening the words so she'd think about them in reference to herself and her future as a foster parent. "Caroline, I was fifteen and hell-bent on get-ting out of the home even though I had nowhere to go. By letting the adoption go uncontested, I didn't have to share a room with ten other boys. I didn't have to share a bathroom or showers like a gym class. I had new clothes, a house I wasn't ashamed of. I didn't let Zane adopt me because I felt some kind of emotional bond or *love*," he stated firmly. "I simply knew a good thing when I saw it."

Disappointment flashed over her expressive face. Disappointment in him, in the sweet, heart-wrenching story she'd probably concocted in her head. But the fact was he'd have said yes to almost anything to not be one of those kids anymore. Even after Zane had adopted them, Liam kept waiting for Zane to change his mind and ship them—*him*—back into the system. It's what everyone else had done, even his mother.

"I'm sorry to hear that," she said, her head tilted to one side, a pitying look softening her gray eyes.

He didn't need this. Didn't need her screwing with his chance to show Jonas that he was more than capable of filling the sheriff's shoes when he retired. He wanted Jonas's support, needed it. Not this.

"Bonds form with time, Liam. You might tell yourself they're not family but I'll bet if you think back to all the time you've spent with your brothers and father, you'll see that I'm right."

He knew she used the words deliberately. *Father, brothers. Family.*

He thought of his old bedroom and how Charlie was now sleeping in it, and found himself taking angry, bitter strides.

Jealous. Was that really jealousy he felt?

He had no right. Carly was correct in one aspect. He couldn't say Zane wasn't family and yet be angry because he'd moved Charlie into his old room. Jealousy was an emotion like love and caring. Liam wouldn't feel so much if he didn't care at all. But was that really a surprise?

Acknowledging that hammered home that he had a long way to go before he could ever consider himself redeemed.

Which is why he had to keep Charlie from hurting Zane, too.

"Liam?"

He wiped his hand over his face and kept walking.

Carly had a good heart, a tender soul, but in the end how would she handle it when some smart-mouthed, hotheaded kid lost his temper and hurt her? When they hit hard and fast, spiraling out of control and uncaring of who they took down with them.

Liam let himself out, careful to lock the door behind him, his strides long and brisk as he left her persistent, too-intrusive questions.

He'd spent the past thirteen years making up for his sins. But if Zane ever found out, Liam didn't doubt the man would sever all ties.

And even though he denied caring, Liam did.

Family didn't do what he'd done to Zane. That was why Liam hoped Zane never discovered the truth.

CHAPTER EIGHT

THE NEXT MORNING, Carly got up two hours before her normal time to get to work early so she could set up a special area behind the reception desk for Sierra.

YPA was her brainchild. After working so hard in high school to make great grades and get accepted by colleges around the country, at the last minute Carly realized she didn't want to go.

It wasn't a matter of fear but of lifestyle. She didn't *want* to work in a corporate office, running like mad and stressed to the gills. She didn't want to travel all the time. She simply wanted a job where she was well compensated, could set her hours and still have a life.

Her stepsister, Skylar, had gone away to school to be closer to her then-boyfriend, Marcus, but Carly had stayed and graduated via an extension branch of Montana State. Two years after earning her business degree, she convinced her father to cosign a loan for YPA, the first single-person office rentals in the area.

Carly rented out office space in the two-story building, and acted as administrative assistant and office manager to her clients, charging them per service. She did their work on an as-needed basis, which allowed them a professional office in which to conduct business without the expense of a full-time employee.

Best of all, even when her clients' months were slow

and they didn't need her to do more than answer their phones, she still collected rent, which meant her bills were paid and she had some extra cash.

Singing a silly song to a fussy Sierra, Carly unfolded the porta-crib, made another trip to the car, with Sierra on her hip, to bring in toys and the diaper bag. Please, God, let it be a good day.

Carly put Sierra on a blanket surrounded by toys. That done, she went through her packed in-box. A half hour later, the first of her clients arrived.

"Congratulations," Jacklyn said, smiling at Sierra. "She's adorable." Jackie was a semiretired attorney, who had resumed practicing law after her husband passed away. She mainly handled wills and deeds.

"Thanks." Carly smiled and tried to ignore the look of panic on Sierra's face as the baby began to crawl toward her at a fast pace.

"I was afraid of this. Where's the sitter?"

Carly forced herself to smile at Dave Adams. Of all her clients, she knew Dave would be the one most likely to have a problem with Sierra accompanying her to work. A financial consultant, Dave lived to crunch numbers and track progress. He didn't care for people or—judging by the look on his face—children. "You're looking at her. But don't worry, if Sierra becomes a problem, I'll take her home."

"How will I get my reports typed up? I'm already a day behind, since you didn't come in yesterday," Dave said.

She kept the smile on her face by sheer will. "I'll make it happen. No worries," she stated confidently, refusing to show any trepidation in the face of Sierra's watery eyes and Dave's less-than-happy glare.

Sierra sat on her rump on the floor and reached for Carly, whimpering louder.

Jackie gave Carly a sympathetic look over her shoulder as she made her way down the hall to her office. Carly wished the older woman had stayed, knowing at least part of Dave's animosity stemmed from Carly turning him down for a date two weeks ago. Separated did not equal divorced in her book, not that he agreed. All he seemed to want was a little office nooky.

Carly bent and picked up Sierra and the closest toy, holding it for Sierra to grasp.

"Why's she crying?"

"She's not crying. Just fussy because she's scared."

Sierra wanted nothing to do with the toy and tried to crawl up Carly's chest, her little fingers gripping Carly's hair. She held the baby close for a moment, then gently but firmly repositioned Sierra on her lap, offering comfort and closeness but not allowing Sierra to strangle her. "Dave, I'll get the reports typed up. Have you given me the recording to transcribe?"

"I emailed the file to you."

"Great."

Another of her renters walked in.

And Sierra's fussiness turned into full-fledged screams.

You can do this. You can make this work.

But as she bounced Sierra in her arms, Carly knew she was going to need backup.

LIAM LEFT THE SMALL cabin he'd spent the past three years building and drove slowly down the winter-rutted gravel road, toward the two-lane highway that would take him into town. Once he reached the straight stretch between his cabin and the ranch house, he slowed even more, spotting Charlie outside the barn. The man loaded tools into the back of one of the ranch trucks.

Liam visually searched the surroundings for Brad or Zane or some of the other hands, but didn't see anyone.

Charlie straightened and turned toward the cruiser when Liam stopped and rolled his window down. "Morning."

"Mornin'." Charlie dipped his head in a nod.

"Looks like you've got plans for the day. What's going on?"

"Just trying to carry my weight."

In tools?

"Shouldn't you be on your way to town?" Zane called out to Liam.

On his way from the house, toward them, Zane carried a couple lunch buckets and a large thermos. "On my way now."

"Charlie's feeling better after a couple nights' sleep so he's going with me to fix the fence that stand of pine trees knocked down during the winter. It'll take the tractor to push the rest of it down but I figure we can cut the brush and limbs out of the way."

Studying Charlie, Liam nodded. He didn't like the thought of Zane working the day away while Charlie was alone in the house, able to do whatever he wanted. "Sounds like a plan. You can keep an eye on him that way."

An uncomfortable silence descended but Liam purposefully ignored it—and Zane's disapproving frown.

"We'd best get to work," Zane said.

Head down, Charlie walked to the passenger side of the truck and climbed in but Zane didn't move, giving

Liam a stare meant to remind him to guard his mouth around his elders.

"He's a decent man, down on his luck," Zane said softly. "You don't have to treat him like dirt because he had a moment of weakness and was desperate."

Liam broke the stare to put the cruiser into gear. "Desperate people do desperate things. My gut says there is something else going on here."

He looked at Zane in time to catch the flicker of a strange expression fading from Zane's face, an expression Liam wasn't able to read. What the hell?

"Anybody ever tell you you're cynical? You see the bad before you see the good. Maybe after Taggert gets back to town and you can breathe a little, you should make a point of coming to dinner here at the house. Get to know Charlie. I bet it would ease your mind."

Not likely. "Drifters are all the same, Zane. Give Charlie time. He'll prove me right."

WHEN THE DOORBELL RANG that evening, Carly swore silently. She couldn't handle another visit from Liam. Not today.

She ignored the chime and hoped he got the hint to go away.

Work had been nothing short of a migraine-inducing hell. Sierra had cried every time one of Carly's clients walked down the hallway. And because people needed to go to the restroom, out to lunch, to the kitchen, to meetings, to make copies, et cetera, she would no sooner calm Sierra when a new episode would begin. The baby had spent the day crying and clinging to Carly like a leech, making accomplishing anything next to impossible.

Sierra was insecure and easily frightened, and who could blame her? But the baby's behavior broke Carly's heart.

"Carly?"

Carly stilled at the sound of the female voice. Definitely not Liam.

She peeled her tired body off the couch and carefully made her way around Sierra's sleeping form.

The moment she'd made it home, she'd changed into a T-shirt and jeans.

Carly smoothed her hair, quickly swiped the smudged eyeliner away and hoped it was the Girl Scout up the street trying to unload a few extra boxes of cookies. Good grief, she needed some peanut butter and chocolate—*now*.

She opened the door and nearly choked on her gasp of surprise. *"Mandy?"*

From kindergarten through seventh grade, Mandy Blake had been Carly's best friend. But in eighth grade all that had changed. She and Mandy had parted ways—Mandy into the realms of the popular crowd, while Carly had remained firmly stuck in her position as a geeky brainiac far beneath Mandy's tolerance level.

So why was she here now?

Other than Mandy making snide remarks to Carly as they had passed in the halls through high school, they hadn't talked since eighth grade. Even though Mandy lived three houses down the street and had ever since Carly had moved in two years ago.

"Hi."

"Uh…hi." Carly remembered when Mandy wore pigtails and knee socks to church. She remembered when they had gone trick-or-treating together and exchanged best-friend necklaces for Christmas, when every weekend was a sleepover.

But more than anything, Carly remembered the way Mandy had turned on her and called her everything from a loser to a bitch and said such nasty things about Carly that for a brief period of time she had wanted her angsty teenage world to end.

Her insecurity over her mother?

Mandy had posted comments online in a popular chat room, been nasty and cruel, the ultimate mean girl who had made it clear to all who would listen that Carly's lack of beauty, style and class was too much for her beautiful mother to bear. "May I help you?"

She'd seen Mandy around over the years, but always from afar. For the first time Carly noticed the deep lines spreading out from the corners of Mandy's eyes, a hard, aged look to her features. Her bitter attitude and party-girl lifestyle had taken a toll on her physically and her expression reminded Carly of the phrase, rode hard and put away wet. Once the prettiest girl in school, Mandy wasn't anymore. But that split-second flash of satisfaction only made Carly feel petty, not happy as she would have thought.

"Yeah. I was going to donate this stuff to the mission but my husband heard what you're doing."

Mandy had trouble looking Carly in the eyes. "Doing?"

"Fostering. We, um, thought you might need it more, so I brought it to you. You know, if you can use it."

It was a laundry basket full of pink and white. Clothes, blankets, shoes. And even though she didn't want anything from Mandy, Carly couldn't turn it away. Not yet anyway. "That's very thoughtful."

And no doubt all the thought had been on Mandy's husband's part. Kyle Benson was husband number two for Mandy, and seemingly a genuinely nice guy, leaving Carly to wonder why he'd hooked up with someone as *not* nice as Mandy.

The world really didn't make sense sometimes, did it? Nice guys finished last, bad girls were revered.

Carly accepted the basket, holding it in front of her. Sierra began to whimper, probably because she'd opened her eyes and Carly wasn't right there.

"Mind if I come in and see her?"

Carly wanted to slam the door in Mandy's face but knew she didn't have enough diva in her to actually do it.

She brings gifts. Behave. "Sure," Carly said, leading the way. "Sierra doesn't like people very much." She set the basket on the couch, then bent to pick up Sierra from the blanket on the floor. "I think she's afraid of everyone after being taken away from her mom."

"Aw, she's cute. Remember when we babysat my cousin's baby? Remember how ugly he was?"

She remembered. She also remembered Mandy calling *her* ugly. And when their gazes met, Carly realized Mandy remembered it, too.

For a second Carly thought she saw a flicker of regret on Mandy's face. But that was ridiculous. She didn't feel regret. Carly had sometimes wondered if Mandy felt anything at all wrapped up as she'd been in her ivory tower with her cheerleading and pageants and parties.

"I have more stuff if you want it. If you can use it. I'd be happy to bring it to you, otherwise it'll go to the mission."

The items in the basket were expensive and of good

quality. "That's very generous." But *why* was Mandy being generous? It had been nearly ten years since graduation, fifteen since Mandy had treated her with anything other than contempt.

Carly forced herself to take a mental step back and assess the situation.

Mandy wanted something. What, Carly wasn't sure of, but something had definitely prompted this visit.

"Kyle is working late tonight. The kids are home, eating dinner, so I guess I'd better get back but I'll bring the rest of the stuff over tomorrow. Around six?"

Carly managed a nod, even though the last thing she wanted was another encounter with Mandy. "If you're sure you want rid of it and can't use it."

Mandy made a face on her way to the door. "I'm sure. Kyle and I have decided we're not having any more children, what with his three and my one."

Four kids. And here Carly was having difficulty handling a single baby. "If you're sure…"

"We are. So, I'll see you tomorrow."

"Yeah, tomorrow." Carly closed the door and leaned against the wooden panel, realizing how lucky she was to not have lived Mandy's life even though in school that was all Carly could think about, almost to the point of obsession.

Once upon a time, she'd prayed to be like Mandy. But now…

Wasn't it funny how thankful one could be for unanswered prayers?

CHAPTER NINE

TWO HOURS LATER, Liam jerked the cruiser to a stop along the curb in front of Carly's house and raced passed the rescue squad in the driveway, toward the front door. His heart pounded hard and fast in his chest, all sorts of thoughts crashing together in his head.

Benny Mayer, one of the local volunteer EMTs, was exiting as Liam hit the porch steps at a run.

"Slow down, junior. The sheriff won't demote you yet. They're fine."

Benny chuckled at his joke and continued down the steps past Liam, lugging two handled containers of medical supplies.

At Benny's words, Liam slowed, stepping into the house where he saw two other EMTs sitting back on their heels as they talked to Carly. She was seated on the couch, and the EMTs had to talk loud to be heard over Sierra's screams.

"Looks like those shiny new teeth of hers cut into her lip some. The cuts aren't deep. They don't need stitches."

"Are you sure?" Carly asked, her face paste-pale as she attempted to hold a bag of ice to the mouth of the straining and twisting and screaming baby in her lap. Sierra's shirt was covered in blood as was the towel lying across Carly's knee.

"What happened?" he demanded.

Carly started and looked at him, two hot spots of color appearing on her pale cheeks. She wet her lips as though to speak. When no words emerged, the female EMT, who had been around for as long as Liam had been on the force, spoke up to fill him in.

"Baby pulled herself up then fell and busted her mouth on the table," Joy said. "She's fine, but Carly saw all the blood and thought there was more damage. It's hard to tell when the kid's screaming and blood seems to be gushing like that."

"She was crying so hard she couldn't breathe." Carly's voice was strained, her gaze not meeting his.

The simple description said it all, though. Liam fisted his hands at the expression she wore.

"Honey, to cry that hard they have to get air from somewhere. She's more mad and scared than anything. You got any flavored ice? Popsicles? If you do, feed her little bits small enough to melt before she can choke. The cold and taste will distract her and help numb her lip. Teething gel will work, too, if you have any of that."

The radios on their belts went off with the dispatcher relaying news of someone's back going out and a request for assistance.

Joy and her partner stood simultaneously.

"She's fine, hon. The good news is she's going to be worn out from all the fuss and sleep like the baby she is once we're all gone."

"Thanks, Joy. Tell Benny I'm sorry about interrupting his dinner."

Joy laughed. "Considering Benny's always eating, he'll get over it."

On the way to the door, Joy glanced at Liam, her

gently wrinkled face creased with worry. "The new mama's a little shaken up," she said for his ears only.

That was a major understatement. He'd noticed the hand holding the bag of ice to Sierra's mouth trembled like earthquake aftershocks.

"You sticking around for a bit? I'm sure Jonas would appreciate it."

"Sure, no problem. My shift's about over. You're positive everything is okay with the baby?"

"Oh, she's fine. No sign of concussion, the bleeding has stopped. She'll quiet down soon. Already has from when we arrived."

Liam said his goodbyes, hesitating in the doorway as the squad pulled out and Carly's nosy neighbors chatted amongst themselves and stared toward the house.

He shut the door with a firm push, his attempt to keep any of the bolder ones from approaching, and waited until the neighbors began to drift toward their houses.

"That's my girl. Yeah, no more crying. How about some fun after all that, huh? That sound good? You like the swing, d-don't you?"

Liam moved so that he could see Carly. She had trouble fastening the belt that held the baby in place. Once Sierra was seated in the swing and the tray was in place, Carly set the swing in motion with a press of a button.

As the swing went back and forth, Sierra quieted even more, until all that remained of her upset were the hiccups he'd noticed the baby seemed prone to after a crying jag.

Carly didn't move, didn't stand. She simply sat and watched the swing.

"She's so tiny she still fits. The doctor said she's only

in the twentieth percentile for her age, that she'll only be around five feet tall."

His gut knotted because of Carly's tone. Unease settled deep within him.

Carly's nostrils flared as she inhaled, her expression vulnerable and sad. Defeated? "Caroline...?"

"I didn't even know she could pull herself up. I should've known that."

Carly shoved herself to her feet and moved to gather the bloodied rag that had fallen to the floor.

"All I've seen her do is crawl, but that's the next step, right?" She clenched the towel in her hand. "I looked away for a *second* and when I looked again— She fell because of me."

"Kids fall all the time. Unless you hit her or shoved her, you're not to blame."

"No, I am. I was so surprised to see her standing I—I think I gasped. I know I made a noise because she jerked her head toward me. I startled her. That's why she fell."

He watched the baby's eyes take on a drowsy look. Sierra shoved her thumb into her mouth and began to suck. Other than a wince when her swollen lip and thumb met, the baby didn't show any sign of being in pain. She was fine. At the moment, Carly was the one who suffered. Before his eyes, her confidence struggled to right itself.

Liam followed her into the kitchen. She dumped the bag of ice into the sink before she carried the plastic and the towel to the trash. Retracing her steps, she moved to the sink to wash her hands, giving the task more focus than it required.

"Caroline, talk to me."

From where he stood, Liam saw her close her eyes, noted the tightly woven tension hiking her shoulders to her ears. But even though he made the request, she didn't have to say a word. He knew what she was thinking. "You have what it takes, sweetheart. You're not your mother."

A husky, sorrow-filled laugh left Carly's throat. "No? Because it sure seemed like it tonight."

He flipped the tap off and pulled her around to face him.

"Liam, don't. Don't say it. Don't try to soothe me. I screwed up. Tonight could have been a disaster."

"But it wasn't, and you know why? Because you did what any good parent would do. You called for help. Carly, kids get hurt. You think she's never going to get another bruise? Kids fall down, they hit their heads, blacken their eyes. You can't keep that from happening."

"I know but… It just makes me think. Maybe I *am* like my mother. She could never handle stuff like this. Blood and tears." A wry twist formed on her lips. "Not unless they were *hers*. Maybe what happened tonight was a sign I…shouldn't do this."

They were the words he'd been waiting for her to say, the indication her confidence was eroding beneath the strain of caring for the baby in the other room.

Staring into Carly's face, Liam knew he could play off her fears. He had been a deputy for eight years now. He knew how the system worked. She had an emergency number to call. The kid could be gone tonight. Within the hour. All he had to do was egg on Carly's self-doubt.

But looking at her and seeing the pain and fear, remembering what she'd said about wanting to—*having to*—prove herself... To prove *to* herself that she wasn't like the mother who'd abandoned her... He couldn't do it. "Maybe it is."

She swallowed audibly, her lashes lifting to reveal the turbulent, storm-tossed gray of her eyes, the shadows of the past. They had more in common than he'd ever realized. "Or maybe," he forced himself to continue, "it's a sign that you *can* do it."

Using his hands on her shoulders, Liam turned her around and nudged Carly across the floor until Sierra and the swing were centered in front of them. "Look at her," he ordered, keeping his voice low so as to not disturb the baby.

He was surrounded by Carly's scent and he breathed deep, because he could. Because she was Jonas Taggert's daughter and determined to steer clear of cops so a breath was all he could have. "She's sleeping peacefully, isn't she? And look at her mouth. It's a little puffy but I don't see a bruise."

"It still happened."

"And I guarantee it'll happen again in the future when she plays ball or falls off her bike or—" he couldn't help but smile "—trips going up the steps at the high school."

His comment pulled a reluctant laugh from her chest. "I was such a klutz. And to add insult to injury, we had a test and I screwed up the formula. I never understood why you took the blame for the fire when it was my fault. You came to my rescue then, too."

"You were up for scholarships. I wasn't." And they'd veered from the subject. "The point I was trying to make is that I might not agree with you doing this on your own, but I understand your reasons."

"You do?"

She turned her head, and when she did it placed her mouth way too close. He had to swallow before he could speak. "Yeah, and I don't have a doubt in my mind that if you want to do this, you can. I'll help you."

"*Help* me?" She shook her head, looking dazed and more than a bit confused. "Why?"

Why, indeed. The only answer he could come up with was that this was important to her, because her reasons were deeply ingrained, personal, and now he really did understand. He understood her drive and desire and hunger. He'd been trying to prove himself for years, to make up for what he'd done to Zane and his other foster families and no longer be the kid who'd been given up, given back. On that score, he and Carly were the same because they both had been made to feel like someone's unwanted trash.

"I don't expect you to help me, Liam. That's above and beyond the call of duty."

"Maybe, but you'll let me," he insisted. "Until Jonas gets home." Once Jonas was back, he could handle her, protect her. Do the things that fathers and family did for one another.

Carly laughed wryly, the sight of her smile doing things to his insides Liam couldn't allow himself to overthink.

"Yeah, well, at this point I'd be crazy to turn you down."

CHAPTER TEN

LATE WEDNESDAY AFTERNOON, Carly hit the garage-door button and waited impatiently for it to rise, praying Mandy didn't see her arrive home. Of all the things to top off her day, another visit from Mandy could very well send Carly running for the gallon-size carton of Chunky Monkey.

Parked, she pressed the button once more and turned off the lights and engine, simply sitting there in the quiet.

What a day.

The overhead timed light clicked off, the interior of the garage darkening to suit her mood.

The morning had been fabulous. Sierra had slept through the night and awoke in an especially good mood. She'd eaten her breakfast instead of shoving it away, and when Carly had packed Sierra into work, the baby girl had sat at Carly's feet and played, crawling close whenever one of her clients walked by but not crying like yesterday. The only time Carly had heard a peep from the child was when Sierra was getting hungry or sleepy.

Carly had been able to make a dent in her work, and even managed to eat lunch while Sierra took a two-hour nap. Things had been going well. So well, in fact, she should have known something was about to happen.

Glancing over her shoulder to the empty car seat behind her, Carly's heart constricted in unshakable loss.

Sierra was gone now—with her father. And this was exactly what Liam had warned her about.

Dragging with fatigue, Carly got out of the car and unlocked the door to the house. She was carrying in the porta-crib, swing, toys and diaper bag when she heard a knock on her front door.

"Carly? It's me, Mandy."

Carly slung the diaper bag to the floor. Didn't Mandy know that after a day of working people needed time to unwind? At least a few minutes?

"Carly, are you sick?"

Crap. Mandy would have to pull the sympathy card. "Coming!"

Carly composed herself as she walked through the kitchen to the front door. Mandy breezed in, her arms full of an overstuffed garbage bag.

"There you are. I brought the stuff. This is just the first load. Don't close the door. Two more are coming."

Carly swallowed, her patience nonexistent. "Two more? Uh…Mandy—"

"Excuse me," said a childish voice.

Carly turned to see an awkward-looking girl, about eleven or twelve, standing on the porch, loaded down with another garbage bag. A handsome teenage boy was behind her, picking on her by pretending he hadn't seen her stop. He shoved the box he carried into the girl's shoulder. She gasped softly in pain, glaring at him.

Carly stepped out of the way so the little girl could get into the house, but determinedly placed herself between the kids so the tormenting would end.

She hated bullies. And yet here she was sharing her

living room with the very woman who'd made her teenage years hell. What was up with that?

"Don't worry, we're not dumping it on you. I thought you could sort through and take what you like. Then when you're finished, we'll take what you don't want to the mission. Elysee, put that here with the rest of the clothes, and, Derek, put that box over there against the wall so it'll be out of the way."

The girl quietly made her way to do as her mother ordered, while Derek took two steps, dropped the box with a bang and kicked it closer to the wall. "Gotta go meet Tim and give him the stuff he left at practice."

"Come straight home."

"No friggin' way. The guys are going to a party. I'll be home after that."

Mandy put her hands on her hips. "I said come straight home. Today's your dad's birthday. He has to work until 6:30, but we're having dinner together as a family."

"You invite my mom?"

Mandy gave the boy a cool smile. "No, I did not."

"Then I guess you didn't get him something he really wants for his birthday." That said, the teenager headed out the door.

Carly stood silently in shock. Wow. What the heck was that?

Mandy glared at the teenager's retreating form. "Kids, huh?" she said with a strained laugh. "Mr. Popular can't quite accept that his dad has moved on."

From what Carly had witnessed, that was the understatement of the year.

"Mom, can I go? I need to study."

Wait a minute. Carly blinked, feeling as though she

had a minor case of whiplash. The blond-haired, good-looking boy was Kyle's son and the poor, awkward girl was Mandy's?

"You've studied since you got home from school. Why not take a break and call Taylor?"

"She's busy."

Mandy waved a hand toward the door, making a face Elysee couldn't see. "Okay, fine, honey. But lock the door. I'll knock for you to let me in. I'm going to help Carly sort through this real quick and then I'll be home."

"Okay."

Whoa, wait—what? Mandy wanted to stay? Do this tonight?

Together? "Oh, you don't need to do that. I can handle this."

Mandy was focused on her task but she lifted her face and Carly barely managed to suppress a gasp. Tears rolled down Mandy's cheeks, and her expression begged for help. "I—I mean, if you want to stay, that's great. If you have time."

The moment the door shut behind Elysee, Mandy dropped into a chair and buried her head in her hands.

"Um…Mandy, are you all right?"

A tear-strangled laugh emerged from Mandy's throat. "No. I'm not. But I have to give you credit for asking. You're a regular saint, aren't you, Carly?" Surprisingly the question wasn't sarcastic. More like a statement of fact, resigned and softly spoken.

"Hardly."

"No, it's true. You let me in, you've been nice to me. When we both know you have every reason to hate me."

"I don't hate anyone." Carly lifted her shoulders in a shrug. "Life's too short to spend it hating people."

"That statement only proves my point." Mandy inhaled, then sighed. "Fine, but you have to admit you don't *like* me."

"Is there a point to this?" Carly asked, choosing to avoid the question.

"Yeah. The point is it's okay to say you don't like me. I deserve it and, after the way I treated you, I don't blame you."

This was way more drama than Carly wanted to deal with after the day she'd had. "Mandy—"

"I probably wouldn't have opened the door if I were you," she said, leaning forward over the bag closest to her to pull out a little girl's jumper. "I mean, really— *sainthood,*" she said drily. "This was Elysee's." She held it up. "Pretty, huh?"

Carly blinked at the change in topic. She *so* didn't have the energy for this. "It's beautiful."

Mandy held the jumper to her chest, smoothing the material down with her perfectly manicured hand. "Okay. Confession time. I had an ulterior motive for coming here yesterday."

Like that was a surprise? Carly might not have known *why* Mandy had shown up but that she'd had a reason was clear. BFFs they weren't. "I suspected as much."

"Pretty obvious, huh? But... I should just say it, right? You probably noticed Elysee is...different."

Different?

Carly pictured the girl in her mind and remembered Elysee's awkwardness, the way she'd walked out of the house with her shoulders hunched and her feet dragging, her clothes loose and baggy and not quite as stylish as Mandy's or her stepbrother's.

"Elysee's my baby girl and I love her—" Mandy couldn't make eye contact "—but she doesn't— She isn't— The kids at school make fun of her."

That was the reason for the big apology? "I'm sorry to hear that."

Mandy lifted her head, giving Carly a glimpse of her emotion-torn features. The tears were back but they weren't crocodile. And for the first time since middle school, Mandy scored points for being human.

"Some of the things they've said and *done* to her," she whispered raggedly, "are unimaginable. The kids have been so cruel. Carly...I know it's years too late but I'm sorry for what I did to you. What's happening to Elysee has made me realize how badly I treated you. I'm sorry."

Fifteen years after the fact, the apology was heart-felt, and therefore accepted. Carly only wished it hadn't taken Mandy's daughter getting picked on and bullied to make it happen. "Hey, it was years ago and I survived. What doesn't kill us makes us stronger, right? For a while there, I wasn't so nice myself," she admitted.

"Oh, please," Mandy said. "You had a few weeks of rebellion. That hardly qualifies as not nice."

"Trying to take your boyfriend wasn't nice."

Mandy made a face. "No, it wasn't. But we both know he was a jerk and not really mine so..." She rubbed her palms over her jeans. "I've always wondered something. How did your dad take your big makeover, anyway? The night of the school dance, he was fit to be tied."

Strange though it was to be having this conversation, Carly laughed wryly. "He wasn't happy about it, especially when I'd snuck out to..." She shrugged.

"To hook up with Travis," Mandy finished. "What a loser."

"We weren't saying that then, though, were we?" Carly murmured.

"Nope. Since I'm on a roll, I should probably apologize for sending your dad after you that night, too."

Carly waited but the words didn't come. "Why did you?"

"You pissed me off by going after my boyfriend," Mandy said, shaking her head. "Of all the girls in school who liked Travis, you were the one I thought I *didn't* have to worry about."

"Because I wasn't any competition." Carly was getting nervous again. Subjects like the current one were often best left in the past for a reason.

"No, that wasn't it. I still remember when you showed up to school on Monday after your birthday makeover. I was so jealous because you looked so pretty and everyone was talking about you. Instead of being a loser as one of the last ones to wear makeup, you wound up making a huge entrance. You were the new toy everyone wanted to play with."

But then her new look had gone to her head and Carly had set out on a mission to make Mandy pay for all the mean things she'd done to Carly once their friendship had dwindled into who was popular and who was less-than-human geektoid. "Some experiences are worth their weight in gold. Ever since eighth grade, I've been more aware of how I treat people."

"Yeah, well, it's taken me a lot longer to learn that

lesson but I'm finally getting it now that Elysee is on the receiving end," Mandy said softly. "Elysee is hurting and angry and withdrawn. I can't get her to talk to me. She says I don't understand because…" Mandy shrugged. "She's seen pictures and heard stories about how—"

"You were always popular," Carly finished.

Her teen years had been filled with angst the same as any other young adult. But where Mandy had been a cheerleader and athlete and prom queen and so many other things that brought more and more attention, Carly had been the geek with her nose in a book—until that fourteenth birthday.

That year, she'd wised up and asked for a makeover that would change everything. It *had* altered everything—but not in a good way.

Her new look had achieved her goal of attracting football star Travis's attention. But when her newly made-over self became too big for her britches, a school scandal involving her, the football team and a group of other unpopular girls quickly brought things into perspective.

In her bid to get Travis to like her, she'd overlooked his sudden interest in her the same way she'd overlooked how some other unpopular girls in class were suddenly all that.

Until news of a sordid bet surfaced and it was revealed that the football player who "popped the most cherries" won tickets to a state game.

The truth behind all of their sudden popularity?

There weren't many virgins among the popular girls.

"Anyway, I was packing this stuff up and talking to Kyle and telling him how ashamed I am of what I'd done and he said maybe you could…help," Mandy said with a wry expression, her eyes dark.

Help? How? "Mandy, this is between you and Elysee. I don't know what I could do."

"You could talk to her. I know it's asking a lot," Mandy said quickly. "I *know* it is, and I know I have no right to ask and you have no reason to help me. Except that you understand and maybe…she'll be able to sense that."

"Can't you just tell her?"

Mandy looked aghast at the thought. "I can't. I can't, Carly. I don't want Elysee to look at me and see those girls who have been so mean. Moms are supposed to be loving and helpful, not…not like one of the people hurting Elysee every day."

But Mandy was a mean girl. Or at least, she had been.

"Think about it?" Mandy begged. "You don't have to decide now. I know you have your hands full with— Carly, *where's* the baby?"

CHAPTER ELEVEN

LIAM MADE NOTE of the minister's car parked outside the First Christian Church as he drove through town Wednesday evening. The man was hammering a stake into the ground, the sign listing the dates of the upcoming vacation Bible school.

Liam lifted his hand as he drove by, continuing on until he spotted Brad's truck outside McKenna Feed. He swung the cruiser into the parking lot, taking the opportunity to speak to his elder adopted brother while he could.

Charlie had been in town since Sunday but with everything going on, Liam hadn't been in touch with Brad, and by the time Liam arrived home in the evenings, it was too late to call. Brad was definitely a sunup-to-sundown type.

The smell of fertilizer, dog food and floor wax assailed his nose the moment Liam yanked open the door. This time of day, the store was quiet, a perfect time to corner Brad and Chance and get a second opinion on Charlie's presence at the ranch. "Hey," he said the moment he spotted Brad behind the cash register. "What are you doing back there?"

"Dooley's wife went into labor two weeks early. If it wasn't his first kid, I think I'd have told him to visit her after work," Brad grumbled.

Liam smirked because he knew Brad was all bark and no bite. "Tough break."

Brad hated working at the store. Normally Chance ran the feed-and-tack store, while Zane and Brad worked the ranch, but whenever their youngest adopted brother wasn't in town, Dooley was in charge as the assistant manager. Whenever Dooley wasn't in charge…

"Got that right. I came in to close out the drawer but a few customers showed up and I wound up staying. I should've been home an hour ago."

Liam frowned at the stack of receipts in his brother's hand. "What are you trying to do?"

"Get the damn drawer open again. I took these out to make some change and forgot to put them back in. I hate these machines."

Liam watched with no small amount of amusement while Brad's hammer hand punched at the keys, every beep sounding angrier than the one before it.

"Where's Chance? Thought he was supposed to be back already." The thrill-seeker of the family, Chance had gone on a big climb at Long's Peak over the weekend.

"Who the hell knows. Dooley said Chance texted to say he needed a few more days. Still hasn't shown his face."

"So call him and tell him to get his ass home now. It's branding time. He knows better than to be taking off at this time of year."

Brad continued to mutter to himself as he fought with the register, losing patience enough to smack the machine once before he resumed stabbing at the keys.

"I mentioned it but Zane doesn't want to set Chance off. At this rate, by the time he gets here we'll be done."

But not without Brad, Zane and everyone else taking up the slack Chance left by not being around.

Liam removed his hat and rubbed the heel of his palm over his eye, swearing silently.

The youngest adopted McKenna brother was a free spirit and extreme adventurer. Rock climbing, white-water rafting… For as long as Liam had known Chance, he was pulling stunts, risking everything for a rush. Zane equated Chance to cowboys of the Old West, always needing something to fire up his blood and remind him he was alive.

But Chance was also a shrewd businessman and bookkeeper with a head for money. His acuity had played a huge role in giving the ranch a stable financial base, not to mention making the store a success. That all meant as a family they cut him a lot of slack whenever the sudden urge to take off and go adventuring struck. The only thing that kept the rest of their tempers in check was the fact that Chance worked harder when he was in town than most men did all year. So they knew not to tie him down too much or else they'd risk him potentially tossing in the towel and making his adventures a permanent pursuit.

If that happened, they'd be up the creek. Not only because the feed-and-tack store supplemented the ranch's income during the downside of its annual cycle, but also because Chance's ease with the customers kept the cash register ringing. "He's usually careful about when and how long he's gone so this doesn't happen."

"I don't care. I'm going to kick his ass for not being here." Brad smacked the machine again. "How the hell do you open this thing?"

"The red one," Liam said. "Bottom button on the right."

Brad punched it several times in rapid succession and the machine blared out a beep loud enough to rival Liam's siren.

Brad's muttering had Liam smiling, glad he'd stopped in for the comic relief if nothing else.

"Can you get off work tomorrow?"

Brad wasn't the only one who didn't like working the store. "Nope. Sheriff's out of town. This is all you, big brother. You want help? Call Chance."

"If you're not here to help me close, why the visit?" Brad asked, sounding like a grumpy bear.

"I want to talk to you about Charlie."

"What about him?"

Liam watched Brad's face turned redder with his frustration. "For the love of— Move over."

Brad quickly got the drawer open.

"Great. Now tally it for the day. I'll post a sign that we're closed until Monday due to branding and a baby delivery. It's only a couple of days."

Liam shook his head but didn't argue the logic. There was barely an hour left to be open now. Fridays and half-day Saturdays were fairly busy days but little could be done about it. Brad was needed at the ranch. Everyone knew how hectic things got this time of year.

Considering the added stress and importance of a birth among one of the McKenna employees, all would be forgiven. Still, it would be easier if Chance simply got his ass back to town and pitched in.

But at least this way Brad would be on the ranch as a buffer between Zane and whatever tall tale Charlie might be spouting. "Did Zane tell you Delmer caught Charlie shoplifting?"

"Say what?"

Liam glanced up and caught Brad's surprise. "Come on, after all these years working with drifters and cow-pokes, is it that hard for you to believe?"

Brad's green eyes were the color of ponderosa pine and presently filled with dubious speculation. "Guess old Charlie never struck me as a thief."

"Yeah, well, Delmer didn't press charges but I think Charlie needs to be watched over, seeing as how Zane set him up in the house."

Brad nodded his agreement, and Liam found himself breathing a sigh of relief. At least Brad was seeing the wisdom, even if Zane wasn't.

"What did he steal?"

"Does it matter?" Liam demanded.

"Suppose not but it still doesn't seem like something Charlie would do."

"You'll keep an eye on him, though?"

"Yeah, sure." Brad shifted his size-thirteen feet. "You available to help with branding?"

Branding a few calves wasn't a big deal. But branding a thousand, give or take? "I'll be there early but I have patrol later."

"Sounds good. Unless that's your excuse to patrol a certain redhead in town."

Liam swore when he lost track of what he was doing. What did Brad know about it? *How* did he know?

"She in some kind of trouble or are you finally taking notice?"

Taking notice? "How long have *you* taken notice?"

The question reeked of jealousy but Liam couldn't

help it. Brad wouldn't be a bad choice for a woman like Carly. He was a homebody, stable. Liam could easily picture the two of them with a half-dozen kids.

The thought didn't sit well.

"Just noticed. Saw her coming out of the bank last Saturday. She looked good. So?"

What, did Brad want to stand there and gossip like old women? "Carly was approved to be a foster mother," Liam said, going on to explain the story as briefly as possible. "She's in over her head and, until the sheriff gets back, I...said I'd help her out."

"Doing what?"

"Simple stuff. When I was over there she hadn't gotten it together enough to mow her grass or even take out the trash."

"So you're doing it for her?" Brad asked, his eyebrows raised high.

"The sheriff *ordered* us to keep an eye on her."

"Huh. Interesting."

"No, it's not *interesting*. She's the sheriff's *daughter*."

"And smokin' hot when she wants to be."

Liam hit the buttons with a little more force than was strictly necessary. Yeah, that she was. Keeping an eye on Carly was one thing, but now that he'd volunteered to help her he had to figure out a way of keeping his thoughts—and his hands—off her.

"You kiss her yet?"

He hesitated but knew it was no use. Adopted or not, Brad could read him too well. Maybe he would have some ideas on how to keep things professional? "Yeah."

"And?"

Liam shot Brad a look no red-blooded man could misinterpret. "*Smokin'* hot."

HALF AN HOUR LATER, the door to Carly's house opened before Liam had a chance to knock. Liam blinked, shocked at the sight of Mandy Blake Whatever-her-current-husband's-name-was on the other side.

"Oh, thank God. It's about time. Get in here." She reached out and grabbed Liam's arm, tugging him inside and shoving him toward the hall. "I didn't think you'd ever get here."

"What's going on? Stop shoving me, dammit." He turned when she dropped her grip but the sight of Mandy wasn't all that comforting. She'd been crying. Her makeup was smeared and something black was smudged on her cheek. And since everyone who had attended North Star Middle and High School knew Carly and Mandy hated each other's guts, what the hell was she doing here? Had she and Carly gotten into a fight? "What happened?"

"I don't have time to explain," Mandy told him, keeping her voice low but not holding back when it came to chocking her words full of exasperation. "I have to leave and go check on my daughter. I've left her alone too long as it is. Get in there and *do* something. Kyle said you've been sniffing around all week so tonight you can do that thing guys *do* and give Carly a shoulder to cry on."

Liam chose to ignore the "sniffing around" comment and focus on the order to comfort Carly. "Why does she need one? What did you do?" He listened closely but all he heard down the hall were soft thuds and mutters.

Mandy rolled her eyes. "Nothing. Look, she'll explain. Just don't leave her, okay? Not right now. I think I dumped more on her than she could handle because I didn't know." She took off for the door.

"Didn't know *what?*"

But she was already gone.

Determined to get to the bottom of whatever was going on, he turned on his heel and went in search of Carly. He followed the sound of mutters and entered the smaller of the two bedrooms. "Caroline?"

She looked up and gave him a smile so strained it reminded him of the time she'd studied the wrong chapter in science and got a C on a test right before a big dance she wanted to attend. "Hey."

He looked around the room. There was a box of toys and blankets on the floor, a half-empty trash bag and mounds of clothes stacked in front of her. Only one thing was missing. "Where's the kid?"

"Gone."

Gone?

She shoved a pile of clothes into a too-small drawer, pressing down on the stack to compress it. "Yep. Her caseworker called me at work and within fifteen minutes she was gone. Sierra's father took her in. But it's okay," she said, "because Abigail assured me that he passed the inspection. Of course, Abigail didn't do the inspection herself so who knows if the other caseworker actually *performed* an inspection but..."

Growling in frustration, she sat back long enough to survey her work and shoot him a dirty look. "Well?"

"Well what?"

"Aren't you going to say it? You know you want to."

Yeah, he wanted to say it. He wanted to tell her this reaction of hers was what he'd tried to help her avoid by trying to convince her to say no to fostering. He wanted to rant and lecture but he couldn't.

Because one glance at her face stated loud and clear that she was once again questioning the whole foster situation herself, and a comment from him might muck the results she was coming to.

Carly gave the clothes one final push, then slammed the drawer shut. "You're wondering about all this stuff, aren't you?"

"Among other things. Where did it come from?"

"Mandy gave it to me."

Mandy? Looking at the items tossed over the side of the crib, he noted the tags in the collars and the emblems on the pockets. That was some donation.

"It's ironic, huh? Before I had a kid and not enough stuff, now I have enough clothes to outfit a small classroom and no kid."

Irony wasn't what she was feeling in regard to Sierra or Mandy. "Get your shoes on and grab your purse and a jacket."

She didn't move. "Why?"

"Just do it."

"You're not Nike," she said, wrinkling her nose. "And I'm not in the mood to go anywhere."

"You'd rather stay here and stare at all this?" he asked, noticing more and more about the room Carly had obviously prepared to house a child. The furniture included a crib, dresser and a change table. White trim framed the walls that were painted a neutral light brown and sported kid-oriented pictures of a rodeo with horses and rodeo clowns. The sight of them sent a blast of resentment through him.

"Something wrong?"

He'd had a similar room once, one with nice things, pretty pictures. Until he'd screwed it all up. "No. You and Mandy friends again?"

"I wouldn't go that far."

He focused on her, rather than the past. "Mandy seemed concerned about you when she left."

That comment drew a wry laugh from Caroline. "Yeah, well, she's only being nice because— She apologized but I'm not sure if it was real. I'm not sure what to think. It's a long story."

With Mandy and Carly involved, it usually was. "So are you with me? I got the impression Mandy was coming back after she checked on her daughter."

Carly stiffened, her head tilted to one side as she contemplated the pair of miniature cowboy boots in her hands with a wistful expression that broke his heart. She put them in the bottom of the closet and shut the door.

"What are we waiting for?"

CHAPTER TWELVE

CARLY DIDN'T TALK much when he got her in his truck, so while she stared out the window and worried her lower lip with her teeth, he drove them through town and kept going.

Restless himself, he turned up the radio to fill the silence, leaving Carly to ponder the dilemma she faced. He knew what he wanted to say to her but he was afraid she'd dig in her heels and fight him on principle alone. He figured sometimes saying less really did mean more.

Almost at their destination, Carly suddenly straightened.

"Are we going to The Rock?"

The Rock was a boulder the size of a small building, located at the base of a mountain. Covered in peace signs, the names of rock bands, graffiti and initials and hearts, The Rock had once been the happening party spot before parents began allowing their underage kids to stay home and party—often supplying the alcohol themselves in some sort of twisted thinking that it was better for the kids to drink supervised instead of making the kids put forth an effort to get plastered and caught. Parents thought they were doing their kids a favor instead of encouraging them to bend the rules and setting them up to fail.

Regularly patrolled, Liam couldn't remember the last

time he'd busted up a party here. In town was a different story. "You been here lately?"

"Not since high school."

The truck bumped and bounced along the road until he guided the vehicle to the side and stopped. "Don't get out until I tell you to."

Carly shot him a quizzical look. "What? Why not?"

"Just don't." Liam got out and opened up the rear door of the extended cab, grabbing the duffel and the hard case he needed.

The few people who knew about his pastime were usually surprised by it. He wondered what Caroline would think. At the back of the truck, he quickly assembled the equipment, knowing the tailgate would keep Carly from seeing what he was doing. Once everything was ready, he moved to the passenger door and opened it. "Come take a look."

Caroline wore her troubles on her face as she slid out of the truck. She hugged her arms around herself and followed him.

"Liam, why are we here? Take a look at what? No one could've painted anything on that rock that hasn't been there before."

"We're not here to look at the artwork." He lifted his hand to indicate the sky, watching her so he'd see her reaction. "We're here for them."

THEM WERE LIGHTS. Not city lights, not stars, not planes, not anything she'd seen before but…lights. Small, bright and amazingly quick, they zigzagged across the sky at differing speeds. "Holy cow. What *are* those things?"

"I have no idea. But they're fun to watch," Liam said, his teeth flashing as he smiled at her.

"You've seen them before?" she asked, moving closer to him because, while she wasn't a believer in aliens of the green and freaky kind, the lights above were unlike anything she'd ever seen or heard of and were, well, *freaky*.

"You spend enough time outdoors and you see a lot of things you can't quite explain."

She couldn't help but gape. It was so *weird*. Montana had always been known as big sky country but something like this had never factored into her understanding of that description. She watched Liam lower the tailgate of the truck and lift the telescope into the bed before he retrieved one rolled sleeping bag and foam pad from the backseat. While he made them a comfortable place to hang out, she stared up at the lights.

Whatever those things were up there, it hammered home the fact how small a role she and everyone else played on earth.

This thing with Mandy... Why was Carly letting something as juvenile as Mandy's behavior fifteen years ago or her mother's abandonment get to her now? Why was Carly doubting everything she'd been so convinced she wanted—no, was *destined*—to do?

"Need help?"

Help? Oh. He wanted her to climb up and look at the sky. With him. On a sleeping bag. There was a time when she wouldn't have considered it but now a part of her felt reckless and needy, and sitting beneath the stars with Liam appealed way more that it should. They were friends, so what was the harm? "I thought you were more into science."

"I'm into anything that interests me," he said simply.

Did that include her?

To distract herself from pretty much everything, including memories of *the kiss* outside the theater, Carly turned her back to the tailgate and used her palms to try and do one of those jump-push moves. It didn't work. The truck was too high and her upper-body strength sucked.

And with Liam watching her attempts?

Carly's cheeks heated with a blush and she was thankful it was too dark for him to see. "Help?"

His hands settled on her waist and he lifted her as though she weighed nothing. But that wasn't the most startling thing to happen.

No, finding herself seated above him with his chest suddenly wedged between her knees sent her pulse skittering out of control. "Thanks."

"Take a look in the eyepiece and tell me that's not cool."

She did as ordered, gasping softly at what she saw. *"Wow."*

"Yeah," he said softly. "You had a bad day."

"Understatement of the year."

"But, if you take a deep breath and look up, you can lose yourself. All the cares and worries in the world slip away."

Maybe it was his voice. Maybe it was the yearning she felt inside her to experience what Liam described, but she was taken off guard when her pulse slowed its pace and became a low throb in her ears. The breeze rustled the limbs of the newly greened trees, whistling softly, soothing.

While Liam made himself comfortable on the sleeping bag beside her, she stared through the lens at the mastery above her, the sky bigger and broader, the stars brighter than she had appreciated before, and the stress of the day fell away exactly the way Liam said it would.

Sierra would be okay. Somehow. She was with her father. Abigail said the man hadn't known he was listed on Sierra's birth certificate but that he'd immediately shouldered the responsibility of being a dad. That said something about a man, right?

"See what I mean?" Liam made a few adjustments to the telescope. "Okay, now look. There's Pegasus up close. And if you look a little lower... See those faint stars? That's Lacerta."

The night sky demanded respect. They starred the atmosphere with reverence because of the power and glory it was.

"What do you think? Glad you came?"

A shiver racked her but it wasn't because of the chill of the cool spring air but the gravelly sound of Liam's voice. They didn't have to speak softly. No one was around for miles. And he didn't have to stay so close but he did. She liked it. "Yeah, I'm glad I came with you."

Because she was. She'd needed this in the worst way.

Carly pulled away from the eyepiece and stared at Liam, confused by her feelings, confused by his behavior. Maybe he'd asked her to join him tonight only to distract her from Sierra being taken out of her care today. But to share this?

She got the distinct impression he didn't show many people this side of himself, and the fact he was willing to let her see it touched her deeply. Liam wasn't only the boy she'd known in high school or one of her father's deputies. He was a man more tender and caring and special than he let on, all because of what the world had done to him.

"Look at that thing go."

Jerked out of her thoughts, she focused on the sky and where Liam pointed, her mouth open in awe as one of the unusual lights zipped across the dark expanse from one end to the other before racing halfway back again in a split second. "That's so weird."

Liam's chuckle sent another shiver through her because of the way his breath hit her ear. "Yeah, it is. But you're not worried about Mandy anymore, are you?"

His low voice and soft drawl had her watching his mouth, remembering the kiss...

"Caroline?"

"Huh? Oh. No. No, not at all. Being beamed into space, on the other hand," she quipped, liking the way his eyes sparkled in the light of the moon and stars. Her thoughts were going haywire as she fought to focus on facts, to steer clear of kisses and lips and gravelly voices that made her skin tingle. "Liam? Um, I was wondering, if you like science and astronomy so much, why become a cop?"

CARLY'S QUESTION SENT a spike of unease through Liam. Why a cop? How could he explain wanting to be something totally opposite of what he was? Where he'd come from?

Now that the kid was gone and Carly had had some time to think and experience the drama of returning a child into the system, should he talk more about his past? Hope it got her to see what she was doing? Maybe if he did, she wouldn't put herself through this again.

"My dad always said he was born a cop. When I was

little and he didn't know any girl games, he used to give me his handcuffs and we'd play cop. I always got my man."

Now, that was funny. He could see Jonas making his baby girl happy by allowing her to handcuff him and Carly forgetting where she'd left the key. He'd bet good money it had happened more than once. "I played cops and robbers with the kids in the home."

The memories of his past had him leaving the telescope. He stretched out and watched Caroline as she moved the instrument this way and that. After a few minutes she tired of that and sat beside him, her legs crossed.

"Were you always the cop?"

"Not quite. I was always the robber who got away with whatever I'd done because I could run faster." Sometimes, it felt as though he was still running, too. He just didn't know to where.

"Oh, *really?* Does Dad know this about you?"

"I was a kid. I didn't know any better." He could feel Carly's gaze on him and knew he'd said too much.

"Why didn't you know any better?"

She shivered in the cool night air and he shifted until he could lift the edge of the unzipped sleeping bag for her to pull around her shoulders. Doing so required that she scoot closer to him.

"My dad took off after I was born. I never knew the man. The only references my mother ever made to him were that he was a lying sack of manure who never paid child support. Then again, she had a lot of other men in her life who possessed the same qualities so…she could've been talking about them, as well."

She turned toward him and her knee rested against

his thigh. "What happened to her? Why were you up for adoption? You don't have to tell me. But if you do, I won't repeat it. You have my word."

She meant it, too. He stared into her glimmering eyes and earnest expression and knew his history would be safe with her. It wouldn't be bantered about town as fodder for the gossip mill.

"My mother was always on the lookout for the next love of her life. What she really wanted was someone to party with, but to her they were the same thing. After my father left, one of the men she was involved with got her doing more than shots on a weekend out and C.S. got involved."

"I'm sorry. No kid wants to be taken away from their mother."

Or left behind. She didn't say it but he knew she was thinking it.

"No, I didn't, and when it was all said and done, she cleaned up her act and even married one of the losers. They had a kid. I was with them for a while but they split up…."

"And?"

"And I was seven when she left me alone with a one-year-old. She totaled her car driving home, the cops came and we were both taken to Children's Services. That was my second time."

"How long?"

"Three months. She kept her act together three months, convinced the officials she was okay. But the last time…my mother decided *I* was the root of her issues with my half-brother's father, and if I were out of the picture everything would be fine."

"Liam." Carly lay a hand on his chest, her head shak-

ing slowly back and forth in stunned disbelief. When that wasn't enough, she lowered herself to his side and wrapped her arms around him, her head on his chest.

"Caroline, don't be upset."

"Shut up. I want to hug you and you need a hug so just shut up and let me."

What he needed was to vault over the side of the truck and put some distance between them. He'd known coming here was a bad idea. But he also knew he couldn't stay at her house and they couldn't be seen in town together without causing more talk. Some people had nothing better to do than to stare out their windows and gossip about their neighbors, and he didn't doubt Carly's neighbors were doing plenty of that already.

But he also didn't want her pity or for her to look at him the way she was right now. All he wanted was for her to see that, having been one of those kids, he understood more than she thought he did.

When she didn't let go, when she buried her freckled nose in his chest and snuggled closer and when she shivered from the cold, he couldn't stop himself from reaching out and wrapping his arms around her. Hesitant, he lowered his face into her hair and breathed deep.

"What happened next?"

CHAPTER THIRTEEN

LIAM DIDN'T WANT to relive the past, not now. He wanted to freeze time, this night, this moment.

"Liam?"

It took him a while to answer. "She signed over her parental rights allowing me to be adopted."

"And your brother?"

"He was the chosen one. She kept him," he said, liking that Carly wasn't looking at him when he admitted his mother had chosen his stepfather and brother over her firstborn.

Seconds ticked by, the silence nearly more than he could bear. He didn't want to be the dream-crusher crying foul on Carly's plans but some of those kids she wanted to help were angry and they had reason to be. *He* had reason to be.

"What happened to you?" she asked, her voice husky with bottled anger.

The hint of emotion got to him, made him hold her a little tighter. "Foster care. The good homes only made the bad ones seem all that much worse."

"So that's why." She swallowed audibly, her hand rubbing across his chest once, twice. The third time she did, Liam captured it and held it in his. He brought their clasped hands to his mouth, his lips against her cold fingers. He didn't allow himself to kiss her, though.

"That's why you're so upset with me. Do you think I'll give them a good home and—and make them feel worse?"

He knew she would. That was why he protested. But there was also more to his protest. "You're missing the point. Caroline, I was a pain in the ass. It's the only way to describe me, my attitude. My actions toward the people trying to help me."

"So? Who wouldn't react to all you'd been through?"

"You're not getting it," he said, frustrated because she was taking what he said personally rather than laying blame where it was deserved. "The caseworkers would put me in a decent home and *I'd* push back ten times harder. I pushed at the foster parents until I got *sent* back. Every damn time," he whispered, wondering how he wound up muttering the words against her forehead, her cheek. "Now that I'm an adult, I can see what I did to those people and I don't want that for you."

Carly raised herself onto an elbow beside him, her weight on his chest, her mouth too close. "I don't want it, either. But if you can tell me you did it, why not tell me how to keep that from happening to me? Why not help me so I can counter that fear in the kids I foster?"

"Because you can't. I did what I did because I knew there would be a point when they would get fed up or tired or bored and send me back anyway. If I pushed, I was in control. Me, not them. Do you really want to be on the receiving end of that?"

"What did you do? How did you push?"

Leaning over him the way she was, Liam let his fingers drift over her soft cheek once more. Her skin was like velvet, her lips cherry-red.

He focused on the words that would drive her away. "I almost killed a kid."

Her shocked inhalation spiked his anger. Dammit, he didn't want to get into the gory details. He'd wanted to distract her, make her feel better, get her to back off the whole foster-mommy thing. But not like this.

"Tell me."

"There was a concert in Helena. I wanted to go but was told I couldn't. That was mistake number one, telling a hotheaded kid he couldn't do something. So I decided to sneak out of the house and bullied another foster kid, Deacon, into going with me. On the way home, we cut across the highway. We saw this car coming slow but didn't think anything of it. We still crossed. Then the guy swerved and hit Deacon."

Her body sagged against his. "That's not your fault."

"Of course it is. I disobeyed orders, I bullied the kid and the accident nearly killed him. We landed at the boys' home again because of what I'd done. The couple had talked about adopting us and it was a decent home. The guy had a heating-and-air business and he needed cheap help more than anything but it would have been okay. One stupid decision on my part cost us both a family and it nearly cost Deacon his life."

"He made the decision to go."

"To this day, he has to walk with a cane. He didn't want to go, didn't even like that style of music. I threatened him. Called him a coward and a chicken and said I'd get him into trouble until he finally agreed to go."

"You were a teenage boy *being* a teenage boy." Carly lowered herself again to rest on top of him, her hands on his chest.

"Stop." He sucked in a breath. His body reacted instantly to the warmth and hollows of hers. "I'm not some poor sucker with a bad life. I knew what I was doing."

"I disagree. Teenage boys don't generally have that level of deep emotional thinking. You were reacting to what was happening around you—scared but afraid to show it," she said softly. "Truth or dare?"

"What?" He blinked at the change in subjects. "I'm not playing some stupid kid's game."

"Chicken?"

He froze at the taunt.

"Did you deliberately set out to hurt Deacon?"

Flat on his back, with her in his arms, the blood left his brain. Suddenly there was enough heat between the two of them to incinerate The Rock. "No."

"Did you shove him into the path of the car?"

Push her away. Load up and get back to town. Don't think about what you're thinking about.

"Fine. You're right. Not my fault."

"Smart man."

That said, she smiled into his face, stilling when she caught on to what he was thinking, feeling. And before Liam could push her away like his brain ordered him to do, she lowered her head the rest of the way, slowly, and pressed her lips to his, closing her eyes after they made contact and releasing the air from her lungs.

Maybe she meant it as a "good job, you agreed, we're just friends" kiss. But that's not how he received it. Even though his head said one thing, his body thought another, and Liam wrapped his arms around her and rolled until he was on top.

He leaned his weight on one arm and slid his free hand under her jacket and shirt, up along her ribs to the fullness of her breasts. He groaned when he made contact, squeezing until he couldn't stand it anymore and moved beneath her bra to be skin to skin.

"This isn't the place for this." Or the time. Or the woman.

"The aliens might be studying us," she whispered huskily, a throaty, nervous-sounding laugh in her throat. "Maybe for scientific research, we should show them how it's done?"

"One kiss wouldn't hurt." One kiss. He could do that. Stay in control.

Liam lowered his head and Carly parted her lips, letting him inside. She gripped his hair in her hands and before he knew how it happened, one kiss became deeper, longer, more passionate than any he'd ever experienced. It left him too weak to move away, too turned-on to stop.

Common sense tried to enter but with every swipe of her wicked little tongue in his mouth, Liam's mind shut down a little more. He worked hard, did good things for the town, deserved good things. And Carly was definitely good. Willing. *Hot.* She was kissing him, not ending with one kiss.

The moment his mind gave him permission to kiss her until she stopped him, all bets were off.

Liam tossed the top half of the sleeping bag aside and snagged the end of her shirt and jacket. Her jeans were next, the moonlight bright enough he could see the masses of freckles on her pale skin and the starkness of Carly's matching black lace underwear. "Do you always wear things like that?"

"They make me feel sexy."

She didn't need anything to be sexy. "Any sexier and I'd keel over now."

Unable to help himself, he let his hand cover the areas in question.

Her husky moan filled his ears and set fire to his blood. She shoved herself up and tried to unbutton his shirt. Considering he was desperate to get her naked, his hands kept getting in her way but her clothes were disappearing as fast as he could make them.

"Wait! Protection?" she gasped against his mouth.

"Wallet." Because even though he hadn't needed a condom in forever, for some reason he'd found himself recently purchasing a box, just in case.

CARLY KNEW LIAM TRIED to go slow, tried to give her time and let her body adjust since it was a tight fit. But she was hot and achy and more than a little frantic herself, unable to hold back those little moans, sounds that seemed to urge Liam on, given his reaction of holding her head in his palms, kissing her and moving inside her until she couldn't breathe. All she could do was wrap her hands around his biceps and hold on.

Sensations took over and she got quiet, knowing Liam stared at her, watched her. She wasn't entirely comfortable knowing she was so visible with the moonlight bathing them both like a spotlight, but Liam was so beautiful she found herself unable to close her eyes as he made love to her, wanting to remember every stroke of his body, every kiss.

She arched her back, an intense and fiercely sensual strike of pleasure shooting through her out of nowhere but not quite enough. *"Liam."*

Wearing a seductive, totally masculine hint of a smile, Liam lowered his head and licked the tip of her breast, suckled her, still moving, holding her climax at bay, building the sensations in her until she couldn't stand it anymore.

Groaning softly, he kissed her, his tongue on hers as he matched his movements. His strokes quickened, harder, deeper, until pleasure suffused every nerve in her body and sent her zinging into the heavens above like the lights they'd come there to watch.

CHAPTER FOURTEEN

SHE'D HAD SEX with Liam.

Before her heart even had time to slow, the reality of the moment hit Carly. One kiss had turned into much more and she'd had sex, glorious, fantastic, make-me-scream sex.

With *Liam*.

"You okay?"

Liam's husky voice rolled over her senses, matching the gritty yet tender feel of his work-roughened hands. His body was still connected to hers, still deep inside, and even though common sense prevailed and she knew he had to make an exit, the darkness of the night, the warmth of his body and the stars overhead, made her wrap her arms around his neck and not let go. "Just a second more," she said, knowing he'd understand the request, because he seemed to understand her moods better than she did at times. More than anything? She didn't want to face him yet and, with his head buried in her neck and his body over hers, she felt...safe.

Liam's arms bulged as he hugged her. Carly shifted until she could feel the thickness of his biceps, her thumb and fingers not even coming close to meeting. She turned her head and rubbed her cheek against the surprisingly velvety feel of his inner arm, the muscle tensing even more against her face when she pressed a kiss to his skin. In response, she felt him flex inside her.

"Caroline."

She'd always hated her name. It was too old-fashioned, too hokey and very grandma-ish. But when Liam said it like that, she actually liked it. He made her name, he made *her,* feel like the sexiest, most beautiful woman on earth. If only the panic inside her wasn't bubbling up and trying to choke her. What had she done?

Liam pressed a lingering kiss to her lips before locking his arms straight and shoving himself away from her. With efficient discretion, he took care of the condom to dispose of later, but nothing could hide the frown on his face.

Pain hit her. As surprised and confused as she was, it hurt to see that Liam regretted what they'd done already. Couldn't he have waited a little longer? And how could she be hurt that he regretted it when she felt the same way? "Don't look like that. It's okay." Because if they both regretted it, well… No one would get hurt and tonight could go down in history as the best sex she'd ever had. Period.

He closed his eyes briefly. "Jonas trusted me to look after you."

Carly sat up beside him, her body achy, empty. Satiated and yet hungry for more. But only because it was him. Somehow, on some elemental, feminine level, she felt as though she should have known it would be this way. That kiss in town…

Why Liam? Why now, after all these years of knowing him and never thinking of him as more than a very handsome friend? "And you did," she heard herself quip, "very, *very* well."

She tried to sound casual, sophisticated.

The feeling she had nothing to lose and everything to gain was strong within her. She slid her arm around his shoulders, shifting until her legs were draped over his lap.

With a growl, Liam snagged her by the waist and pulled her the rest of the way. "You know as well as I do that this is a mistake. Carly—"

"I like it when you call me Caroline."

"Caroline," he said, exhaling, "we shouldn't have done this."

"But we already did," she whispered, "which means it's okay if we do it again."

"You don't mean that."

"I do. One kiss, one night. Then everything goes back to normal because—" this took a deep breath to get through "—we both know we'd never make it as a couple."

In that instant she got a split-second flash-forward image of getting involved with Liam, then opening the door one day to find her father on the other side in official mode telling her something bad had happened.

No, she couldn't go there. Maybe in one sense her biological mother was right. Lea Taggert had used Carly's father's profession as an excuse for her abandonment of them but in reality the law-enforcement profession *was* an issue for Carly. The constant worry. The danger. She didn't want to live in fear, always wondering if some idiot would pull a gun or something.

She and Liam had long passed the point of should-we or shouldn't-we. But they were adults. Maybe it was true that Liam wanted no ties, whereas all her life she wanted to be anchored so deeply to town, to family, that nothing could pull her away like whatever had allowed her mother to walk out the door and abandon them so easily. Still, that was neither here nor there.

Right here? Right now?

She felt safe and secure in Liam's arms. She wanted him despite his profession, despite his brooding, despite everything tomorrow would bring. She wanted him. No one else.

"Your father will skin me if he finds out about this."

"So don't tell him." She nuzzled her face into his neck, drawn to the musky scent of his skin. "I'm a big girl, Liam. I don't normally do this type of thing but... I'm not sorry I did."

He sucked in a harsh breath when she pressed her mouth to his, and she was fascinated by the way his eyes darkened and glittered with sexual hunger when their tongues melded together. It was cold, the temperature dropping little by little. It didn't matter. Not when she could press her bare breasts against his chest to warm them, when his hands slid up her back and his arms were so engulfing and so hot she was encased in perfect heat.

And even though she told herself to retreat and let things end now, she couldn't.

She needed to be with him again, to know the power of physical desire combined with caring and tenderness. Because even at the age of twenty-seven, she'd never experienced this feeling, this rush of want and need and tenderness. It was heady. It was powerful.

Because it felt so special and that was the most frightening thing of all. One kiss and she wanted more from a man who—based on what he had told her of his life— was too afraid to care for anyone. But denying this moment wouldn't change things between them. They'd been friends since day one of their freshmen year in high school. More than acquaintances, but never really close. Simply friends. Total strangers hooked up, friends shared more. Friends shared...*this*.

"God knows I should make you get dressed and take you home but..."

Carly shifted on the sleeping bag, Liam's hands helping to position her just so. "But I don't want to go." She brushed her mouth against his. "And you don't want me to, either."

THE NEXT MORNING, Liam arrived at the ranch house to start branding, even though he'd had only a few hours of sleep. At the end of the barn's aisle he saw a man in Major's stall, but it wasn't until he nearly reached them that Liam realized it was Charlie, not Zane, saddling the horse. "What are you doing? Major doesn't like strangers."

Charlie's hand stilled on the animal's back, then resumed his task. "Doesn't seem to be minding much."

Liam glared at the hired hand. "Where's Zane?"

"He's finishing up a call in the house." Charlie's gaze settled on Liam, surprisingly frank. "Any other questions, Deputy?"

"Yeah, there is. What's going on here? The truth."

"Zane's a decent man, so I'm trying to work to earn my keep," Charlie muttered, his gaze on the horse in front of him.

"The way you earned what you stole from Delmer Frank?"

Charlie's hand slowed and Liam felt a twinge of guilt when Charlie lowered his head. It was a low blow but one that had to be dealt with. Given Liam's mood after tossing and turning all night, getting to the bottom of Charlie's presence gave Liam the argument he needed to release a little steam.

"I'm not proud of that. Devil came over me and I started shoving food in my mouth. Never stole anything before."

"I find it hard to believe that was the first time."

"It was. God's truth."

Liam narrowed his gaze on Charlie. The man seemed to be genuinely sincere, but good liars lied well.

"There a problem here?" Zane called out from the entrance of the barn.

Not sure what to believe and only knowing his mood was as dark as Major's coat, Liam shook his head. "No. No problem."

"You got in late last night."

And Zane had apparently noticed. Who had noticed him dropping Carly off at her house last night? What if someone got suspicious? "I had some things to catch up on."

The least of which was figuring out what he was going to do now that he'd slept with the sheriff's daughter. He'd driven Carly home in virtual silence, the music on the radio covering the awkwardness he felt once he'd stopped thinking with his lower head.

He'd taken advantage, even though he hadn't intended to.

Carly had been upset last night and she'd wanted comfort he was only too ready to provide.

Giving her a shoulder to cry on was one thing. In the light of day, he knew she would rethink what happened and remember he wasn't the picket-fence type. He didn't doubt she would regret sleeping with him.

He'd had a hard time looking himself in the mirror this morning. Carly had been vulnerable, upset over Sierra. And he'd showed her the stars.

Working with Carly's father, seeing her at station functions—talk about screwing himself. He could lose his job over this. What then?

"Best not stand here all day. Let's get those branding fires going so we're ready when the others arrive."

CARLY HAD THOUGHT IT hard to concentrate with Sierra distracting her at work. Getting through *the day after sex with Liam* when all she could think about *was* sex with Liam? Nearly impossible.

The inability to concentrate ranked right up there with sugar highs, caffeine trips and family drama, all rolled into one.

She went for a walk on her lunch break in an attempt to clear her head but even the pretty day couldn't help her regain focus. Throughout the afternoon, she made numerous typos on contracts and forms and legal briefs, and it took her twice the usual time because of having to double-check and repair everything.

Finally five o'clock rolled around. And because she was determined to hold her head high and let Liam make the next move—if there *was* a next move—she decided to go to her Thursday-night book-club meeting at the library as scheduled. Not that she'd had time to finish the book, given how busy she'd been the past few days.

Getting out of her car, she pressed the button to lock the doors and listened for the beep before clutching

the unread book to her chest to make her way into the
building. The moment she stepped over the threshold,
the smell of old books, coffee and fresh pastry hit her.
Yeah, getting through the evening without at least one
doughnut was going to be an issue.

"Carly? I thought that was you."

Carly turned to find her client Dave giving her a
slow, totally creepy once-over from his position beside
the copy machine. "It's me. Hi, Dave."

His bald spot gleamed beneath the overhead lights,
the little hairs that remained sticking up like the last
weeds of summer blowing in the breeze of fall. Didn't
guys get that it was just better to shave them off? Bald
was way better than looking like one of those ceramic
heads with grass growing out the top.

"I didn't know you belonged to the group. You
weren't at the last meeting."

"No, I didn't make it." And she seriously doubted
Dave had read this month's selection. The book was all
over the bestseller lists but a total chick-book and not
Dave's he-man-beat-my-chest-and-eat-raw-meat type
of thing.

"Well, it's good that you're here. I suppose you heard
the news?"

"News?" she asked, wishing she'd gone home,
changed clothes and worked in her yard, since Liam
couldn't be bothered with calling her. They'd had sex—
twice!—and he didn't *call?* There were names for guys
like that but she wouldn't have thought Liam would be
one of them.

*You said it was for one night and didn't speak to him
all the way home. Why would he call?*

"Kate filed for divorce today. I'm a single man, see?"

he bragged, lifting his left hand sans the wedding ring he wore only when it suited him. "So I thought, what am I waiting for? Here I am."

It took everything in her not to burst out laughing. Yeah, there he was.

Dave could be a fairly decent guy on occasion, but he was in the midst of a midlife crisis and Carly couldn't blame Kate for bailing out. No wife should have to put up with wandering eyes. "Well, I hope you enjoy your bachelorhood."

"You want to sit together?" He leaned closer to her, smiling as though sharing a secret. "I didn't read the book. Couldn't get past the first page. You probably did, though, right? I'll bet you stayed up late to finish it."

She wondered what Dave would think if she told him what she had been doing last night. "Actually, I just remembered something I have to do before work tomorrow. I'm sorry but I need to go."

"Need some help? I could come with you."

In your dreams. Dave needed to get a clue. And stop staring at her boobs.

As a teenager, she'd wondered if she'd ever have enough up top to attract a man's attention but she'd since learned the fact she possessed breasts at all was enough for some men—like Dave. "Thanks, but no. Enjoy the evening."

Before he could come up with another excuse, Carly fled the library, checking to make sure he didn't follow her to her car.

To fill the time—because she really didn't want to go home and stare at the walls of her empty house without something to soothe her—she stopped by the grocery store and stocked up on emergency ice cream.

The phone was ringing as she unlocked the door and she raced to answer it. *Don't sound too eager.* "Hello?"

"Hey, sweetheart."

Carly tossed the bag onto the counter, kicking herself for the shaft of disappointment that shot through her. Every single time the phone rang at work today her heart had jumped into her throat. Now this?

She really had to stop and reevaluate. "Hi, Dad. How's the trip? Are you and Rissa having fun?"

"It's beautiful. I'm glad you two ganged up on me and made me come. Wish you were here to see it. Rissa said to tell you hi."

She smiled despite her mood. "Tell her hello back."

"Something wrong? You sound funny."

"Nope," she said, putting her purse away on the desk and sorting through her mail. "Must be the connection." And the letdown she felt because Liam wasn't the man she'd thought him to be.

"You're sure?"

"Positive. Please tell me you didn't call me to worry?"

She heard him release a gusty, telling sigh.

"No, I didn't," he said, amusement in his voice. "I called to check on you and see how things were going. Did you fix lunch for the guys?"

He would have to ask that. "I didn't, actually. Something came up but I'll make it up to the men this Sunday."

As soon as the words were out of her mouth, she winced at the thought. Last night was a one-night thing. A product of the moon and stars and whatever those little lights were in the sky. After nearly twenty-four hours of silence, she got the message that Liam wasn't interested. Loud and clear. And neither was she, not given his profession. Talk about worry. But she'd have to figure out how to handle seeing him now because in a town the size of North Star and considering Liam worked at the station with her father, there was no way to avoid him.

You couldn't have thought of that last night?

Over the phone line, she heard a loud knock and a muffled call.

"That's room service. Hang on."

She knew an out when she heard one. "No, Dad, I need to go. My groceries are melting. Go answer the door and you and Rissa have fun, okay? I love you and I'll see you when you get back."

"I love you, too. Yeah, put it over there, thanks. Carly—"

"Bye, Dad! Enjoy your trip!" Biting her lip and grimacing at her wholly fake enthusiasm, Carly hung up on her father and stared at the portable phone several seconds after setting it down. "I'm probably going to regret that."

She put the groceries away but held on to the container of ice cream, her hand hesitating over the lid. "It'll go to your hips."

But she had to do something. Eat. Clean.

Why hadn't he called? Even to say "hey, it was fun"?

Determined, she shoved the carton into her freezer and headed down the hall. Liam wanted to act as though nothing had happened?

Fine. She could do that, too—without scarfing down enough ice cream to serve a family of four.

Last night she'd let passion and chemistry get in the way of common sense and she wasn't going to do it again. Liam wasn't the guy for her. He was a cop, his hours sucked, he didn't like her taking in foster kids. They wouldn't work because the saying about opposites wasn't true. Who wanted to fight over everything? No, it would be best to call it a fun night and leave things at that.

So *why* was she freaking out over not hearing from him?

It didn't take a genius to figure out that Liam was afraid of relationships due to his past. Parents could really do a number on their kids, and his issues about his mother's abandonment were radically apparent to someone who had them herself.

Which brought up another barrier. How would things work between them when neither of them trusted one hundred percent?

Liam might try to fool himself and say Zane and the others weren't his family but anyone with eyes could see they were. Liam was in denial. No other word for it. He tried to keep a wall between him and hurt.

What kind of relationship could they have with him acting that way, while she tried to figure out if she was mother material? Disaster with a capital *D,* that's what.

She'd even say he was afraid to want things like a real relationship or *love* because he was too scared it wouldn't last.

What had he said about pushing his foster parents away? About being a good cop because he had no familial ties? Her heart broke for the boy he'd been, but he was an adult now. He had to realize he couldn't shut everyone out completely, and last night she'd watched the roadblocks going up on the silent drive home.

Knowing what she did about Liam and yet choosing to ignore it made her less than intelligent on the man-scale. To be smart about it meant cutting all ties and forgetting last night ever happened.

So there—that was her choice.

Carly showered and put on her pajamas, leaving the lights off but turning on the television and inserting her favorite movie into the DVD player.

She might not be a psychiatrist but she knew certain things. A deciding factor in becoming a foster parent had been her need to overcome her past. To turn a bad thing into a good one and move forward.

Being with a man who couldn't deal with his own past wasn't moving forward.

Still, in the dark of her bedroom, she couldn't bring herself to walk away. Liam was...more than a one-night stand. More than a high-school friend. He was a good man. Was she going to sit back and let him call the shots? Or was she going to prove to him that, while they'd had sex and maybe were destined to be only friends, it didn't mean she didn't care about him.

Because last night proved to her she did.

CHAPTER FIFTEEN

LIAM SPENT THE ENTIRE MORNING helping to brand the last of the calves.

Brad and his crew had spent the past week herding the calves in from the open range. It took Brad, Zane and the rest of the hands plus neighbors to get the massive job done. They worked steadily and, although it was back-breaking labor, they managed to finish around noon.

The neighbors who had shown up to help drifted away, heading to their own ranches to catch up on the chores they'd ignored to pitch in at the Circle M. It was unspoken but understood that when their branding took place, the favor would be returned.

Liam had to head out, too. But first he needed coffee and a big dose of it. A little lunch wouldn't hurt, either.

"Look who's here," Brad muttered under his breath as they were packing up the supplies and tools about an hour and a half after the last calf had been released.

Liam turned to follow his adopted brother's gaze and found Chance surveying what remained of the portable pens.

Not a man on the ranch wasn't tired, filthy and wearing a day's work, except Chance. And from the sound of Brad's tone, he wasn't going to let Chance forget it.

Brad packed up the supply of vaccinations, syringes

and fly tags they'd used. Closing the container of meds, he grabbed it, causing the plastic and glass bottles inside to bump together. The sound drew Chance's attention.

Chance headed toward them but Brad turned on his heel and stalked to the oversize metal building used more often than the old-fashioned barns closer to the house.

With a nod of welcome, Liam grabbed the last of the containers and prepared to follow.

"Hey. How did it, uh, go?" Chance asked when he got close.

"Twelve-twenty-three," Liam said, giving him the total number of calves moved through the pens in the past two and a half days.

Liam watched as Chance slid a sheepish glance into the depths of the building.

"Sorry I didn't make it. Something came up, otherwise I would've been here."

Brad exited in time to catch the last of Chance's statement, but he kept right on walking toward the house without a word.

"Man, I hate it when he gets like that," Chance said.

"Doesn't happen often—and never without reason." Liam couldn't help but jump to Brad's defense. Chance should have been there. That he'd chosen climbing a few rocks over his duty to the Circle M and Zane wasn't right. It wasn't right that everyone else had busted their guts in the mud and muck. That's what had Brad's boxers in a knot.

"I smell Zane's coffee from here," Chance said, obviously trying to make conversation.

Liam carted the container into the building and set it with the other one. "Zane needed it strong to get through a rough couple days." And because he had to, Liam added, "He could have used your help."

"I know. And I should've been here. Come on, Liam, you couldn't have been around that much with you filling in for the sheriff."

"All the more reason for your ass to be here." He headed for the house now, too. He needed a cup of the stomach-burning brew to face down Carly.

Chance swore, keeping pace with Liam. "I said I'm sorry."

"Tell that to Zane."

They'd reached the house and Liam opened the screen door.

"Tell me what?" Zane said the moment Chance stepped over the threshold. Zane stared at Chance a long moment, then nodded. "Welcome home, son. Whatever it is can wait. I'm tired and hungry and I don't intend to spend my lunch listening to you three mutter and complain."

Liam headed straight for the coffeepot. Now that he'd gotten his two cents in, he wasn't going to jump into this dogfight.

"I texted you, Chance," Brad said. "You knew we were branding but you didn't come home from wherever the hell you were. Now you show up? Bet your ass I'm going to complain."

"How did I know Dooley's wife would go into labor early?" Chance argued.

"Boys." Zane's fork clattered against his plate.

Liam moved toward the door. Skip eating—he'd get something in town.

"Where do you think you're going?" Zane demanded.

"The food's hot. Sit down and eat. Whatever it is can wait."

"Can't," Liam said, pausing because it gave him a chance to sip the too-hot brew. "I'm on duty tonight, and I have to shower and change."

"That," Brad said pointedly, "is what I mean. Liam knows that for calving, branding, haying and market seasons we need as many hands as we can get around here. He doesn't *plan a vacation in the middle of them.*"

"Boys, you're ruining my dinner and Charlie's, too," Zane growled. "Shut up or take it outside where I don't have to listen to you."

Once more, Liam headed toward the door. At the same time Brad turned from the stove with his loaded plate and, because it was a small kitchen with five grown men—Brad the biggest of them all—in it, Liam sidestepped to get out of the way. Chance moved, too, and Brad wound up knocking Chance off balance, into the old butcher block.

Brad ignored them all and continued on his way to the table but Chance caught Liam's attention when he cursed under his breath and paled, one hand braced on the waist-high wood block while the other wrapped around his ribs protectively.

Liam zeroed in on the move, and decided he had a few more minutes to stick around.

The kitchen chair creaked under Brad's tall frame when he shifted to get more comfortable, his back to Chance and his focus on the plate in front of him.

But Liam wasn't going to let Chance's reaction slide. "Broken or bruised?" Liam demanded, earning a wrathful glare from Chance when the query had all present turning toward him.

"I'm fine."

"Not quite believable when you say it through gritted teeth," Liam observed.

Brad swallowed a mouthful of food and swore, shaking his head.

"Not at the table," Zane ordered, the warning an old one they'd all learned to heed—or else they earned the punishment of shoveling manure and hauling rock.

"Sorry," Brad said, managing to look sincere.

"Answer the question," Zane continued. "You hurt?"

"Some bruised ribs, one broken. It's no big deal," Chance replied.

"It's big enough that while we work our asses off, you went missing," Brad said.

"I'm here now, aren't I?" Chance glared at his brother. "I came as soon as I could. The store will be open tomorrow."

"That's fine but you're not off the hook. You were hurt and holed up somewhere and we didn't even know about it," Zane grumbled, wagging a finger. "How bad's that bruise on your noggin?"

Chance looked down at the floor. "Concussion. Doc wouldn't release me to drive and I knew you all had your hands full. You didn't need to be worrying about me."

Zane went into lecture mode. Chance had it coming but Liam didn't have time to stick around, or the energy to dwell too long on Chance's preferred hobbies. The thought of him free-climbing thousands of feet into the air and getting hurt miles from medical care pissed them all off.

Liam, especially, since he could very well be one of the lawmen pulled from his patrol to aid in a rescue effort, which meant precious resources wasted on someone smart enough to know better.

Carly's words swirled in his brain as Liam lifted his hand in a silent goodbye to no one in particular and headed out the door.

Carly had blamed his past for his views on family but what was Chance running from whenever he pitted himself against a sheer rock face with no ropes? Why did Brad ride off into the open range after a bad day, and why did Zane keep the entire house plastered with pictures of a daughter he never talked to?

They all had their reasons—and their demons.

The sooner Carly understood that and stopped trying to get Liam to open up and share his feelings as though he was a guest on one of those talk shows, the better.

When Liam arrived at Carly's house much later that night, the lights were off, her car nowhere to be seen—probably parked in the garage.

Liam sat outside like a damned stalker, hating himself for being such a coward. What should he do? Go? Stay? Did it even matter now that twenty-four hours had passed and he hadn't even picked up the phone to call?

He put his cruiser in gear, imagining he could smell the scent of her perfume in the air, on the seats.

He hadn't intended to not call. He'd planned to drop by her business once the branding wrapped up. But all of that had taken longer than he'd anticipated and he'd barely made it to the station in time to start his shift. Then a routine traffic stop outside town had turned into an involved drug bust that needed processing.

He'd resumed his regular patrol and noticed Carly's car parked outside the library. He'd paused long enough to see her through the window, chatting up some ass who couldn't stop staring at her breasts, his thoughts visible on his sleazeball face.

Liam had circled town and when he passed the library again, Carly—and the sleazeball—were nowhere to be seen.

It was none of Liam's business what she did with that guy from the library.

Not when he hadn't called her, hadn't connected after sleeping with her. If she found someone else, it was just as well.

Carly wanted too much. House, kids. Hell, she probably even wanted a minivan instead of the small SUV she drove. And she'd made it clear she didn't want a cop for a lifetime. So what could they have but one night as she'd said?

She'd be better off without him. He couldn't be with her and not want the things she wanted. It wasn't right. And he couldn't keep her from having what she wanted because if he did, she'd be miserable and she'd blame and resent him. From the sound of things, that's what had happened between her mother and father. Liam didn't want to repeat the past. Carly didn't deserve that. No one did.

Growling to himself, Liam let off the brake and got the SUV moving.

Some things couldn't be undone.

All he could hope for was that Carly would forgive him eventually.

CHAPTER SIXTEEN

CARLY THREW HERSELF into work the next day, making up for the delays and mistakes of yesterday. It was Friday, the end of a long, *long* week and she had plans for the evening—a birthday party for one of her friends.

As far as hearing from Liam...nothing.

So what did sitting outside her house in the middle of the night *mean?*

She'd almost missed him. She'd dozed off somewhere in the middle of the movie, but woke up at the sound of an engine outside. Hoping against hope, she'd jumped out of bed in time to see the briefly lit image of Liam's face before he drove off into the night.

But he'd come to her house. Come to her. Even if he hadn't come inside or called.

Not calling him and asking him to come back had almost driven her insane. Then again she'd have to have his cell number, and calling the station to get it would raise way too many questions.

But she'd considered it.

Which was simply more reason to believe she'd gone over the edge. Sleeping with Liam when he wasn't the guy for her wasn't a smart move. All the old reasons for not being with him still stood, but now she'd thought of a few more. Such as how he was...hard when she wanted soft.

The second that thought registered in her mind, Carly stopped brushing shadow into the crease of her eye and groaned.

What a thing to think. She liked Liam's hardness. Every, um—yeah. That wasn't what she meant. At all. What she *meant* was that he lived out on the Mc-Kenna ranch when she was an in-town girl who liked those conveniences. She wanted picket fences and quiet neighborhoods, whereas he spent his days driving Montana's highways and back roads, looking for danger. She couldn't help but see that preference as yet another way Liam avoided making emotional connections.

Again, not her type. She was a smart girl. She needed to chalk the experience up to a learning one and *deal*.

Her father had always told her to look at the facts. So…fact: she and Liam had little to nothing in common except that he was a deputy and she was used to that sort of thing. Maybe that was the draw? That he was familiar?

She grabbed her blush brush and fluffed it over her cheekbones. Next up, eyeliner. Smoky eyes were a must. She was pulling out all the stops for her night on the town because nothing was going to hold her back.

That done, she scanned her handful of lipsticks and chose the perfect shade.

Familiarity was *not* the reason. She wouldn't lie to herself. If anything, that sense of sameness knocked her off kilter because of how sticky the situation could become if her father found out she and Liam had seen each other *nekkid*.

No, familiarity was a whole other reason sleeping with Liam was a colossal mistake rather than one of the reasons she was drawn to him.

Smoothing gloss over the lipstick, she pursed her lips and made a kiss face in the mirror. *Kiss off, McKenna.*

Fact: she wanted a nice guy. One who *called* after sex. Not someone who labeled one of the most amazing experiences of her life a mistake.

But coming by her house...*that* meant something, didn't it? Maybe Liam simply wasn't ready to admit it yet?

Air huffed out of her chest when Carly realized how badly she wanted it to be true. Now that she knew a bit of his background and childhood, how could she blame him for panicking?

You've gone off the deep end, making excuses. He didn't call. Face that fact!

But he wanted to see her, otherwise he wouldn't have been outside her house. He wouldn't care who she dated. None of her father's other deputies were as interested in her love life as Liam.

She smoothed the frown lines on her forehead and stared into her eyes in the mirror.

Fact: sex meant something to her, more than physical release. Sex was personal, intimate, and not to be shared with any guy who came along, which meant she *had* to own up to Liam not being just any guy. If she didn't like him, she wouldn't have slept with him. *Fact.*

But until she could get him to own up to his own feelings—

Hell-o, he's a guy and it was sex. How do you know it's more? How do you know you're not making it out to be more?

Her shoulders sagged a bit before she determinedly squared them again.

Call her crazy, but she knew.

She'd known him a long time, and he was not the type of guy who did something he regretted later. If anything he was overly cautious, siding with *not* doing those types of things.

So, the way she looked at it, a girl needed to know her strengths and her weaknesses. When to play defense and offense. That meant she had to stand up for herself and not let a man freaked out by his own feelings send her into a junk-food coma.

Instead, she mused, shoving her fingers into her hair to fluff it up, the post-sex-no-call woman needed to put on her dancing boots and go have some fun. See and be seen.

And her friend's birthday party at the Wild Honey was just the thing to get her over the no-call hump.

Is it? Or are you going because Liam might be there?

She fluffed her hair again, unable to shove the thought aside.

A run-in with him might mean having to somehow pretend the lack of post-sex contact meant nothing—if indeed their night meant nothing to him—*but* that was a risk she had to face because...

Fact: maybe she could overlook his profession. She didn't like it, but she *was* used to the life and if—she *had* to stand firm on this—he offered up a compromise regarding his take on kids, well, she might reveal the fact she would reconsider her stance on the cop thing.

What *would* she say when—if—she saw Liam tonight?

Enough already. Go. Dance. Have fun and enjoy the evening. Do you think he's driving himself nuts thinking about you?

Carly refused to contemplate that question and turned away from the mirror.

Fact: Liam's behavior was not going to keep her from having a good time. With him or without him.

But hopefully with him.

THIRTY MINUTES LATER, Carly shivered when the cool spring breeze blew under the hem of her dress. She wore one of the cute, thigh-length strappy dresses she'd picked up in Helena on a shopping spree paired with a jean jacket and her cowgirl boots. She'd spent extra time on her hair, getting it just so, and that bit of shine on her legs came from the hint of shimmer in her body cream. Maybe it was overkill but it was barely visible and she knew it made her legs look a little smoother. So why not?

She was out to paint the town Carly.

Parked outside the Wild Honey, she grabbed the prettily wrapped presents, one from her and one from Rissa, to carry inside, where country music blared and people shouted to be heard. Small towns might be slow during the week but on a Friday night everyone came out for some fun. *Like ants to a picnic,* her dad often said.

Every station picnic, fundraiser and social event, she and Holly hung out together, commiserating over having cops for dads. But tonight there would be no commiserating on tap. Tonight was all about celebrating Holly's twenty-ninth with her gal pals.

Inside the bar, Carly quickly spotted the others and joined them at the tables grouped together in the corner. Holly wore a light-up tiara reading Birthday Girl in fake rhinestones, and it looked as though the women were well into their second round.

Carly released the breath she held, determined she would not turn around and go on a Liam hunt through the crowd—or worse, through town.

She hated feeling like this. All out of sorts and wound up and anxious.

This was a perfect example of why she'd always pictured herself with someone less edgy. Someone more relaxed. *Fun.* How like her to pick the wrong guy.

If someone had asked her six months ago or even a week ago who her ideal man was, Liam wouldn't have even made the list.

Now he was suddenly the only man on it?

The news left her stumbling a bit as she neared the table but she managed to cover her awkwardness and force a smile, placing the gifts on the grouped tables and greeting the women despite the knot of unease in her stomach.

How could she fall for someone so opposite of everything she'd always wanted? Was she setting herself up for disappointment? Heartache?

"Whoa, Carly! Girl, don't you look *hawt!* I think someone's on the prowl, since daddy's out of town."

Carly laughed at the joke, accepting the ribbing in good fun, even though the image of Liam automatically popped into her head.

Fact: Liam was the only one on her list. Liam had come through for her, helped her when she needed it, kept her company even though he'd thought she was doing the wrong thing. "That I am."

Her comment created a chorus of cheers, go-get-hims and raised glasses, but she meant what she said.

Fact: she was her father's daughter—which meant one way or another, she was going to get her man.

CARLY'S DRESS WAS too damned short.

With a Coke in his hand, Liam watched from the sidelines of the Wild Honey while some yahoo twirled her around on the dance floor. Each and every time he did it, every man in the room held his breath and looked to see if that was the twirl that showed them more than her long legs.

More than that, every twirl made Liam wonder if she was wearing that pair of lacy underwear again. The black, slinky thong she'd had on the other night?

The thought alone left him scowling and he downed the cold Coke in four long swallows.

There should be a law against a group of females holding parties in a bar on a Friday night. Every ranch hand and drifter in the area was on the make, and they zeroed in on that table in the corner as soon as they walked through the door.

The guy made a show of spinning Carly again before the song ended. The moment it did, five guys stepped forward to be next in line.

Before he really knew what was happening, Liam had set his empty glass aside and was crossing the dance floor.

"Want to dance?" the guy closest to Carly asked.

Liam swore to himself. He'd arrested the man twice in the past year for DUI. "Sorry, bud." He put a hand on the guy's shoulder to hold him back. "She's dancing with me."

CARLY GLARED AT Liam when he stepped into the picture. The entire time she'd been dancing she'd felt him watching her, and stamped down the thrill that came at the fact that not only was he here, but also that his tone

held more than a smidgen of jealousy when he spoke
to Hank Billups.

"Back off. I was here fir— Uh, hey, Liam."

Liam closed the distance between them and wrapped
his arm around her waist, ignoring the mutters of the
others. Not that she cared. Liam was here and he was
holding her close and the spark of jealousy she'd heard
was reflected in the smoldering glint of his eyes.

Best of all?

The sight eased the tension inside her. Liam wasn't
as unmoved and uncaring as he tried to appear.

The proof was in the possessive way he held her.
Score one for Team Carly.

"Are you trying to get yourself hurt? You're attracting too much attention." He practically growled the
words.

She knew what he was saying. The bar was packed
with ranch hands and locals, some drifters. Men who
liked to drink and party on the weekends because they
worked so hard during the week. But she knew to watch
herself and be careful.

By dancing with every guy who asked?

She hadn't danced with— Well, okay, she *had*
danced nonstop for a while but only because during
the first dance she'd spotted Liam glaring at her and
she couldn't help herself. Sometimes men needed a little kick in the pants to remind them not to take certain
things for granted.

But the truth was, Liam was her only danger. No
matter how much she'd like to pretend she was worldly
and experienced, she wasn't. Not when it came to men
and sex and potentially getting her heart broken. And
the fact he was so upset over sleeping with her wasn't

good. She'd never backed down from a challenge but she wasn't a mountain climber like Liam's brother, either.

Nor was she a coward.

Without a word, Carly slowly slid her hands up Liam's arms, pausing long enough to squeeze his biceps because she couldn't pass up the opportunity. She was pleased when she saw the pulse at his throat pick up speed in response. "Oh?" She smiled up at him, moving until her breasts touched his chest and her thighs brushed his with every step.

His glance strayed low, and she didn't need to look down to know the deep neckline of her spaghetti-strapped dress dipped if she moved a certain way and revealed more than a hint of cleavage. She wound her arms around his neck, the act giving him an unprecedented view, and the sound of Liam's ragged inhalation strengthened her determination. "I hadn't noticed."

He smoothed his hands up her arms, fingers locking around her wrists—but he didn't remove them.

"You're going to cause talk."

"Like they're not already talking about that little stunt you just pulled—or you stopping by my place every day after work?"

"Everyone in town knows the sheriff asked us to watch over you and how you took on a foster kid the moment your father was gone. There are no secrets, Caroline. You need to remember that."

"Ah. So I suppose that means they also know about you sitting outside my house last night?"

She watched as a wary look filled his chestnut-colored eyes. Liam was trying to hide his reaction to her words but she wasn't so naive or inexperienced that she didn't know a bluff forming when she saw it. Her heart tugged in her chest because she could swear she saw longing and sadness in his gaze. And because she was sure she wasn't misreading his stare, she forged ahead. "Why didn't you come in?"

"You know what would've happened if I had."

Her heart beat too fast in her chest but at his words it tripped a bit and pounded harder. "And that would have been bad?"

Swaying on the dance floor, Carly realized how scared Liam was, though he'd never admit it.

He pushes before you can, remember?

Well, she wasn't his mother or one of his foster families who would send him back or reject him. And no doubt he had to be at least a little worried about that. Everyone knew getting dumped sucked, and for someone like Liam, that thought alone would put him on edge.

As big and strong and handsome as Liam was, she recognized vulnerabilities in him she'd never have thought possible. Instead of making her leery, the presence of those emotions made her feel even closer to him, probably because she saw those same weaknesses in herself. Was she totally off base where Liam was concerned?

She didn't think so. No, she knew so. But how could she convince him to take a risk when he'd obviously been hurt many times over?

"I owe you an apology, Carly. I should have called you. We should probably talk about what happened the other night."

"Yes, we should," she said firmly, knowing she couldn't mince words when he would be sure to keep his time with her brief to avoid the gossip they both knew was stirring.

Standing so close, feeling the heat of him, she wanted more. Time to sit and talk to him the way they'd talked in the back of his truck. Time alone without worrying about gossip or arguing over fostering because she knew it was too late to worry about talk, seeing as how she clung to his neck and they barely moved.

"We can't talk here."

"We could go outside, sit in your truck. Or to my house."

He was silent so long she knew he considered it.

Finally he shook his head. "Meet me at the cross-roads. It's on your way home and we can settle things there."

Settle things? On her way home? That sounded like a brush-off—which she wasn't going to accept. Meeting him at the crossroads meant leaving the birthday party and bar early. It also meant they had no true privacy. At least The Rock was so far off the beaten path they didn't have to worry about being discovered.

Liam probably thought they could have their talk and he could send her on her way.

As if she'd make it that simple for him.

Okay, maybe if he truly wanted nothing to do with her, she'd pick up her dignity and go when their conversation was over. But that wasn't the vibe she got from him. Call her crazy but her female intuition said Liam tried to deny himself, deny her—but he struggled because of his past and fear. Totally justifiable. But why stop what could be a very good thing because of that?

If they didn't click, fine, she could accept that. But she would not accept him using a bad childhood as an excuse. It had happened to him, but it wasn't who he was. Liam could get over himself already. "I'm scared, too, you know," she whispered as they swayed back and forth in time with the slow song.

"Not here, Caroline."

The heat of his breath so close to her ear unearthed a shiver of awakening need deep inside her. "Fine. But I want you to think about something until we can talk more, okay?" Her arms tightened and she lifted her mouth so that she couldn't be overheard. "Before you tell me how we shouldn't be doing this—" did she dare say what she was thinking? "—I want you to remember how it felt when we were together, because I know you'd like to feel that way again."

His hands tightened at her waist and his entire body hardened against hers. She drew back enough to see his face and caught her breath at his expression. Desire and want, need. Not sexual but...the need for closeness, for a connection. For her.

No, she wasn't alone in feeling the way she did. She was simply the braver of the two at the moment. And that was okay. For now. Her words were getting through to him and, even though Liam held back emotionally, maybe time was the answer.

The music ended with the country singer carrying a high note to the heartbreaking end. Carly stepped back, her body missing the hard, sexy warmth of his. "I'll be at the crossroads," she said, "but if you keep driving... I'll follow you home."

CHAPTER SEVENTEEN

LIAM PULLED OVER TWICE. Changed his mind no less than a dozen times.

He even forced himself to wait a full ten minutes after Carly left Wild Honey before he let himself get behind the wheel of his truck.

But as he came upon the four-way intersection where Carly had said she'd be and spotted her red SUV idling in the dark of night, he experienced such a sense of relief his chest felt tight and his hands shook at the thought of her waiting for him while he'd jacked around trying to make up his mind.

Doubts and excuses and all the reasons why he needed to keep his hands to himself circled around and around in his head like vultures ready to strike but the sight of her car...

When he'd suggested meeting, all he'd wanted to do was talk. Now that he was here, he wanted— He didn't know what he wanted besides her. Besides the promise he'd heard in her voice when she'd whispered that last remark before leaving the dance floor.

He took his foot off the gas and pressed on the brake but something inside him rebelled. Propelled him on. He flashed his lights at her, slowed down but didn't stop.

He rolled slowly by, his hands tight on the wheel.

Maybe she'd follow him as she'd said. Maybe she wouldn't.

Maybe that was his answer.

Behind him, Carly pulled onto the road. Liam rolled to a stop at the sign, his gaze on his rearview mirror as he made the turn to go to his cabin. He hoped Zane wasn't up to notice the second set of headlights but if he was...

Blood pulsed through his veins, loud in Liam's ears.

Carly came to a stop.

Hesitated.

Began to move, inching forward.

Finally she turned, her lights behind him as she increased her speed to catch up.

And Liam released the breath he didn't know he held.

ARE YOU SURE ABOUT THIS?

Carly gripped the wheel a little tighter, every fiber of her being screaming a resounding *yes* as she parked behind Liam's big truck and turned off the ignition.

But that niggling naysayer was also there because she was adult enough to know that sex didn't necessarily change things between them no matter how much she now wanted it to. Would making love with Liam get her what she wanted? Maybe. Maybe it would bring them closer as a couple, because the first time could be written off as unexpected.

But to do it again? She gathered her purse and keys.

Yeah, the second time—now—could only be considered deliberate. *Premeditated.*

Which meant she ran an even bigger risk that Liam might redouble his efforts to keep her at arm's length once the desire faded with dark of night, replaced by the light of reality and all that stood between them having a relationship and making it work. She was ready—but was he?

Liam walked toward her door, his long stride loose and fluid, that of a man with purpose. And she knew what that purpose was.

Her.

Her heart hammered in her chest and she couldn't get enough air. He opened her car door, looking big and imposing due to the frown on his face. She smiled at his expression, her pulse tripping because she could tell he wasn't happy feeling what he did.

But that was okay. For now.

Silent, he held out a hand for her to take and she did so without hesitation, letting him draw her from the warmth of her car, hold her hand all the way to the plain-looking cabin. The cabin itself was made of new logs, chiseled and pieced to fit perfectly.

But there were no pots for plants on the porch, no pretty outdoor furniture, no softness to the hard, rigid lines of the structure. The exterior matched Liam perfectly—plain and simple but complex beneath, a puzzle of interlocking pieces.

He released her hand long enough to unlock the door. The interior was dark, no little lights or lamps to show the way. The only images she was able to make out were of large, thick furniture, a hulking shadow of a television cabinet, a fireplace made of rounded rock that rose from the floor all the way to the ceiling.

With every detail about his home she noted, anticipation built inside her. His silence added to the feeling when the closing of the door and the latch of the lock shut out the moonlight and everything else.

The last what-if niggles of doubts fled entirely, replaced one hundred percent by the awareness that she was with the man she was supposed to be with. Broken, bruised, guarded. Liam needed her. Even more than she needed and wanted him.

He wrapped an arm around her waist and brought her flush against his body. Without a word, he tugged the jean jacket off her shoulders and let it drop, the metal buttons pinging as they hit the floor. Eyes dark and glinting with a purpose that made her head spin, his mouth claimed hers in a kiss so hot, so sensually thrilling, she had to grip his arms to hold herself upright.

Dazed, she didn't realize Liam had physically turned her, until her back met the solid wood door and she was held in place by his hard, mouthwatering body.

Another thrill shot through her when his hands slipped low, the hem of her short dress teasing her thighs as he bunched it and pulled.

"What are you wearing beneath this? Eh, Caroline? I've been wondering all night."

She blinked her eyes open, glad they'd finally adjusted to the dimness. She didn't want to miss a moment of what was about to happen. "Find out for yourself."

She couldn't quite grasp that the sexy, throaty voice taunting him was her own. But she'd never felt this way for anyone before, so why should she be surprised her need for Liam was so obvious? Her body hummed from being close to him. Actually having to talk? Now?

Impossible.

"I intend to," he murmured.

He pulled the dress all the way up, slow at first, making no bones about tilting his head to see what he revealed, then fast and quick, over her head, as though he simply couldn't wait. The removal of her dress left her in her comfortably worn boots and matching steel-blue bra and thong set.

Yeah. Before leaving the house, she'd hoped to see him and had planned ahead accordingly. "Like what you see?"

"Have *mercy*." He ran his rough hands over her, lingering, squeezing. The way he kissed and touched her, she thought he planned on making love to her standing up and leaning against the door, but the second the clasp of her bra gave way beneath his questing fingers, Liam swung her up into his arms and carried her through the house.

"I want a bed this time."

The words barely registered before he dropped her.

Carly couldn't contain a shriek when she fell through the air. She hit the mattress and bounced lightly. A part of her wanted to say "I'll get you for that" but a bigger part of her was thrilled because she'd never been on the receiving end of so much passion.

A lamp switched on at the twist of his fingers, bathing the room in light. Normally she would have been curious about his home because she felt houses were such a reflection of their inhabitants, but all she could do was stare as Liam yanked his shirt over his head and toed off his shoes.

She was way too aware of being panty-naked in front of him, though. Modesty reared its head and she really wanted to cover herself with her arms.

"Don't move," he ordered. "Not even an inch."

"Or?" she asked, unable to keep from issuing the throaty challenge.

"Handcuffs."

Oh, now that was definitely a pro for dating a cop, she mused.

Liam left her on the bed and disappeared into what appeared to be a bathroom. Seconds—literally before she could pull herself together enough to challenge his order to stay put—later he returned with a box of condoms.

His gaze drifted over her, his hands stilling on the buttons of his fly as he looked at her with an expression she knew she'd remember to her dying day.

"I always knew you were beautiful but…I like you there."

In his bed. And, *oh,* did she like it, too.

When he looked at her the way he did, she felt beautiful. She forgot all about the freckles she hated, her wild red hair. The little lines that had started to appear around her eyes and mouth and the way she carried her weight in her belly and thighs and nowhere else. None of that mattered now. Not when Liam looked at her the way he did right at this moment.

He lowered himself to the bed, close enough she could feel the heat radiating off his body. He held his weight off her as he kissed her mouth, the sensitive skin of her neck.

She wrapped her hands around his corded biceps, feeling the rock-hard solidness of muscle beneath surprisingly soft skin.

"Do you know how beautiful you are?"

She slid her hands up, around his head. Tried to guide his mouth to hers again. Liam had other destinations in mind, apparently. He shifted to nuzzle her breasts instead, his arms bulging as he continued to hold himself just out of reach.

"I dreamed about you like this. All sprawled out and mine for the taking."

Carly couldn't stop the whimper of sound that escaped her at his words. She closed her eyes and tried to gather herself to do a little exploring of her own, only to gasp when Liam fastened his mouth over her breast, shifting onto his side so his free hand could shove the scrap of stretchy material she wore low.

Between the kissing and the way he touched her so intimately, she was more than ready for him by the time he finally donned a condom and covered her with his body. The hair on his thighs tickled the inside of hers as he pressed down, joined them, his weight welcome as he began a slow ebb and flow that kept the tension coiled tight, without giving too much.

She moaned into his mouth, her hands gripping his arms and shoulders, pulling him, urging him on, until the intensity grew and the bed frame squeaked and the only thing she could do was lock her knees at his waist and hold on.

She cried out her pleasure when her body tightened, splintered, the force too much.

She was vaguely aware of his groan, aware that he'd pulled back enough to watch her lose herself in him. He continued moving, carrying her along to the very end of completion before he buried his head into her neck and followed.

Carly felt every ragged breath he took, every fast-paced slam of his heart thudding against her.

But it wasn't until she lowered her legs from around his hips that she laughed.

His entire body tensed. "Something funny?"

The insulted pitch of his voice widened her smile. She rubbed her calf along his and waited.

"What the—" He broke off with a rusty-sounding chuckle and he lifted his head to shoot her an ornery look. "Guess we were in a hurry."

"Yeah, I guess we were."

A point proven by the fact he had taken her to bed—with her boots on.

"YOU'VE GONE QUIET AGAIN."

Liam stared at the ceiling in his darkened bedroom, ignoring the itch of Carly's hair snagging in the whiskers on his chin. Her breath was moist on his chest from where she lay with her head tucked beneath his jaw, bare body soft and warm and lush against him.

"I have?"

"You did that in school, too. Got quiet whenever you were…thinking about something important."

She smoothed her hand over his chest, along his shoulder to his arm.

"If this is about my father, stop worrying. He'll be fine. He respects you, Liam. It won't be a big deal."

Maybe. Maybe not. The feeling of respect was mutual, but every man had his limits and Jonas was protective of what was his—Carly especially. "I'm fairly certain the words 'I wish he'd take advantage of my daughter' have never left your daddy's mouth."

A sleepy laugh escaped. "You're probably right but can I just say now that I'm *very* glad you did?"

Liam smoothed his hand over the waves in her long red hair, drawn to the softness of it and how it felt drifting over his skin.

"Stop it, already. You're making me nervous. What are you thinking?" she demanded, lifting her head from his chest.

He stared into her eyes. In the dark, they looked like gray smoke. "We have to be realistic, Caroline. This can't go far. No further than this right here. You know that."

Now she was the one who grew quiet. Her lashes dropped over her eyes and Liam wanted to kick himself for saying what was on his mind when they'd just finished doing what they'd done.

He cursed himself silently and shifted, rolling until he stared down into her face. "I'm sorry."

"A little bit ago you couldn't wait to be with me," she reminded him. "Now—"

"Now I *still* want to be with you, but I don't want to hurt you."

"Oh, Liam. Then don't."

"It's not that easy."

"It could be if we let it be."

"That's wishful thinking, sweetheart."

"Why? Why does being together have to be difficult?"

Even in the darkness, he could make out the pattern of her freckles on her chest and collarbones, the way they almost disappeared beneath the makeup she wore. But nothing could hide her hurt and the disappointment he saw on her face. "Caroline, you want things I can't give you. This is as far as it goes. We can't be anything more than what we are right now."

"That's a crock of bull, Liam McKenna. What can't you give me? And just so we're clear—what are we now? Because from where I'm lying, I'm thinking making love with you *one time* might be passed off as one of those things that can never be. But twice? No way. But that's what's making you so nervous, isn't it? You're upset because you want me…"

The tic in his jaw was back. He ran his hand over the spasm. "*We* are a bad idea, Carly."

"But?"

"But I can't—" He rolled onto his back and ran his hands over his face. "I can't…stop thinking about you. Is that what you want to hear?" He dropped his hands in time to see a sweet smile reveal the flash of her teeth.

"Yeah, as a matter of fact, it is. Because I feel the same way. Liam, that's *good.* It means we're both on the same page."

Unable to let the pretense go on when her desires and plans were crystal clear, he said, "Hardly. You're all about home and family and kids and—I don't want that. I don't want kids."

She blinked twice and swallowed. "You mean, right now? Right away. Right?"

"I mean, ever." Guys like him weren't meant to have kids. Raise kids.

Everyone knew the statistics. Children of abuse were much more likely to abuse. And even though he knew he'd never physically abuse a kid, what about emotionally?

It wasn't too much of a stretch to know he'd be hard on any kid he might ever have because he'd been such a wild kid himself. And to be a cop on top of that?

He'd always be suspicious, distrusting, because he already knew the worst things they could do. He'd seen it all. Hell, he'd done some of it, too. And even if he had good kids, what were the odds he'd screw them up by always questioning their every move as if they were criminals? He didn't see a way around it. Because no matter how hard he'd try, he knew his past would trip him up.

"Liam…"

He heard the surprise in her voice. The shock because, as he'd known she would, her mind had gone down that road. "Carly, you need to listen. I do not ever want to have children and that will not change. Being a parent isn't for me."

She sat up in the bed, holding the sheet to her chest. "I don't believe that. *Ever?*" she repeated. "Because of your past."

It was a statement, not a question. And he forced himself to answer honestly. "Yes. Because of my past."

"You don't think that's a bit extreme?"

Extreme? No, not for him. But it was another reminder that she saw the best in people, not what they were underneath. She didn't know everything he'd been through so how could she think his response anything but an overreaction? "Your childhood and mine aren't comparable, Caroline."

"Maybe not on some levels but we all have issues. We were both abandoned and I can understand why you'd be afraid of passing your fears on to a child but—"

"You're not getting that it's a hell of a lot more than just that. It's more than being shoved into the system. It's more than being neglected, or being smacked around or rebelling against everyone who tried to do something nice for me." She didn't understand and she never would. He didn't want her to know, either. Not when he'd worked so hard to put his childhood in a box and lock it away forever.

"Liam, you're not the same person now as you were then. I know you wouldn't treat a child that way. I couldn't—I *wouldn't*—be with you if I thought that. You can't give up on something before you've tried it."

She sat on the edge of his bed, her bright red hair spilling down her back. Such a contrast to her milky skin. "That's the point I'm trying to make, Caroline. I don't want to try. I do not want kids."

CHAPTER EIGHTEEN

I DON'T WANT TO TRY. I do not want kids.

All day Saturday, Liam's words repeated in her head. She'd left his cabin at the break of dawn, after he had fallen asleep and she could do nothing but lay there and try not to be hurt by his words. She'd known working out a compromise wouldn't be easy, but she hadn't expected to hit a solid wall.

Liam now knew she wanted kids so by saying he didn't, he was setting a boundary and letting her know it. She couldn't fault his honesty, nor could she cry foul later if things progressed. But how far could she let things go now?

Pursuing her interest in him meant giving up on something very important to her. When she began fostering, she wasn't sure if she wanted a family, but now she *was* sure. Worse still, she wanted Liam's children but knew now that would never happen. Her eyes were wide-open in her relationship with him, like it or not.

Maybe taking such a hard stance was his way of pushing her away again. Maybe it was his way of giving her an out. Maybe it was simply how she felt—he had been merely stating a fact.

Maybe, maybe, maybe...

Regardless of his reasons, she was so into him she wasn't sure how to respond. She wanted a future with him. But did she want it enough to give up having children?

He wasn't bluffing. He'd *meant* what he'd said. She could tell from his expression. The sorrowful look in his eyes because, no matter how much he wanted her, he had his limits and he wasn't going to let her push him on a subject like this.

So either she accepted Liam as he was—because she wasn't one of those women who fooled themselves into thinking she could change a man—or she stood up for her own desire for children, abandoned any hope of being with Liam and moved on. Yeah, that was an easy decision to make, she thought with a groan.

Shaking her head at the confusion she felt, Carly opened the Rav 4's rear door and grabbed the first of the flats of flowers she'd bought at the local nursery.

"Need some help?"

Carly turned at the question and saw Mandy's daughter staring at her from behind thick but stylish glasses.

Oh, not what she needed today. But the poor kid— she looked miserable.

Carly wasn't sure what to think about Mandy wanting her to talk to Elysee about not fitting in. On the one hand it took a lot of nerve, something Mandy had never lacked, but on the other hand Carly had seen the desperation on Mandy's face. Desperation that couldn't be faked but the kind produced only by maternal instinct.

Mandy was worried about her daughter and because Carly had screwed up at that age herself, she knew Mandy probably had reason to be worried Elysee would find a way to act out. "Sure. There are some in the front of the car, too."

Carrying the flat to her porch, Carly passed Elysee

on the way back to the car. "So what have you been into today?"

"Nothing."

Carly grabbed another tray of flowers. She loved playing in the dirt and watching things grow. Last year, the garden club had voted her flowers the prettiest in town. She'd won a basketful of bulbs, garden tools and gift certificates to local businesses. Come to think of it, she had one in the house for McKenna Feed that would expire if she didn't use it soon.

"This is a lot of plants."

Elysee's doubtful expression drew a smile. "It's only a start, actually. I love the color and shapes and textures. They're a lot of work but I like that, too, being able to see something grow. They make me happy."

Once the flats were distributed between the locations where she intended to plant, Carly was about to go inside and change when she realized Elysee stood there and waited, looking awkward. "Does your mom know you're here?"

"Yeah. She told me I could come over. I was on the phone with her when you pulled in. She's stuck at the dentist and I don't want to be home with my step-idiots. They're jerks."

Carly's heart tugged at the girl's words and the hopeful expression she wore.

She was close to her stepsister, though not as close now as they'd been in high school. Ever since Skylar had broken up with her then-boyfriend, Marcus, and moved to New York, they rarely saw her unless they traveled to New York. Luckily, spending a few days in the Big Apple wasn't a hardship. "Well, I need to change into work clothes. Why don't you go do the same, then you can help me plant these? If you'd like to, that is."

"Really? You don't mind?"

"Be back in ten minutes."

Elysee took off toward her house and despite the quiet street and safe neighborhood, Carly watched her go to make sure the girl made it home okay. She didn't need to be babysitting Mandy's daughter, of all people, but the girl's loneliness cut to the quick and Carly couldn't turn her away.

How could she, when she felt she was staring into her own eyes at that age?

Half an hour later, Carly sat back on her heels to stretch. Planting went a lot faster with Elysee's help, but the girl's presence and company had done nothing to clear up the confused state of Carly's thoughts.

Throughout the tilling and digging and planting and mulching, her thoughts circled the same issue like a wagon train circling to defend itself from attack. Only, her *train* was circling around to defend her want of a family.

There were things about Liam she didn't know. She needed more information about his past but what she wanted to know could only come from him—and she didn't see that happening anytime soon.

Then, there were things she knew and didn't like. His job, mainly. His stance on children—definitely.

That was important. Never wasn't a matter of timing or compromise. It was...never.

What was wrong with wanting a family? Sharing your life with someone? Couldn't Liam see how far he'd come? How far he'd grown as a person from where he'd been as a child?

No, he couldn't. Liam was putting the future of their relationship on her. Pushing her away, even though he admitted he didn't really want her to go.

How was that fair? Was she reading too much into his actions versus his words? Overthinking the way he'd held her, touched her and treated her—versus what he'd said about children?

It was enough to drive a girl insane. There were *so* many things to draw her to Liam but when he set up a roadblock, boy, did he ever make sure it was a doozy.

Like the night beneath the stars, he tested her steadfastness, made the next step her decision, as though he was complacent and didn't have a say. A part of her resented it. But a part of her also understood why.

If she made the choice to walk away, then the blame was with her, not him. And deep down in her soul, she knew that all the protests and walls and words of warning were his way of protecting himself because he'd apparently always had to.

Because he *believed* she'd balk. Leave.

She was stuck between a rock and a hard place, and the sides were closing in. But she couldn't give up.

Regardless of the hurt that might be looming in her future, regardless that she'd snuck out after he'd drifted to sleep because she'd needed time to think, more than anything, she wanted to show Liam how good it could be. What he was *missing* by holding everyone at arm's length. Not only her and what they could share, but Zane and his brothers, too.

Sticking around when she knew it meant no children was her doing the hard stuff Liam wasn't able to do right now. It was her taking the hard road, assuming all the risks, if Liam didn't come around later and decide he wanted more. If he didn't change his mind.

Fact: she was ready to risk everything on the chance he would have a change of heart. And it terrified her because she was in way over her head where he was concerned.

Resolve firmly in place, Carly turned to watch Elysee carefully tapping dirt around the stems. Once again Carly felt a bittersweet connection with this awkward, clearly intelligent girl.

Was this what it would be like to plant flowers with her daughter one day?

Or was this what she'd miss if she stayed with Liam?

"Carly? Is this okay?"

Somehow she managed a smile. "Those look great."

"Are you sure? You're looking at me awfully funny. Did I do it wrong?"

She shook her head and smiled. "I was thinking about something else. It's perfect. You're quite the landscaper." She hoped the girl didn't notice the forced cheeriness behind the words. "I appreciate your help, Elysee. You're doing a wonderful job."

"Thanks. This is more fun." Elysee shrugged. "There was a party today my mom wanted me to go to but I didn't want to go."

Carly managed to hide a cringe. Did she really have to get involved with this? Now? "Oh?"

"Jordan Sands. She's...not very nice. But my mom talked to her mom, who invited me, so Mom wanted me to go even though Jordan didn't want me to. Mom thought it might help what happened this week."

Don't ask, don't ask. "What happened?"

"I aced a test and Jordan told everybody I was to

blame for Mr. Peters not grading on a curve. Now nobody is speaking to me and some of the kids…" Elysee's words trailed off. She began digging another hole with the spade, hitting the ground with sharper intensity.

"I'm sorry that happened to you, Elysee. That sucks."

Elysee looked surprised by Carly's choice of words. "Mom said you used to be a geek like me."

Carly wasn't sure whether to be insulted by the bold truth or pleased she'd apparently outgrown her geekdom. "Hate to tell you this, sweetie, but once a geek, always a geek. We are who we are inside."

Elysee looked horrified by the news.

"Elysee, listen. You know what? I'm glad I was— *am*—a geek. Geeks are special people. Geeks are the ones who grow up humble and considerate of other people's feelings. As a group, they're pretty nice people."

"I hate being a geek."

She'd hated it, too. "Come on, you can't say it isn't a little fun to know the answers most days. Admit it, you like knowing you're smarter than Jordan, at least a little?"

A small smile pulled at the girl's lips. "Well, yeah. But it's not fun when people laugh and make fun of me."

"People with small minds behave that way."

"Anybody ever make fun of you?"

For a split second, Liam popped into Carly's head. He hadn't made fun in the classic sense, but he definitely didn't agree with her dreams, which made it seem like he mocked her. "Yeah, they did."

And things were getting sticky conversation-wise. She shoved the dirt in around the roots of a snapdragon and tried to formulate a subject change.

Elysee was silent, a frown pulling her eyebrows low

as she broke up a clod of dirt. "How did you make them stop?"

"I didn't." Feeling the girl's gaze on her, Carly shrugged. "I stopped," she explained. "I realized the more I responded and got upset over the things they did, the more they did to me. So I stopped reacting. And, no, it didn't work or make them stop. They did and said worse things, trying to get a reaction from me."

"So what happened? Did you tell the school? Change schools?"

"Nope. I changed me. I became like them. New clothes, makeup, hair. But it wasn't a change for the better. In fact, I wound up in more trouble because it took a while for me to get the fact that I didn't really want to be like them. I didn't know it at first. And I soon found out who my real friends were and when it was over I had a lot of apologies to make."

Elysee planted another flower, silent for a while... Then she asked, "Was my mom one of your friends?"

"No," Mandy said from about ten feet away. "I wasn't. I was one of the kids making fun of Carly."

Talk about a flash from the past. Carly paid extra attention to picking out the right flower for the next hole. She'd been so focused on Elysee's questions that she hadn't noticed Mandy pulling into her driveway down the street or joining them.

"You did it?" Elysee asked, hurt making her voice thready. "You said you were best friends."

"We were. Once," Mandy clarified. "Then we weren't."

"Mom."

"Elysee, it was a long time ago. It doesn't matter now," Carly said.

But it did matter. One glance at Elysee's tear-filled eyes and quivering chin said so. She wasn't looking at her mom and seeing the same person now. Elysee saw her tormentors.

Mandy's daughter got to her feet, her gloved hands fisted. "You treated Carly like they treat me? You were *that* mean to her?"

"Leesee, honey, I didn't understand what I was doing at the time. I didn't see how mean I was. Now I do."

Carly wanted to get to her feet and run into her house but she couldn't force herself to move. Hearing the pain and shock in Elysee's voice, the disbelief that Mandy could have been so cruel was uncomfortable to watch.

There was a reason she hated gossip. During school, she'd been on the receiving end of it way too many times.

Mandy sighed deeply. "Yes, I was that mean. But now I'm not and I *hate* what I did to Carly because every time one of those kids make you cry, I remember what I said and did to hurt her and it kills me."

"What about you?" Elysee asked, her blue-eyed gaze stark and full of anger. "Do *you* forgive *her?*"

"Yes, I do," Carly said. "I have forgiven your mom."

"*Why?* If she was half as mean to you as they are to me, *how* can you do that? She doesn't deserve it!"

"Leesee, please—"

"Shut up! You're just like them!"

CHAPTER NINETEEN

CARLY GOT TO HER FEET, not wanting to be involved and yet totally engulfed in the argument. "Elysee, stop. Listen to me, okay? I forgave your mom because I wasn't going to let her win. Being angry and upset all the time? Hating her? It got me nowhere. And even though it wasn't easy, even though it felt totally wrong and completely unjust and I didn't *want* to do it, I had to because not doing it gave her power. It held me back and it will hold you back, too. The best revenge isn't getting even or not forgiving them. It's being successful and taking the high road and having people talk about you for good reasons, not bad ones."

"They call me h-horrible names."

"Be nice anyway," Carly said softly.

"They make me drop my books or hide them in the boys' *bathroom*."

"They're jealous," Mandy said. "I always was."

Carly looked at Mandy in surprise because she would not have believed Mandy would own up to the emotion publicly, much less to her daughter.

"It's true. Carly was smart and she was pretty without makeup. People were starting to notice, the boys especially. And even though her mom had left, her dad wanted her around. So, I was jealous. My mom only wanted me around for the child-support check my dad sent, and he...couldn't be bothered with me. Carly's dad loved her, *everybody* loved her," Mandy said with a wry twist to her lipstick-coated lips, "because she was so nice. I was jealous and that's why I was so mean."

Carly forced a smile at Elysee. "It's not easy to rise above the meanness and pettiness. But if you can, you'll see that in the long run what they say hurts so much because you let it. You give it power. As to how to fix it...are there other girls getting made fun of?"

Elysee nodded. "A few. Why?"

"Because during the worst of it, I met a girl no one liked and we became best friends. After that we even became sisters."

"What if you invited those girls over?" Mandy suggested. "You could watch movies, hang out."

Elysee needed friends, a support system. Carly hadn't had one until Rissa and her daughter, Skylar, had moved to town and befriended her. Once they had, everything had changed. Most especially her outlook. Elysee needed that, as well. "I'm only extending this invitation to you but I'd let you use my hot tub. I don't let just anyone in, but for you and your friends, you can. If your mom says it's okay."

"Oh, that'd be *awesome*. Really?" Elysee's eyes sparkled again, not with tears but with excitement. It was quite a change from minutes ago. Ah, teenagers and their hormones.

"Sure. Give me a little advance notice, okay?"

"Oh, Carly, thank you!" Elysee ran over and gave Carly a hug before releasing her and running past Mandy without stopping. "I have to call Ashley right now. She's new," Elysee called over her shoulder, "but she seems nice. Okay, Mom?"

Mandy laughed. "Now she asks," she said to Carly. "That's fine. Have her mother call my cell if she wants to talk to me."

Carly watched as Elysee ran all the way home.

"I can't remember the last time I saw her that excited," Mandy said. "Thanks for offering her the use of the hot tub. That's very nice of you."

"She's sweet, Mandy."

"Yeah, she is. Total opposite of me, huh?"

Mandy had been nice—once.

Carly kneeled in front of the garden bed and reached for another flower. Mandy joined her, picking up the gloves Elysee had dropped to the ground before racing home. "You don't have to do that."

Mandy nodded. "I know, but I want to."

They worked in silence for a while, finishing the side of the drive before moving across to the other. Gradually they began to talk about the weather, the influx of ranch hands in town, movies, favorite television shows. The book club. Finally the driveway beds were planted and they moved on to the pots Carly kept on her porch and the boxes beneath the windows on either side of her front door.

"So," Mandy drawled. "You and Liam, huh?"

Spending the past couple hours with Mandy gave Carly new insight to the grown-up, mature version of her, the one who hurt because her child was being hurt and who recognized her part in Carly's teenage angst and regretted it. Sometimes you simply had to set things aside and move on. "Yeah…me and Liam."

"It's a little surprising, if you think about it," Mandy said casually. "I mean, after all those times you complained about your dad being a cop and having to ride in his car, his schedule."

"Yeah. I did that a lot." Even now it bugged her. Liam didn't want the same things she wanted, and he was being so darn stubborn and *male* about it all, so why was she still tossing it around in her mind?

If she were smart, she'd have a fun time with Liam until her father came home, then cut her losses and... and end it. That way, no one would be hurt.

Yeah, right.

"And? What changed?"

Carly shrugged, at a loss for words. "Truthfully? Nothing, which is why I'm questioning everything. Liam and I...we don't have the same outlook on life."

"Who does? Carly, get real. Liam's great and you know it. And he's hot. So what if he's a cop? Use it to role-play," Mandy said suggestively. "You can be the bad girl he has to pat down."

Carly felt her cheeks heat because she could *so* see them doing that. And enjoying it. "But what about all those things I said? All those things I *hated* about growing up with my dad? If I couldn't handle being a cop's kid, how could I handle being *more?*"

"I don't imagine it would be easy but you've got to admit your childhood was way better than mine. My parents were both insane. If they thought they could get one over on the other, they'd lie or cheat or whatever to do it. Cop or not, your dad wasn't like that. He was always stable and honest and honorable. A good guy, who always tried to do what was best for you because he loved you."

"I know that but—"

"But nothing. Okay, you want brutal honesty? Today

seems to be the day for it," Mandy said with a sigh. "The way your dad loved you is partly why I didn't *like* you. You had this dad who was so good and you complained about him when I just wanted mine to give a damn about me. All my father wanted was for me to shut up and stay out of his way. He'd make me stay with him every summer because some stupid divorce paper said I had to. The only reason he did it was because it ticked off my mom, not that she wanted me home with her all summer."

She packed down another plant. "Look, if you're worried about being with a cop and having a life, think about growing up from a different perspective. Your dad was great. North Star isn't that big and he was always around. And, yeah, there's a danger to the job but, again, it's North Star. The only thing I see holding you back is yourself."

She was right.

Carly was letting her own fears get in the way of what she wanted. But what about Liam's? Even though her mind and heart might have adjusted to the thought of being with a cop, his *I don't want to try* was black-and-white. If she managed to set her own insecurities completely aside, what about him? She didn't want to be with a man who had to be convinced to be with her. What kind of relationship was that?

SHE'D SNUCK OUT. Liam knew he'd surprised Carly last night by his no-kid declaration, but he hadn't expected to wake up alone. If she'd gotten out of bed and walked out at the time, yeah, but when she stayed he'd thought… He wasn't sure what he'd thought but he'd figured staying meant she was more accepting of the idea.

Granted, he could have picked a better time to bring up the subject but it was best she know where he stood regarding things like that. If sneaking out in the wee hours of the morning while he slept was her way of dealing with it, so be it. Now he knew.

He wasn't about to change his mind on the topic of kids. Maybe whatever they'd shared would be over now. And if it was, maybe it was for the best.

But if that was the case, why did the thought leave him with a knot in his chest?

He ignored the sensation and turned down Harper Road. He drove a couple miles before he turned up a driveway leading to a dilapidated house. He'd been there many times over the past couple of years to check on things. Between all the guys who patrolled this section of road, someone stopped by at least twice a week and visited with Pruett Murphy, an eighty-nine-year-old man living alone. Pruett made the best coffee around.

Parked beneath a big shade tree, Liam heard Buster barking long before he knocked on the door. "Pruett? It's Liam McKenna."

Inside, Pruett's dog whined, his claws scraping along the inside of the wood entry.

Liam waited on the porch, noting a couple of boards that needed to be repaired. On his next day off he needed to run by and fix those so Pruett didn't trip and fall.

Liam turned and surveyed the yard, not noticing anything amiss but the fact Pruett wasn't answering the door. The old guy was hard of hearing but Buster's bark would alert him. "Pruett? Deputy McKenna. Hope you've got coffee." Liam knocked again, tried the handle, not wanting to frighten Pruett in case the man was in the bathroom or had his pistol nearby.

The door opened with a twist of the knob and Liam's gut tightened when Buster continued to bark, the sound frantic.

He stepped into the smelly living room, swearing when he saw the debris on the floor where Buster had tried to claw his way out of the house.

Liam petted the frantic animal and tried to prepare himself for what he knew he'd find given the tinge of death in the air. "I know. I know, it is bad, isn't it? Where is he, boy? Where's Pruett?"

Buster whined pitifully and led the way down the hall, stopping at the bathroom door where more claw marks showed Buster's attempts to get to his master.

Liam opened the door to see Pruett prone on the floor. There was no need to feel for a pulse. Buster whined louder, longer, a mournful wail that sent chills down Liam's spine.

The dog shoved himself between Liam's legs and lay down on the floor, his head on Pruett's chest, the whining growing louder. Liam literally had to drag the poor dog out of the room. "Come on, boy. Come on. Let's go call this in and get Pruett to where he needs to be."

LIAM WAS NEVER AS glad to see a shift end as that evening. He'd put Buster in his cruiser and brought the dog back to the station. The animal had done nothing but lay on the cool tile floor, his bowl of water and the few treats of meat donated from the deputies' various lunches lying untouched beside him.

Liam had been so busy he hadn't been able to call the animal shelter. He hated to take Buster to the over-

crowded and underfunded place when Buster had literally been a man's best friend. What kind of treatment
was that for three years of loyalty?

His workday over, Liam got up and knelt by the dog,
patting Buster's head. "Come on. Let's go home. You
play your cards right and you might get to stay. Zane
had a soft spot for old Pruett."

Whistling for the dog to follow, he led the way to the
station door and commanded the dog to jump into the
cab of his truck. "Let's go get you some chow and see
if Zane will keep you, eh?" Liam scratched the dog's
ears and stared into his big brown eyes. "Don't look at
me like that, Buster. It ain't gonna happen. I'm never
home and I'm fairly sure you're not K-9 material."

Liam drove through town, noting the Gleasons were
back from their winter home in Florida and the Parkers
had put a for-sale sign in their yard. Word had it they
wanted to move closer to their daughter in Phoenix.

He pulled into Frank's Grocery, trying to ignore the
way he scanned the parking lot for Carly's car. She'd
left. She hadn't called. He'd leave it up to her to make
the next move.

Liam was on his way inside when he noticed Charlie bending over to pick up a coin. Once the piece was
in his pocket, he grabbed the handle of a shopping cart
and pushed it into some others as though he worked
here.

What the hell?

He gathered up all the carts and shoved them into
a line. That done, he ambled over to pick up a bag left
near one of the light posts.

Shaking his head at what he saw, Liam entered the
grocery, determined to talk to Delmer. He didn't have

far to search. Delmer stood at the front, watching Charlie out the window.

"Liam. Good to see you."

Liam nodded in greeting. "What's going on? What's Charlie doing here?"

"Don't that beat all? He showed up this morning, saying he was going to pay me back for what he'd eaten. Said it was only right. A half hour would've settled the little bit he ate. But he's been here all day, picking up trash, hauling groceries, gathering the carts. I've told him twice he's done more than enough, but he says he owes me a full day for not pressing charges. You gotta admit, that's not the way most of those drifters would've responded."

No, it wasn't. Even Liam had to respect Charlie's decision to settle his debt.

"What can I help you with today? You shopping early for lunch tomorrow?"

Crap. He'd forgotten about lunch at the station. Shoving that aside to deal with later, he rubbed the back of his neck. "I'm actually here for dog food. Any idea what kind Pruett Murphy bought for Buster?"

"I do. Why are you—" Delmer sighed. "What happened?"

"Most likely a stroke but who knows, given his age."

"And you got Buster?"

"Didn't seem right to turn him over to the pound. Pruett trained him well. Just can't tempt him to eat. Never seen a dog in mourning until now. Hasn't drank or eaten since I found him."

Delmer made a sound of sympathy. "I remember

Pruett talking about Buster being finicky and only wanting his food and nothing else. Come on, I know what you need."

CHAPTER TWENTY

CARLY SHOWERED OFF the dirt and sweat of a day spent planting, dressed in jeans and a snug T-shirt that accentuated her assets and drove to Liam's. She was waiting for him when he pulled up to his house.

Due to years of betrayal she'd been careful of what she'd said to Mandy, but talking about the complications of dating one of her father's deputies had clarified a few things.

One, who couldn't use a friend like Liam? Especially one who understood how hard it was to overcome what they'd both experienced. Whatever happened between them, she needed to remember that.

Two, life was too short and something bad could happen to Liam or to any man she might date at any time. Why hold back, when Liam could be around many, many years? When what she felt for him was growing stronger every day?

Three, she didn't want to live a life of regret. And while she was pretty sure she wanted kids and a family, she wasn't a hundred percent sure, so until she figured it out, why not be with Liam? Have fun? Enjoy his friendship and companionship a day at a time? She'd kissed her share of frogs along the way so why not keep on kissing the one who made her heart race?

Which led her to realization number four—

"What are you doing here?"

Carly stood from her seat on the steps. Liam held the truck door open and a dog jumped out. Once it did, he grabbed a bag of dog food from the backseat.

Spotting her, the dog's tail began to wag and he came over to her to investigate with a sniff. "Hey, you. What's your name?" she asked, scratching his ears and getting her wrist licked as a thank-you.

"That's Buster. He belonged to Pruett Murphy."

"*Belonged?* Did Pruett give him to you?"

He looked away, and for the first time she noted how tired he seemed.

"I found Pruett dead this morning. The Murphys didn't have any kids or family left, so…"

"Oh, Liam, I'm sorry."

"Yeah, me, too."

Her heart melted then and there. He really was an honorable man, a caring man. He rescued damsels in distress and animals, too.

"What are you doing here?"

"I wanted to say I'm sorry I left like I did. I needed to think and I thought it best if I left before someone saw my car here or saw me pulling into my house, wearing the clothes I'd worn last night."

"Ranch hands haven't all left for the day. They could see you here now," Liam stated reasonably.

Too reasonably?

Did he want people to know? But why say the one thing guaranteed to upset her if that was the case? "I thought you'd be relieved. Wasn't that why you said you didn't want kids? So I'd get upset? So we'd argue and I'd leave?"

He couldn't quite meet her eyes, which said more than words.

Liam ignored the question and unlocked the door, carrying the large sack of dog food like it was paper cups.

"Come on, boy."

She and Buster followed Liam into the house.

"Look, I came to see you because of number four."

"Am I supposed to know what number four is?"

She wasn't explaining this well. She wasn't doing any of this well, but how did you tell someone you wanted to see how things would go? *Where* they would go?

She managed a weak smile. "I needed to think about what you said, Liam. Does that strike you as all that surprising?"

A muscle spasmed in his jaw. "No. What's number four?"

"That I'd rather be sorry than safe."

"What?"

"It's a good thing," she said in a rush. "Really. You surprised me with saying you don't want kids. Now, I'm not saying I do or don't. I'm here because I don't know, I'm not sure yet. And until I am sure one way or the other, why shouldn't we see each other? We get along, we have…chemistry. So, yeah, I'd rather take a risk and be sorry than play it safe and walk away now. That's what I'm saying. That's number four."

She forced herself to move closer, hoping she wasn't making a fool of herself and he was about to turn her away, laugh at her. All she knew was that she didn't want to miss this opportunity when it was…whatever it was. Because it was strong, undeniable. Powerful, and scary, too.

Liam closed the distance between them, his steps slow and measured, as though he gave her time to change her mind—maybe wanted her to? But she stood her ground and waited.

Waited, until he lifted her face with a hand under her chin and lowered his head, the kiss going from zero to a hundred thousand miles per hour in a split second.

Yeah, she'd *so* rather be sorry than safe.

LIAM WOKE IN THE middle of the night and swore. Carly was gone again.

He tossed the covers back and swung his feet to the floor, grimacing when he stepped on something sharp. Wait a minute—those were Carly's jeans.

She wasn't in the bathroom but when he left the larger of the two bedrooms and ventured down the hall, he found Carly dressed in his shirt and curled up on a blanket on the floor, Buster snuggled tight and snoring softly. As though sensing his stare, Caroline opened her eyes.

"Hey."

A slow smile pulled at her lips. "Hey."

She was such a softy. Which made being with her all the more tricky. "Comfortable?"

"Not very."

Buster snuffled out a sigh.

"I couldn't help it. He was whimpering and crying in his sleep. When I petted him, he stopped."

Because the dog knew a good thing when he had it. Which made Liam wonder why he was pushing Caroline away if she was willing to stay. If he left it up to her, let her make the decisions, whatever happened happened. When she wanted to move on, she could.

Carly drowsily ran her fingers through Buster's fur. "Are you going to keep him?"

He didn't hesitate. "No."

"No?" She petted the dog with a long stroke. "Oh."

He could see her disappointment. He smiled, amazed how easy it was to be with her, to read her when she lay there, soft and at ease.

What better way to help cure her loneliness? Give her a companion, something to baby?

He walked over and squatted beside them, placing his hand over hers. "I'm not keeping him—you are."

"What? No, I can't."

"Why not? He's fully trained and he'd make a good guard dog for a woman living alone. Zane's got several dogs already on the ranch so Buster wouldn't get a lot of attention."

"He wouldn't?"

Liam shook his head. "He'd have to stay outside, too. Zane doesn't like dogs in the house."

Carly was silent for several seconds as she thought over his words.

"I suppose I could keep him. He's awfully sweet and gentle natured. I'll take him but I get to return him to you if there's a problem."

He held out his hands and when she placed hers in his, he pulled her to her feet and swung her into his arms. "Deal."

"So what's it to be tonight?" Mandy asked from the chair in the corner of Carly's bedroom Tuesday evening. "Where are you going?"

"No idea." Carly stared into the depths of her closet

and hated everything she saw. "He said to dress comfortably."

"Men don't have a clue, do they?"

"Nope." Carly sighed. How was she supposed to dress when she didn't know what they were doing?

"Thanks again for letting Elysee and her friend come over and use the hot tub. She hasn't stopped talking about this for days."

The girls were in the hot tub now, located on Carly's screened-in back porch. Every now and again, she and Mandy would hear a giggle and splash. "No problem. I'm glad my suggestion to buddy up with someone else who was getting picked on instead of taking it on alone worked."

"Me, too. I'm going to go check on them. We'd better get out of here if we're going to make the big movie premiere. Vampires suck," Mandy said, tongue-in-cheek.

"That they do. Have fun." Carly grabbed a T-shirt with a healthy V-neck, jeans and paired it with a form-fitting heather-blue hoodie that darkened the color of her eyes.

She entered her bathroom, Buster hot on her heels. The poor dog stayed glued to her side at all times, following her from room to room and whimpering and howling when Carly closed Buster out of the bathroom while she showered. Carly had resorted to closing the bathroom door but talking to the dog the entire time so Buster would relax and settle down.

She dressed quickly, touched up her makeup. She was straightening her hair when Mandy returned.

"Nice and casual, but with sexy hair. I like it. Haven't seen you wear it that way for a while. Want me to help?"

The words emerging from Mandy's lips gave Carly

pause. How could it not after so many years of animosity? It was...*weird* to have Mandy acting like a friend again. Carly couldn't help but wonder if things would change once Elysee was no longer having trouble.

But then another part of Carly was disappointed in herself. Being an adult meant letting bad things go. She could totally understand teenage drama and mistakes. Not once since Mandy's reappearance had she given Carly reason to believe her motives were anything but aboveboard.

It was nice, actually, having Mandy around again.

Most of Carly's friends were married and busy with their families and young children but Mandy's family was old enough that she was able to visit. And if she and Carly could let bygones be bygones and get along well enough for Mandy to be a semiregular visitor, maybe there was also hope that Liam's feelings about family would change? At least *his* family. How could he share a house with Zane and his brothers but *not* consider them family? "Sure."

Twenty minutes later, Buster was snoring on the couch and Mandy and the girls were leaving as Liam arrived to pick Carly up.

"Have fun, you two," Mandy said as she prodded the blushing, ga-ga-eyed girls down the steps. "Don't do anything I wouldn't do," Mandy added with a teasing smile.

Noting that Elysee glanced over her shoulder for one last blushing look at Liam, Carly had to agree. He was definitely hot. Dressed in faded jeans, a black shirt and boots, her cowboy-cop looked good enough to eat.

Liam's gaze swept over her, lingering on her chest

and the cut of her shirt sans jacket. Awareness zinged through her, making her want to fidget.

How odd was it that she'd slept with him several times now but was so nervous at the thought of going on an actual schedule-it-ahead-of-time first date? Not that they were calling it that. Heaven forbid they use the *D* word.

"What wouldn't she do?" he asked, his voice low and full of sensual innuendo.

But not for Mandy. For *Carly*. "Nothing I can think of," she said, moving down the steps.

"And you?" Liam leaned close as she passed and brushed a discreet kiss across her lips, an oh, so sexy sparkle in his eyes.

She flashed him what she hoped was a seductive smile and moved on, so close she felt the hair at her temple catch in the five-o'clock shadow on his chin. "Still have those handcuffs?"

CHAPTER TWENTY-ONE

By Wednesday, Liam had to admit he liked spending time with Carly. As soon as his daily shifts were over, he'd hurry home or else to an agreed-upon meeting place outside town and spend the evening with her. More often than not, they'd wind up at his cabin, anything to keep from being spotted in town and causing more talk.

At the same time, he also couldn't help but think his plan to distract Caroline was working. She hadn't mentioned the foster program recently and she'd become totally obsessed with making Buster feel at home in her house. She'd bought a dog bed big enough for a mastiff, a basket full of toys and a half-dozen treats until she found one the picky Buster favored.

Liam tossed the last of the hay bales into the truck bed to haul into the storage area at the back of McKenna Feed and raised his arms over his head to stretch out his back. He was getting soft sitting in a patrol car all day.

"That it?" Charlie asked as he entered the barn where Liam worked.

"Yeah. I'm heading out. Tell Zane I said goodbye, would you?"

"He knows." Charlie opened the passenger door of

the truck and grabbed the handle at the top of the cab as though to pull himself inside the vehicle.

"What are you doing?" Liam asked, confused.

Charlie hesitated a split second but then continued his climb into the cab. "Going to town with you."

"Why?" He didn't want to be stuck with Charlie, and he wasn't planning to drive back to the ranch anytime soon. Where was the old man going and how would he make the return trip? Zane didn't pay him to ride to town and hang out.

"Zane made an appointment with an eye doc for me. Told him it wasn't necessary but he said I couldn't drive until I'm tested."

"Insurance is hard to get these days. Zane can't afford to have an employee get in an accident in one of the ranch vehicles. He'd be liable."

"That's why I'm going to see the doc," Charlie said through the still-open passenger door. "Zane said you'd drive me."

Liam glanced outside the open barn doors, wishing Brad or one of the ranch hands would appear and take over the chore.

He'd hoped to swing by Carly's business to see her and Buster before heading to the station to keep an eye on things and catch up on paperwork until Carly closed for the day. But as luck would have it, there wasn't another soul in sight.

He jumped off the bed and shut the tailgate. He took his time walking to the front, hoping someone would appear before he climbed behind the wheel.

Fifteen minutes later, he and Charlie were halfway to town and neither of them had spoken a word. Finally Liam couldn't take the silence anymore. "Saw you working at Delmer's last Saturday."

"Saw you, too."

Liam glanced over at Charlie before turning his attention to the road. Yeah, this was comfortable. And no doubt Zane had planned this trip the moment he knew Liam was taking the hay to town. Zane was all about the ranch running smoothly, and the fact Liam didn't like Charlie's presence was probably a burr in Zane's saddle. "That was a good thing you did, working to pay Delmer back."

"It was the right thing to do." Charlie lifted a hand and scratched his scruffy face. "Mighty pretty girl, the sheriff's daughter."

Liam didn't want to talk about Carly. "That she is."

"Sheriff's a nice man. Met his girl once or twice at the station dinners they have with the fire department."

Was there a reason for this conversation? He didn't know where Charlie was going with his rambling but Liam also didn't care to find out. Maybe the silence wasn't so bad.

"You thinking of marrying her?"

His grip tightened on the wheel. Marriage? To Carly? They had shared some good times but...

Frowning, he realized it was all too easy to imagine Carly in a white dress, a veil on her hair, curls around her face. All too easy to imagine a future with her. Except... "No. I'm not."

"Mind if I ask why?"

Beyond it being none of Charlie's business? "We disagree on some things. Things that are important in a marriage." Liam knew it was best to simply enjoy their moment, revel in being with Carly for as long as it lasted.

Foster care had taught him to live day by day, moment by moment. Because the moments... They never lasted long.

"Seems like if all the other feelings are there, a man might compromise on a thing or two."

"Not this thing," Liam said, not taking his eyes from the road.

"Something in particular?"

"Yeah." When the silence stretched between them and Charlie simply sat on the opposite side of the cab and stared at him, Liam sighed. "She wants kids."

"You don't?"

"Nope. Why would I? I know nothing about being a parent and I don't care to try."

"Could've had worse than Zane."

He wasn't about to get into a heart-to-heart discussion with Charlie about his childhood.

"Afraid you'd fail?"

Liam glanced across the cab.

"At parenting?" Charlie said, as though he had to clarify.

Liam refused to answer the question.

"I know something about that. Failing. I used to think if I could catch a break, I'd conquer the world. And once I did, I could go back and right my wrongs. Never happened, though."

Yeah, that was the example he needed to hear. Liam settled himself more comfortably in the driver's seat, but a glance at Charlie revealed the old man now stared out the window at the scenery passing by, an unreadable expression on his face.

"So what about those wrongs?" Liam asked. "You might not have conquered the world but if they're bad enough, you could try to fix them."

He could only imagine what kind of trouble the man had gotten himself into. In his years as a deputy, Liam had seen it all. Thievery, rustling, breaking and entering of the very homes paying the ranch hand's salary.

"Maybe. I don't know that that's possible now. Time passed, people moved on. Some things are best left alone when you're not sure good can come of it."

He thought of Carly, of his relationship to her. "Amen to that."

IT WAS LUNCHTIME on Friday when Abigail, the social worker who handled Carly's cases, called.

After a slow morning and Friday-itis caused by the beautiful day outside, several of her clients had chosen to pack up early and head home, leaving Carly to answer the phones and little else.

"Carly? Are you interested? He's six years old, quiet as a mouse. He's been physically abused and he needs a loving, nurturing home."

Abigail went on to give more details about the child but Carly had trouble focusing. While Liam had never come out and actually said he hoped or expected her not to take in another foster child, he'd made his feelings clear. Crystal clear.

And what about her dad? He and Rissa were due to return on Sunday evening. By taking in this boy, she was opening up a whole can of trouble.

"He really needs a good home, and you're one of the few on my list willing to accept a child with his issues. I could hand him off to another caseworker or put him in another home but right now you're the only child-free home I have and I think Riley could use the extra attention. Will you take him in?"

Maybe if Abigail hadn't given her the boy's name… She'd always *loved* the name Riley.

Carly closed her eyes and prayed Liam would understand. And if he didn't?

She gripped the phone tighter. If Liam didn't understand, things might end between them before her father ever made it home on Sunday. "Yes," she said softly. "Yes, I'll take him. When will you bring him?"

TWO HOURS LATER, Carly pressed the button on her home phone and ended the call. What was she going to do?

Of all days for an office emergency, of all times, why *now?*

She stared at the little boy asleep on her couch, sick to her stomach at the pain he'd suffered, at the image of his bruises and cuts and burns. If she lived to be a hundred, she'd never get that sight out of her head.

Riley Mays needed more than a good home, and while he was with her Carly planned on helping the child in any way she could. But she knew Liam wasn't going to be pleased, which only made the queasiness she felt that much worse, especially since she now recognized the marks marring Liam's body. He had them on his arms, his chest, his back, a few on his legs. Little white patches of faded skin just like those on Riley.

Cigarette burns, Abigail had said.

Cigarette burns.

Carly pressed her trembling fingers to her lips and closed her eyes, unable to imagine doing such a thing to anyone, much less a child.

And Liam... There were so *many*. It made her sick to think about the pain and suffering he'd endured. Children were to be loved, nurtured. Taught right from wrong, yes, but not abused.

Focus. They're both safe now.

Standing in her kitchen, Carly leaned against the cabinets, weak-kneed and struggling to maintain control of her emotions. Liam was an adult. He'd overcome, became a deputy, a better man.

But what about Riley?

A glance at the clock reminded her that she had to go. The call had been from the maintenance repairman at her office. There was a water leak in her building. Of all days... "Think, think, *think*."

She had to get to the office but she hated the thought of waking the little boy. He'd sat on the couch while she and Abigail had talked, falling asleep as though absolutely exhausted from the ordeal he'd suffered. And no wonder.

Grabbing the phone, she dialed Mandy's number but hung up when the answering machine clicked on.

Her father might not approve but Rissa would have watched Riley in a heartbeat if she were in town. Another option would be taking Riley to the Second Chance Ranch for her aunt-by-marriage to watch over, but that would take too long. She had to get to the office building now.

A knock sounded at her door and for the first time in fifteen years she prayed for it to be Mandy.

It wasn't. Surprise rolled through her when she saw Liam standing on her porch, looking big and masculine in his cowboy hat and shades. "L-Liam, what are you doing here?"

She'd hoped to have more time to come up with a plan on how to break the news to him about Riley's presence in her house. Now words left her and panic set in. He was going to be upset.

He held up a bag from the diner. "It's a little late for lunch but I brought some anyway in case you haven't eaten. Dessert, too. Porter said it was your favorite."

"Oh. How thoughtful. Thank you."

Liam took off his sunglasses, his gaze narrowing on her face. "Something wrong? You look pale."

"No. No, not at all. Come in." She stepped back so he could enter the house. As soon as the door shut, her cell phone buzzed. She groaned at the number and gave him an apologetic shrug as she answered the cellular pest. "I'm coming as fast as I can, Sal." Couldn't the man handle a little water?

"You haven't left yet?" Sal asked.

Her handyman could be such a drama queen. "No, I haven't left yet but—" She looked at Liam, not seeing another way around the impossible situation. "I'll be there in five minutes."

He raised his eyebrows at the statement. "Not unless you want a speeding ticket," he murmured as she ended the call. "But if you let me frisk you, I might get you off," he said with an ornery grin, pulling her close for a kiss.

Stressed to the hilt and knowing he was not going to like what she was about to do, she wasn't surprised when he pulled away and stared down at her because of her lack of response.

"What's going on, Caroline?"

"There's an emergency at my office building and I need to leave. Now."

"Okay. I'll drive you."

She shook her head, wishing there was a way to prepare for the argument about to take place. "You can't." She lifted her chin, dragging in a deep breath. "Because more than anything, I—I need you to stay here."

She shoved her hair out of her face and waited. He'd catch on and the moment he did...

"Why?" he asked with slow deliberation.

Unable to handle the way he stared at her, Carly walked to the kitchen to gather her purse and keys.

He followed. "Carly, what is going on?"

"I wouldn't ask you to do this if there was any other option but there's not. Mandy isn't home, Dad and Rissa are still gone and I don't have time to drive him to stay with my aunt Maura."

"Drive...*who?*" Liam demanded, his expression hardening.

"The boy I—I took in from Children's Services. Liam, I had to. I couldn't say no. I'll explain everything later. Just, please, Liam, stay. I'll be back as soon as I can."

He snagged her elbow in his hand when she turned toward the door, prepared to run so she could be the first one out and he'd *have* to stay.

Yeah, no way does that *resemble your mom in action. Sprinting for the door and leaving you and your dad behind.*

"*Caroline.*"

"Shh. He's asleep. Don't wake him. You have to do this for me. I'll only be gone a few minutes, an hour, tops. Riley will sleep the whole time. You said you'd help me with this, at least until my parents get home."

Liam dropped his hand as though she'd burned him.

"Dammit, Caroline."

The words had barely left his lips when he turned and searched the living room, his gaze narrowing in on Riley, his head barely visible beneath the throw she'd placed over the boy.

"Liam, please. I know you're upset but try to understand. Abigail needed someone to take Riley in and I *had* to say yes," she said in a hoarse whisper, not wanting Riley to wake up to more trauma and drama than he'd already been through. "I'll be back soon. I *have* to go before Sal starts screaming like a girl, but I'll be back as fast as I can."

Liam followed her to the door, swearing under his breath with every step he took.

"Caroline, wait. You can't leave me here with this kid."

She turned and stood on her tiptoes, brushed a quick kiss over his mouth. "For me, Liam. Do this for *me*."

Stepping back, she held his gaze, then hurried out the door.

CHAPTER TWENTY-TWO

LIAM SAT IN CARLY's recliner, taking all the care and effort to remain silent so the kid would sleep.

She had said she'd be back soon. She wouldn't linger, knowing how he felt about the situation.

But after pacing for ten minutes and it doing nothing to work off the excess frustration fueling his blood, he decided a little shut-eye wouldn't hurt, since he hadn't exactly gotten a lot of sleep lately himself.

Five minutes later, he couldn't ignore the sensation of being stared at. The kid hadn't moved but he was awake.

Sighing, Liam grabbed the nearby remote and found a channel of cartoons instead of the rodeo he would have preferred. Rather than watching the show, the boy kept a wary eye on Liam.

Finally he couldn't take it anymore. "You hungry?"

He'd left the sack of food on the counter in the kitchen, and his own stomach growled at the thought. Breakfast had been a long time ago, a morning's chore, a ride with Charlie and now *this* ago.

The boy didn't respond but he sat up on the couch, the blanket Carly had placed over him falling away to reveal bumps and bruises and— Liam sucked in a harsh breath.

Dear God.

In an instant he was transported back in time. He saw the gleam of resentment and hatred in his mother's eyes, smelled the alcohol on her breath until the stench of his burning flesh beneath the cigarette butts she smashed into his skin overtook everything except the pain.

A knot formed in Liam's chest. He couldn't look away from the kid's wounds, both old and new.

Under Liam's scrutiny, the boy drew his knees to his chest and put his head down as though in shame.

Silent, Liam muttered the ultimate of curses and shoved himself to his feet, trying not to notice the way the kid flinched and tried to bury himself in the cushions. "Carly will be back soon. Come into the kitchen and we'll eat."

Stalking ahead of the kid for some breathing room, Liam searched the fridge and found the makings for sandwiches. He grabbed plates, chips and, because he figured the boy would agree to whatever was put in front of him, Liam made a couple of sandwiches, saving the dessert for after. The kid could have Carly's portion.

A soft shuffle behind him alerted Liam to the kid's presence. "Have a seat. Almost done."

From across the room, Liam heard the boy's stomach growl. He was a scrawny little thing, one arm covered in a blue cast, the other so thin Liam made a third sandwich, just in case.

Minutes later, they were both seated at the table. Liam watched as the boy dug in. "Slow down." The words emerged more forcefully than Liam had intended. Dammit, he wasn't good at this. But he remembered eating that fast before—and being violently sick as a result.

The boy's head jerked up and he paled to the color of glue.

"I know you're hungry," Liam said, trying to make up for his tone, "but you'll throw up if you eat too fast. Trust me. Slow down some and you won't get sick."

The boy didn't respond verbally but he began eating at a much slower pace, watching Liam from beneath his lowered lashes.

Liam finished his sandwich, satiated for the moment, and sat back in the chair, unable to look away from the boy's burns, unable to distance himself from the past. "It'll get better."

Riley made eye contact, cheeks puffed out with food even though he had stopped chewing.

His gut in knots, Liam clenched his jaw as he unbuttoned the cuff of his long-sleeved shirt and rolled it back, shoving the length above his elbow. That done, he pointed to one of the many faded spots on his arm, waiting for the kid to make the connection.

It didn't take long.

Riley's green eyes widened and he stared at Liam with new awareness.

Liam searched for words. "You won't ever forget," he said gruffly, "but one day it will all seem like a bad dream and you'll be bigger and older. And because of what happened to you, you'll know better than to hit or hurt…or burn."

Riley's eyes changed. He lost some of the wariness he wore like a shield, and in its place was hope, understanding. Too damn much for a kid his age.

But at the same time it made Liam feel good that he had given the boy some comfort. He suddenly understood in a way and on a level he never had before why

Carly was so passionate about fostering. Why she was drawn to it.

He understood, but it didn't make it any easier. Carly had never been abused and she wasn't sucked into hell at the sight of every mark on Riley.

Not like him. Staring into Riley's gaze Liam saw clear to the kid's battered soul and it ripped Liam's heart out because what he saw... What he saw was like reliving his past—and getting burned—all over again.

CARLY WAS A NERVOUS wreck by the time she made it home. Instead of a few minutes or even an hour, she'd been gone well over four. The water *leak* had been a water *break*. Several of her offices on the first floor had flooded, and her clients were upset and rightly so. She had stayed to soothe ruffled feathers and pitch in on the moving effort. Thank goodness she had two empty offices in an undamaged portion her clients could use while she had the damage repaired.

Carly let herself into the house and walked through the dusk-darkened space, only to find Liam and Riley sitting on her back deck side by side on a lounger by the hot tub. Buster was asleep against the warmth of the tub, his face resting on his paws in total doggy relaxation.

Every now and again, Liam would point at the stars beginning to show themselves in the cloudless sky.

She leaned against the door frame and watched, her heart swelling with so much tenderness she couldn't help but smile.

If only he could see what she saw right now. The patience he exuded, the gentleness of his tone when he spoke to Riley even though the boy didn't respond. She wanted to freeze this moment, absorb it to hold on to. Just in case.

She wanted to be with Liam, not only now, but always. It was totally crazy and much too soon to be thinking such thoughts but she knew what they shared was right. It was real.

After her teenage scandal, her father had tried to explain the difference between sex and love. He'd stressed monogamy and commitment, true caring and tenderness, and what she felt for Liam… She wasn't ready to call it *love* because if he stuck to his declaration about not wanting children, what then?

But whatever it was… Looking at Liam and Riley together, their heads bent so close, she knew deep in her heart she didn't want to go through life without a child in it. Without *children*.

Liam's children?

As crazy and as fast-moving and forward-thinking as it sounded, considering they'd only gotten together recently, yeah. She could see that happening.

But what if he didn't change his mind? Was affection and sympathy and whatever it was she felt for him *enough* to erase the void of not having children? If that was the only way they could be together, could she sacrifice her newly discovered want and still be happy?

Something alerted Liam to her presence. He glanced at her, his expression changing before her eyes. Hardening, angry. All toward her. "I'm sorry. It wasn't a leak but a water break and it took a lot longer than I thought it would."

Liam stood and without a word to either her or Riley, he walked toward her, passing her and continuing through the house toward the door. "Liam?"

He didn't stop.

"Riley, stay right there, okay?" she ordered. "Liam, wait."

"Don't bother."

"Liam."

He whipped around to face her, his eyes blazing with an anger she'd never known him to express. "What? You know how I feel about you being a foster parent, yet you left me here to *babysit* while you took off?"

"It was an emergency."

"Never again, Carly. I agreed to—to mow your damn lawn and take out your trash. I did not agree to spend the night watching some kid. You don't ever do that again."

She was startled by the fury in his tone, the way he looked at her, but she couldn't back down. Wouldn't. Too much was at stake. "Did you *look* at him?" she asked, careful to keep her voice low. "How could I say no? How could I turn him away?"

Liam didn't answer. He walked out of her house, his angry strides eating up the short distance to his truck. But from where she stood, Liam had made it clear he was a million miles away.

"Do you want me to leave?"

Carly closed her eyes when Riley's little-boy voice said the words with such bravery. He had nowhere to go and they both knew it. "No, Riley, I don't want you to leave. In fact," she said, facing him and trying hard not to stare at the visible burns, "I very much want you to stay."

LIAM WAS SO ANGRY he knew he wouldn't be able to concentrate on the paperwork he'd planned to finish up at the station, so he cranked on his radio and headed home, the evening breeze blowing through the windows but doing nothing to clear the haze in his mind.

During the drive to the Circle M, his thoughts kept circling the same track—Carly, kids like Riley. His past. Kids, period.

Liam knew it wasn't fair but he didn't want Carly to be hurt and how could she not be when kids like Riley showed up covered in bruises and burns, silent as ghosts?

It wasn't fair, and it wasn't right. He couldn't help but be protective of Carly, put her first, because she was so open when it came to people. Even in school she'd been too trusting and time and again she'd gotten kicked in the teeth because of it.

This kid? Riley could be the one to really make Carly hurt. And as much as she needed to know the realities of what she was doing, Liam wanted to protect her from it. Once you saw certain things, you couldn't ever forget them. Same thing once certain things were *done* to you.

What was she going to do when Riley continued to show up in the system, older, harder, more bitter and beaten down until the only thing he knew to do was fight? Steal? Show the kind of in-your-face belligerence Liam would bet cold hard cash that Carly had never experienced. What then?

He wouldn't be able to stand it. And the moment the kid laid a finger on Carly, Liam would be hauling his dysfunctional ass to jail while she blamed *him* for taking the kid away.

And even if Riley didn't turn on Carly? Even if the kid kept his cool?

Then he and Carly would be stuck watching the kid come through again and again, every bruise another reminder of the past and how screwed up the system could be at times.

It would eat Liam alive.

He knew the officials did what they could. The system wasn't perfect and the kids paid the price for imperfection. How many broken arms and cigarette burns were in Riley's future?

Shit.

Having taken the long route home to clear his head, Liam was driving along the ranch-house road when he noticed Zane and Charlie sitting on the porch and enjoying the pretty night.

His leg tensed and even though he told himself to press on the gas and keep going, his foot wound up on the brake instead. Seconds later, he was on the porch with them, not wanting to go near the cabin because he knew he'd see Carly everywhere he looked. Especially in his bed.

"Evenin'," Zane and Charlie said in unison.

"What are you doing home so early on a Friday night?" Zane asked.

Not what he'd hoped to be doing. Especially compared to last Friday night when Carly had followed him home. "Been a long week. Brad around?"

Maybe talking to Brad would help. He was the most stoic and stable of the three adopted brothers, with Chance coming in dead last.

"Nope. He and a couple of the boys went to find some fun." Zane nodded toward his truck. "You know where they are," he said, referring to the Wild Honey. "Why don't you go hunt 'em down and join them."

Once upon a time Zane used to tell Liam to get his act together and straighten up. Now he was too strait-laced. And even though he knew Zane didn't understand what had happened to turn the tide and make a difference, Liam was all too aware. "Not tonight."

Charlie stared a hole through Liam's head.

"What?" Liam asked, fixing a glare on the man when the staring didn't stop.

"Something's wrong. You left this morning in a decent mood but it's sour as mountain hooch now. What's troubling you?"

Liam stood. "Have a good night."

He was halfway to the truck before he glanced over his shoulder to see the light from the kitchen spilling out the storm door and encircling Zane.

No matter how much he tried, he couldn't force his feet to take another step. "Why did you do it?" he asked, the words tumbling out of his mouth before he could stop them.

He didn't want to have this conversation in front of Charlie but the whole damn town knew Zane had adopted them, so what did it matter?

"Do what?"

"Adopt us."

Zane's rocker stilled, and he sent a glance in Charlie's direction. "Lot of reasons, I suppose. Which one do you need to hear?"

Zane leaned forward in his chair, his gaze solid on Liam's despite the distance and the darkness. "You boys were good boys deep down. I knew it. I could see it, despite the trouble you'd gotten into."

"But why did you do it? You didn't need us. After

we paid off the damages, why go through the hassle of an adoption?"

"That girl you've been seeing, she get a new foster kid?" Charlie asked.

Liam sent Charlie a glare. "How do you know about that?"

Zane sipped his coffee. "You know how word gets around. As to why..." He inhaled and released the breath in a gusty rush. "I guess I did it because I'd missed out on my chance to be a father. I hoped to make up for it, and you boys certainly needed someone."

Liam understood the reference to fatherhood. Zane had a daughter out in California. One who never called, never visited. Not once the entire time Liam had known Zane.

And considering Zane was a man to respect and look up to, the fact the woman was so uncaring rubbed all of the adopted brothers raw.

But Liam couldn't say much of anything considering he'd work until his dying day to make up for the pain and heartache he'd caused Zane, all the while praying he never discovered what Liam had done the night before he'd finally woken up to the fact he didn't want Zane to send him away.

Liam walked to the porch and sat on the wooden steps in the shadows.

"You like that girl, don't you?" Zane asked.

"No," he said firmly. "How can I, when she knows what it will be like, how she'll feel when she has to send this kid back? I've tried to warn her, help her see what she's doing. I gave her a damned dog to mother and keep her company. But she still said yes to taking in another kid and I don't want to be responsible for picking up the pieces when he's gone."

"There's nothing wrong with wantin' to be a mother," Zane argued.

"She doesn't have to do it like this." Liam ran his hand over his neck and squeezed hard.

"How can she do it, then?" Charlie asked. "You said you told her you didn't want kids. Maybe she thinks this is her only way of gettin' them."

"She's going to get hurt. She's already hurting," Liam said, hating that his voice revealed more than he wanted. "The kid she has now is black and blue and scared of his own shadow."

"Everybody has a calling, son. Maybe this one is hers." Zane set his mug aside. "And getting so mad about it just proves you do care, whether you'll admit it or not."

Fine. He liked her. And maybe fostering kids was her calling but it sure as hell wasn't his.

"Liam?" Zane called.

Liam hadn't realized he'd gotten to his feet and was almost to the truck for the second time. "What?"

"Haven't seen much of you these past couple weeks but when I have you seemed...happy." Zane nodded as though to confirm his words. "Maybe you should think about that."

He didn't need to think about it. Zane was famous for telling them all to go think on things after they'd done something wrong. But Liam hadn't done anything wrong. Carly was in over her head and he had to separate himself from the situation, one way or another.

Maybe he hadn't done half-bad taking care of the kid tonight but he couldn't let himself get sucked in.

Ready to escape the conversation he'd brought on himself by stopping, Liam practically dived into his truck, grateful for the concealing shadows.

He had been happy this week. Happy because of spending time with her. Tonight when he'd seen those burns on Riley's arms, memories long buried surfaced, ones he'd considered too strong to ever share. But he had—with the kid, no less—and he still wasn't sure why.

Liam drove to the cabin on autopilot, glad he knew the private gravel road between his house and Zane's like the back of his hands, because he wasn't paying nearly enough attention to be behind the wheel.

He pulled up to his dark house but made no move to get out, his hands gripping and releasing the leather. He either had to support Carly and help her the way he'd said he would, or get the hell out.

Which would it be?

CHAPTER TWENTY-THREE

CARLY HAD STARED at the ceiling of her bedroom until around midnight, Liam's departure circling her mind until she'd pulled a pillow over her head as though she could hide from the words.

The clock read 12:32 a.m. when she heard a knock at her door that sent Buster bounding down the hall, his nails loud on the wood floor. He growled, the sound bone-chilling, and she knew exactly why the elderly Mr. Murphy had liked having Buster around.

"Shh, don't wake Riley."

As though understanding her words, the dog stopped growling and sniffed the crack of the door. Grabbing the portable phone, she peeked out the nearest curtain. *Liam?*

Carly fumbled to unlock the door and the moment she swung it wide, Liam stepped inside. "What are you—"

His mouth smothered her welcome and she was vaguely aware of him hauling her close and shutting the door. The kiss was hard and fast, totally ravishing—a word she'd never thought she'd ever use in real life—and thorough enough to leave her shaking and unable to stand on her own when he finally lifted his head.

The pretty night-lights left on throughout the house cast enough light to see him clearly. His eyes blazed with hunger but it wasn't only physical hunger. No, it was something else. Something as wild and untamed and desperate as the kiss had reflected. That something made her choice.

Taking his hand, she led him down the short hallway. They both looked in on Riley to quickly make sure the noise hadn't woken him, but once Buster was settled on the rug at the foot of Riley's bed, Carly led Liam to her room and locked the door behind her.

The child's presence in the house forced them to be quiet but their lovemaking was hot and sweet and not quite slow, the kind that left her holding on to his shoulders and breathlessly gasping out, "I love you," when it was over.

On Saturday morning, Carly tried to comfort herself with the fact that Liam had returned to her after their fight.

She would not think about whispering those three little words that weren't returned *or* how she'd woken up alone in her bed. No wonder Liam had acted cranky about her sneaking out of his house. She certainly didn't like that he'd done the same.

The important thing is that he came back.

Yes. Liam had returned despite her taking Riley in, despite having to babysit the child during her emergency. It was progress. And hopefully it was progress she hadn't undone by pushing the cart even faster and saying she loved him. But she couldn't not say it at the time, couldn't not think it.

All this time she'd been searching for Mr. Right and Liam had been right there, first in school, then at the station. Always there, always her friend. But how did he feel about her?

Carly turned and found Riley staring at her, looking more than a little guilty and sad and scared. "Riley, eat your eggs."

He lowered his gaze and took a small bite.

The bacon crisp, she took Riley two strips. As soon as she put them on his plate, his head lowered even more.

"S-sorry."

In response to the boy's words, her cheek throbbed, but until then she hadn't paid it any mind. "It was an accident, sweetheart. You didn't mean to hit me. You were having a bad dream."

A bad dream where she'd found him curled up on the bed, his eyes glazed, crying out for his daddy to *stop*.

Carly stroked her hand over the boy's soft hair, trying to show him the gentleness he so badly needed.

Riley grabbed her hand, not looking at her while he closed her fingers into a fist, then jerked her hand toward his face.

Carly yanked her hand away in time. "Riley, no."

At a loss for words, she dropped to her knees beside his chair. "Look at me. *Riley, look at me.*"

His chin quivered and his eyes were full of tears.

"Honey, I am not going to hit you. Do you hear me? What you did was an accident. A little makeup will cover the bruise right up. But I don't want to hit you. In fact, I won't ever hit you. If you do something you shouldn't do, I'll tell you. And if you do it again," she said, forcing strength into her words when her heart was breaking, "I'll put you in time-out or take away one of your new toys. But I will not hit you. Do you understand?"

His nostrils flared with every breath but he nodded once.

Trust was hard to form after it had been shattered. From the little Abigail had told her, Riley would be placed with a family member as soon as they found one willing to take him in. She couldn't imagine a family being unwilling to accept one of their own, especially a child, but who knew what people thought these days?

All she knew was that Riley was another example of why she had to do this. Maybe she'd agreed to foster because she wasn't sure she could be a parent. But now she knew she had exactly what it took to be a mother. Mothers gave love and protection and care. And foster mothers gave hope to kids who experienced little of it. They gave comfort in a time when a child deemed no one trustworthy or safe.

Riley was merely one example of so many kids. How could she turn them away? How could anyone look into Riley's precious little-boy face, see the pain and the bruises and the torment, and turn him, turn any of them, away?

Taking a deep breath, Carly straightened and cleared her throat. "Eat," she whispered, needing a second to collect herself after what Riley had done.

The boy rubbed a fist over his face before picking up his fork. From her position by the stove, Carly saw that he ate with a little more ease. "You know, it's Saturday and I have the day off. We have to pick some things up for you before school on Monday and I need to check on my office and the water damage I told you about.

But when we're finished that, what would you like to do today?"

At least school or day care wouldn't be a worry. Abigail had assured her the bus would drop Riley off at YPA on Monday around 3:30 p.m. or so. Carly had no doubt she could find something to keep the little boy entertained in the hour and a half until closing. He was so good-natured, so gentle with Buster, and she knew Riley wouldn't be a problem to have at work the short time he'd be there. "Come on, we need to think of something really fun. Wanna go to the park?"

A flash of something—hope, excitement, disbelief—flickered over the boy's face, shattering the remaining pieces of her heart. She'd known it would be a hard journey, and staring at Riley's cast and bruises, she struggled to hold a smile on her face. Being a mother, especially a foster mother, took strength and courage, a backbone of steel and a loving heart.

All the qualities her mother had lacked—and all the things Carly was slowly learning she possessed.

LIAM SLOWED THE SUV cruiser when he spotted the gleam of Carly's bright red hair in the park. No one else in town had hair like her and he'd recognize that wild mane from a mile away.

Carly slid down the slide and hopped off the end like a kid. He smiled at the sight, watching as she turned and waited for Riley. The kid's face lit up during the rush of the drop, his smile making the black eye and cast harder to stomach, even from a distance.

Carly placed one hand on Riley's shoulder and pointed to the swings. While she headed off in that direction, Carly missed the way the kid looked over his shoulder to where three older boys tossed a baseball and played catch. Riley glanced at Carly and ran to catch up, but twice more he looked over his shoulder at the boys, with a longing only a baseball fan could understand.

Liam drove off and continued his patrol, his thoughts consumed by the words she'd said last night.

Carly was a good woman, sexy, smart. Passionate. Only an idiot would turn her away.

But by saying she loved him… He didn't believe in love. It was a fleeting sentiment, one that never lasted.

But right now all he knew was that he didn't want to be with anyone else. Right now, that had to be enough.

THAT EVENING AFTER Liam's shift, Carly looked surprised to see him on her doorstep. "Grab your shoes and Riley. We're going to be late for the early movie at the theater if you don't get a move on."

Caroline exhaled in a rush and wrapped her arms around him. "You're here. I'm glad."

So was he, even if he didn't know what the hell he was doing. Unable to pass up the opportunity, he lowered his mouth over hers and kissed her.

"I love you, Liam."

Hands buried in her hair, eyes closed, he brushed his lips over hers again. "Get your shoes."

"GET YOUR SHOES."

Not exactly the three words Carly had been hoping to hear from Liam. She hadn't planned to tell him she loved him the first time.

Or the second.

When he had shown up to take them to the movies, the words had slipped out naturally and from her very soul. She couldn't hold them back—or be sorry she'd said them now.

She loved him. But Liam obviously had issues with her and trust and foster care—everything about their relationship was a powder keg ready to blow.

But after dropping them off following the movie, Liam had driven to the station for an hour or so to work, then walked back after it was dark. Most of her neighbors had pulled their blinds and called it a night. But it wouldn't have mattered. It was their last night before her father and Rissa came home and they both knew it.

With Riley in bed, she and Liam had made love, then shared a late-night snack before he'd left. When Liam had asked about the smudge on her cheek, she'd waved off the comment and changed the subject, not wanting to ruin the mood and knowing the truth would sour everything. They were already too aware that once her father was back in town, things could change.

"Riley, are you dressed?"

Hearing a footfall behind her, she turned to see the boy dressed in shorts and a T-shirt and looking very apprehensive.

She dropped to her knees in front of him and smiled. Kids were scared of what they didn't know or understand, of what their parents made them afraid of. And in Riley's case, someone made him afraid of the cops. "You look great. Now, don't be nervous. They're police officers but they're my friends, like Liam. You had fun at the movies last night with him, didn't you?"

Riley's head bobbed up and down in a slight nod. "Yeah."

She smiled, glad he was finally beginning to feel

comfortable enough to talk to her. "Good. Now, I need a big favor. Will you help me?"

Another nod, this one more tentative. "How?"

She held up a chocolate-chip cookie still warm from the oven. "I need an official taster. Is this good?"

TEN MINUTES LATER, Carly and Riley carried plastic containers of food from her car into the station in preparation of the weekly Sunday lunch.

Mike Shipley, one of her father's other deputies, quickly put aside his coffee to help.

"Hey, Carly. McKenna's been looking for you."

"He has?" She set the containers on the counter and flipped the oven on to a low temp.

"Anything else?"

"To carry in? Yeah, in my car. The trunk's open."

"Hey, little man. Want to help me carry in the rest for Miss Carly?"

Carly quickly nodded her acceptance to Riley's questioning glance. "Deputy Shipley has a little boy about your age. Go on. And don't forget to get the cookies out of the front seat, okay?"

The moment the two walked away, Carly hurried to put the pans in the oven to stay warm before she went in search of Liam. She found him working on paperwork in her father's office and muttering to himself.

"For every arrest, there are a thousand forms," she said softly, quoting her father's biggest complaint about law enforcement.

Her words drew a smile from Liam that was quickly replaced by a frown.

"That's no smudge. What the hell?"

Oh, no. Apparently she hadn't done a good enough job with her makeup. "It's a bruise. Nothing serious."

Liam's entire body turned to stone. "Where did it come from?"

"Stop it," she ordered. "That's why I didn't tell."

"Tell me what? Where did that come from?" he repeated, moving closer.

"Riley had a bad dream and I mistakenly tried to wake him. It's fine. I'm fine. I didn't tell you because I didn't want you to be upset."

"He *hurt* you?"

"Not on purpose."

The blinds separating her father's office from the rest of the station were drawn but she knew better than to shut the door. She edged over enough so no one could see them and stood so it would bump into her heel if the door was pushed inward. "Look, Liam, my parents... They're coming home today. They'll be here in a few hours and I could use your support. Don't be angry with Riley, okay? It was a total accident."

Liam pulled her into his arms, squeezed her a little too tight.

Carly couldn't help but be happy he looked so torn. Maybe it was too soon to be declaring love for each other but she felt it for him. And Liam...he cared for her. She could tell.

She raised her face to his and relished the sizzle she felt as his lips met hers and lingered, the caress deepening until her breath quickened and her heart thumped with the speed of Buster's excited tail-wagging greeting. Everything disappeared but the two of them.

Liam pulled her closer, away from the door. "Caroline..."

She blinked, hoping, praying she would hear the words she wanted to hear.

What he hadn't told her about his past, she was able to fill in. But that *was* the past, not now. Not her. But as with Riley, Liam was waiting for her to strike out at him, to hurt him. She had to prove he could trust her.

A commotion out in the station interrupted whatever Liam was about to say. He quickly stepped around her. "Stay here."

"Riley's out there," she said, following him.

Both stopped in surprise when they saw her father hauling Charlie into the room. The man was staggering and swearing, mumbling nonsense.

Charlie didn't look so good. He was pale and shaking but red-faced angry all at the same time, and she couldn't help but wonder if he'd taken something.

Her father shoved Charlie into a chair.

"Sheriff, welcome back," Liam said, moving closer. "Charlie, you been drinking?"

"Can't smell anything on him and he denies drugs," her father said. "Give him a Breathalyzer. He was swerving all over the road." Looking at her, Jonas smiled. "Hey, sweetheart. What, no hug for your old man?"

"Of course. You're here early." Carly stepped forward to hug her father, smiling despite the knot coiling in her stomach.

"Our flight got canceled so we took an earlier one," he said, releasing her. "We missed you. Anything happen while we've been gone?"

CHAPTER TWENTY-FOUR

LIAM STEPPED CLOSER to Charlie, his instincts telling him something was off. The sheriff was right in that Charlie didn't smell of alcohol but that didn't mean he wasn't high from something else. "What did you take, Charlie?"

"N-no. Was coming to town to... Was... See the doc..."

Liam inhaled, catching a fruity smell on Charlie's breath.

"Why don't you take him over to the clinic?" Jonas said. "I saw the doc's car there as I pulled in."

Knowing what was about to go down between Jonas and Carly the last thing he wanted to do was leave her. "Maybe Shipley—"

"Keep me posted," Jonas said with a nod, his arm wrapped around Carly's shoulders as he led her into his office.

Liam hauled Charlie close and with a last, lingering glance at her, he herded Charlie toward the door.

"You're good," Charlie mumbled. "Good s-son. Don't want to m-meet my maker." Charlie's words were slurred. "When I can't hold my h-head up— So many mistakes."

Liam half dragged and half carried Charlie across the street to the clinic. It took a few bangs on the door but once the doc saw his uniform, she let them inside the closed clinic.

"In there," she said, waving them toward an exam room.

It took both of them to get Charlie on the table. Charlie fumbled but managed to grab hold of Liam's shirt when he tried to step away.

"So many regrets. Don't you live with...regrets."

"Don't be worrying about that now. You can make up for them later."

Charlie's dull gaze watered and Liam was surprised by the emotional display from the world-weary cowhand.

"I...hope so."

"Charlie?" the doc asked. "When was your last shot?"

Shot? Liam watched as the doc pulled on rubber gloves and removed a small box from a locked drawer. The doc quickly stuck Charlie's finger and waited for the reading to appear. "Doc, you know him?"

"Charlie? Yes. Is he under arrest?"

"Sheriff wanted him checked out for possible DUI."

The doctor checked Charlie's pupils. "No, he's not drunk. Charlie's diabetic." She looked at the screen of the glucose monitor and shook her head. "He's been too long without his meds. He can't afford to get more than a week's supply at a time so we've been trying to help him out." To Charlie she said, "Hang in there, Charlie. We'll get you fixed up."

HALF AN HOUR LATER, Liam retraced his steps across the street. He'd called Zane and Jonas and filled them in on Charlie's diabetic episode.

Fortunately, the doc saw no long-term damage but was going to keep Charlie in the exam room a little longer to monitor his numbers before releasing him. Another call to Chance secured Charlie a ride home in a few hours.

When Liam entered the station, he heard Caroline and the sheriff arguing behind the closed office door. He searched the room and saw Carly's stepmother in the kitchen, looking after Riley.

Liam froze, torn between letting Caroline face her father's wrath on her own or joining them and having it potentially end his career.

"Dad, before you go off on another tangent, listen to me, okay? This was *my* decision."

"McKenna should've called me and told me what was going on. *You* should've called me."

"Why? Dad, I know it's hard to think this way but you're not the one fostering, I am. You're angry with *me*. This is not Liam's fault. He argued against my decision, too. But I'll tell you what I told him, this is about *me*. This is something I *have* to do. It's who I need to be and if you don't like it, fine, but you're not going to change my mind."

She was defending him. Defending him when he was standing outside like a coward.

Liam turned the knob and walked in.

"McKenna, not now."

"Liam can stay. I'm out of here. I'm taking Riley home." To Liam she said, "I'll see you later?"

The sheriff swung away from his position at the window so fast the papers on his desk ruffled in the breeze. Jonas's gaze narrowed on his daughter before shifting to Liam.

When the office door slammed behind Carly, Jonas slowly approached Liam, his gaze heated and narrowed on Liam's face. "Well? Anything to say, McKenna?"

The expression on the sheriff's face reminded Liam too much of the past. Of the foster father he'd had when he was fourteen. The family had a fifteen-year-old daughter ready to experiment in all kinds of ways and she'd enjoyed teasing Liam, getting a rise and reaction from him. But when the girl's father had caught them about to kiss, he'd grabbed Liam by the neck and thrown him across the room. He had been removed from the home by Children's Services within twenty minutes. He'd waited by the trash on the curb for C.S. to arrive.

Nothing had happened between him and the girl. And truth be told, he'd worked up the willpower to say no and was about to step away from her. That's when they'd been caught. But the look on the father's face... That look of betrayal was the same one Jonas Taggert wore now.

"What happened while I was gone? Is there anything else I need to know?"

Liam swallowed. He wasn't about to tell the sheriff he'd slept with Carly, because it wasn't any of the man's business considering she was of age but... "She's good, sir. No, she's great with those kids. You would be proud of her if you could see her in action."

Jonas stared Liam down, and with every second that passed Liam became more and more uncomfortable.

"I'm not going to ask about whatever has happened between you and my daughter," the sheriff drawled slowly. "You want to date? Fine. I don't know that I like it, considering what'll happen if things go wrong. But I respect you, McKenna. I wouldn't have put you in

charge if I didn't. Hell, I *like* you. But get this straight—
you *only* see my daughter if you're serious about trying
to make something of it. She isn't some barfly. Do you
understand me?"

"Yessir."

"Good. Now, gather the men up and get in the brief-
ing room. I have a feeling I've missed a lot these past
two weeks."

MONDAYS WERE ALWAYS HARD. After a too-busy weekend,
her parents' return from vacation, et cetera, Carly was
dragging by the time evening rolled around. She had
made it home with Riley and managed to change into
shorts and a T-shirt when a knock sounded at her door.

She peeked outside to see Liam standing there,
dressed in cargo shorts and a light-colored shirt, a baseball cap on his head instead of the Western-style hat he
normally wore. What on earth? Other than his standard-
issue uniform and jeans, she'd never seen Liam wear
anything else. "Hi," she said, pulling the door wide.

His gaze swept over her and in an instant her body
heated like a volcano.

"Hi, yourself. Got plans for the evening?"

"No. Do you?"

Her words prompted a grin from him and her heart
fluttered at the sight.

"Hey, Riley, you take that spelling test yet?" Liam
asked.

"No. It's tomorrow."

"Ah. You study?"

"He studied at the office," she informed him. "And
he got them all right, didn't you, Riley?"

"That's good. So how about taking a break and you and Carly come with me?" Liam said.

She leaned against the door. "Where to?" she asked, liking this version of Liam. And the fact that he was here. Asking them to go with him.

She bit her lip, hoping it hid her smile because she was so happy Liam was initiating an outing with them regardless of her father's return.

"Riley here has always struck me as a baseball fan. That true?" Liam asked, his attention focused on the child at her side.

"Yeah," the boy said, a wary expression flickering over his face. As though he was afraid to reveal liking it too much.

"That's what I thought. So how about we go catch a ball game? The high-school varsity team is playing tonight. Might not be the pros but they've got a real good chance at the state championships this year. What do you say? Do you and Carly want to go?"

Riley looked up at her, a pleading, hopeful, precious expression on his face. "We haven't had dinner yet."

"Hot dogs at the game," Liam said. "There's nothing better than a hot dog in the stands."

Carly laughed. "Now, that's an invitation, isn't it, Riley?"

The child nodded, his excitement apparent but still reserved.

"So what are we waiting for? Go find your shoes. Quick!" she ordered, laughing as Riley raced down the hall and into the spare bedroom.

Once Riley was gone, Carly tilted her head and regarded Liam, afraid to ask what had come over him, because she knew better than to place too much emphasis on his appearance or else risk what would no doubt be a rapid denial of his feelings. So instead she said, "You look awfully sexy in that baseball cap."

Liam entered the house in an instant, crowding Carly until they were no longer standing in the doorway for all her neighbors to see.

"Sexy?" he said, lowering his head until his mouth hovered over hers.

"Yeah. Very." She licked her lips. "Hi."

"Hi, yourself. Things okay with you and your folks?"

Hearing Riley's thumps as he stomped his feet into his shoes, she knew they only had a matter of seconds. "You want to talk about my father or kiss me?"

Liam's head lowered, his mouth locking on hers—until Riley came running and forced them to pull away.

"I'm ready!"

Carly glanced up and found Liam watching her reaction, and enjoying it, if the glint in his eyes was any indication.

"So am I."

Liam and Riley headed out the door but Carly lingered over the act of collecting her keys and locking up, her heart beating wildly in her chest. Hoping against hope that Liam's *so am I* meant he was ready for more than the ball game.

GET THIS STRAIGHT—you only see my daughter if you're serious about trying to make something of it.

The sheriff's words repeated in Liam's head for the billionth time, but despite their regularity he didn't have a solid response to them.

Going to the ball game had been fun. Riley had broken out of his shell some, going as far as to jump up and cheer when the home team scored the winning play.

It was getting close to Riley's bedtime when the game was over, so Liam had driven them home, not really wanting the night to end because he'd liked sitting on the bleacher seat beside Carly. Liked the way she looked with her sunglasses perched on her freckled nose and the waning sunlight shining in her hair.

He'd intended to leave them at her door without so much as a good-night kiss because too many of her neighbors were out watering flowers and being nosy. But Carly stood on tiptoe and kissed him anyway, holding nothing back, and he'd left wishing he could stay.

But no way could he risk spending the night with her now, not with her father back in town. Wasn't that the point of Jonas's fatherly warning? That Carly wasn't a woman to be used for a bit and set aside?

The next morning, Liam finished the chore of setting the post, and paused long enough to wipe the sweat off his face. He noticed Zane walking toward him.

"Gonna need another twenty or so posts to get it done. I'll get the tractor and meet you on the far end," Zane said.

Liam stomped one last dirt clod around the post hole he had finished filling. "Sounds good. I'll load up the posts."

He grabbed his tools and tossed them into the truck, relishing the bright day and the heat of the sun on his skin.

Any man dissatisfied with his life needed to spend more time outdoors, working hard, sweating and seeing the fruits of his labor.

It took him a while to load the shaved pine logs cut

for the fence line and stacked ready for use. Back in the truck, he took a long drink of water, his thoughts shifting to Carly as they always did. What was she doing today? Was she busy at work?

He picked up his cell, tempted to call, but set it down again. Space was a good thing sometimes and Zane and old Charlie were waiting.

Liam would call Carly later, once the job was finished. Riley would be home from school, and the boy had been nervous about his spelling test this afternoon.

Shoving the truck into gear, Liam rounded the various buildings, two of Zane's favorite ranch dogs running alongside the truck but careful to steer clear of the tires. Liam was a quarter mile from his destination when he saw Charlie in the field. The old man tossed down the shovels he carried and ran as fast as his legs would carry him toward the tractor. The tractor was on its side, something blue, the color of Zane's work shirt, beneath it. *"Shit."*

Liam floored the gas and drove through the fence in his way, uncaring of the damage as he plowed through the spring-damp field as fast as the truck would go.

He made it to Zane the same time as Charlie.

"Is he alive?" Charlie asked, gasping from his run.

Liam couldn't respond, all he could do was fall to his knees beside the only man to ever care whether he lived or died. *"Zane?"*

Zane's face was whiter than the clouds overhead.

"Zane, talk to me. Where are you hurt?"

Zane's gloved hand lifted and lowered in a feeble move, indicating his chest. The tractor pinned Zane from his belly down.

"Where's your phone?" Charlie asked. "We need help."

There was no time. Zane's chest and stomach were hard, swelling fast. "Hang on," Liam ordered. "I'll get the truck, pull the tractor off."

"Liam…" Zane's voice was raspy and weak. His eyes dull yet full of awareness. "Come here, son."

No. No, this couldn't be happening. Internal injuries and miles from help.

Dear God, no. God, please. Not Zane. Not like this.

"Dammit, Charlie, *help me.* We've got to get him—"

Zane put his hand over Liam's and gripped it tight. "Stop."

Liam froze at the word, at the gurgle that emerged with it. Blood seeped from the corner of Zane's mouth, staining Zane's white mustache.

Liam's heart stopped cold. His training, everything left his head and he was no longer an adult man but a boy with not enough sense and too much anger at the world, the boy Zane had taken in anyway. "Don't do this. Come on, Zane," Liam begged. "We'll get you out."

Zane's mouth formed words Liam couldn't hear. He bent over Zane, his chest so tight he couldn't breathe for the pain.

"You always made me proud."

Liam pressed his forehead to Zane's, his eyes closed as he tried to will strength into the man.

"You worked…so hard."

"Zane, just hold on."

"Always tried to prove… You were worthy. Love." A sad smile flickered. "Always have been."

"No." The word came out thick, hard, the emotion of a boy in the voice of a man.

"Yes. Stay a family. All of you. T-take care of each other. Promise."

"You're not going to—"

"Charlie…?" Zane shifted his hand and Liam's protest came to a stop when Charlie grasped Zane's palm in his arthritis-gnarled hands.

"Make it right. Liam, you…you help Charlie. Let him…make it right."

"Make what right?" Liam gripped his father tighter but Zane's lashes had drifted down, stayed closed. "Make what right? *Zane?*"

Charlie placed a hand over Zane's chest, his fingers slowly clenching into a fist.

"He's gone, son. Zane's gone."

CHAPTER TWENTY-FIVE

IT WAS NEARING 9:00 p.m. that evening when Liam found himself parked in Carly's driveway once more. Now he wasn't sure why he was there but, feeling the way he felt, Liam didn't want to be anywhere else. With anyone else.

Her blinds were drawn and there were no lights glowing from within the house, unusual for her, since she had a tendency to stay up late. Maybe she was around back, in the hot tub.

He walked up to the door and frowned when he found it partially opened, unlocked. Buster immediately noticed his arrival. Barking, running and skidding toward the door on the hardwood floors, the dog's tail wagged steadily.

Buster sniffed Liam's leg and the bag Liam carried and immediately quieted when Liam petted the dog's head and scratched behind his ears. "Where is she, boy?"

Buster led the way to the living room, where Liam saw her curled up on the couch in the dark. "Caroline?"

Her eyes glittered when she looked at him and the knot that had formed in his gut this afternoon tightened like a noose. After the day's events, it had seemed more important than ever that Riley get the items in the bag Liam carried but now...

"My dad swears he didn't call Abigail but I can't help but wonder," she whispered, her voice thick.

Rubbing a hand over his chest to ease the ache, Liam's other hand tightened on the sack. "You're saying...Riley's gone, too?"

She blinked and lifted her face enough that he could see she'd been crying. Hard. The eyes-swollen, nose-red crying that came when someone grieved as though their heart had been broken.

"What do you mean, *too?*"

"Zane's dead." His throat felt as though it had a mass the size of Texas in it, dry as sandpaper.

Zane was dead, Riley was gone. All in one hell of a day.

Carly closed her eyes and squeezed them tight, rising from the couch and moving toward Liam as though she sought comfort as much as she tried to offer it.

But it was comfort he couldn't afford to give—or receive. Not now. Not at a time like this.

He took a step back.

Carly stopped, her mouth parting as though he'd sucker punched her.

"Liam?"

Somewhere along the way he'd started to become involved, attached, to care. Not only for her but for Riley. Zane. Liam had forgotten the hard-learned rule he'd lived by for so much of his life. The rule of survival.

No ties, no entanglements, no feelings.

He'd barely gotten to know Riley, had barely spent time with him, but Liam felt the loss. What would he feel if something happened to Carly? The way it had happened to Zane?

She needed someone able to love her the way she loved. And he wasn't that guy. He took another step back. "Your father told me that I shouldn't be with you unless I was serious about a future. Caroline, I can't do this."

Her eyes widened in hurt and horror, but he forced the words out. "I can't be the guy you need me to be. I can't stand by and watch you get your heart ripped out every time a kid goes back into the system. I can't pretend it doesn't matter to me."

And if Carly could, if she could handle sending those kids back? How could she ever really be his, knowing what it did to him? What would keep her from replacing him as quickly? Maybe some men could handle it, maybe they were more worthy and understanding of her love, but…not him.

"Liam, don't do this. I'm *so* sorry about Zane but you can't shut yourself off like that. And what about us? I l—"

"Don't say it again," he ordered. "Goodbye, Caroline."

Outside, Liam dragged in deep breaths as he rushed toward his truck, tossing the bag across the cab where it hit the passenger-side window. The bag opened, the contents spilling onto the seat.

The ball bounced off the cushion and rolled into the floorboard but the mitt Zane had bought him stayed put until Liam tossed it into the darkness of the floorboard where he couldn't see it.

Out of sight, out of mind.

Wasn't that the saying?

He prayed to God it was true.

CARLY DROVE LIKE an old woman who really shouldn't be behind the wheel, her thoughts on Liam, Zane's death, Riley's departure.

So this was what it felt like to have her heart ripped right out of her chest while she was awake and watching and able to feel every nerve shred.

She turned into the driveway that led her to her father and Rissa's house, knowing before she pulled to a stop beside the sign advertising Rissa's helicopter charter business that her father's cruiser was parked outside the station in town.

The large two-story garage door was open, a light on inside.

Drawn the way the lost usually were, Carly climbed out of her car and walked toward the glow. Every bone and muscle in her body protested the movement but as she neared the structure where Rissa housed her prized helicopter, her stepmother's thin frame stepped into sight.

"Carly? Hey, what a surprise. Your dad's not home yet but— Oh, honey. What happened? What's wrong?"

Head down, heart shattered, Carly dived into Rissa's open arms. Her stepmother staggered a bit from the force but she clutched Carly to her, murmuring nonsense and stroking Carly's hair the way she had when Carly had been stood up for the first time.

Right now nothing mattered but the pain. It consumed her, but it wasn't enough to make her numb. If only it would. It took everything in her to simply breathe. To inhale and exhale as though everything was *fine*. To hold back the tears, because if she shed a single one the dam might break and she'd never be able to stop. "Thank you." She managed to squeeze out the words.

Rissa's arms tightened around Carly. "For what?"

Gathering herself, Carly pulled back, loving the way her stepmother looked as she smoothed Carly's wild red hair away from her hot face. "For being my mom when mine didn't want me."

"Oh, Carly." Rissa's expression softened even more, her eyes sparkling with tears she didn't try to hide. "Riley's gone, isn't he? Back into the system?"

"Abigail picked him up after school today." Her voice broke getting the words out but she stopped long enough to clear it. "And…Zane McKenna died this afternoon. Or evening. I'm…not sure which."

"What?"

Rissa's shock at the news was evident. Carly explained what she knew, which wasn't much. "Everything is so messed up. There I was licking my wounds when Liam showed up. He needed me to—I don't know—*comfort* him, but as soon as he found out Riley was gone… Liam couldn't handle it. It was too much. I was too much, so he…left."

"It's a lot for anyone to handle, but whatever he said, you have to ignore it." Rissa straightened one of Carly's curls. "Carly, you said yourself Liam came to you for comfort. I know you're hurting but Riley is in a safe place and Zane is gone."

"I know."

"Good. Then you know you can't take whatever Liam said or did personally."

How could Carly not take it personally when she knew Liam meant every word? "Rationally, I know that. But that's just it. When I agreed to foster kids, he tried to warn me how much… How much this would *hurt* but I did it because I had to know if I have what it takes to be a mother."

"Oh, Carly. Honey, you will make a wonderful mother. How could you ever doubt that?"

"*You* are a wonderful mother," Carly said. "But I had some things I had to figure out."

"Did you?" Rissa asked, linking her arm through Carly's and tugging her along toward the screened-in gazebo adjacent the pond located down from the house and garage.

Carly gathered her hair in a hand to pull it off her neck and wished she had a band to control it. Sometimes it seemed as if her hair reflected her emotions. Wild and all over the place. Or more rarely, tame and calm. "I thought so."

"Is Liam upset that Riley is gone? Or that you're hurting?"

Carly breathed the crisp night air. "Both, I think. But it's more, too. He doesn't want to be a parent. Not… ever."

"Oh, honey, then why did you get involved with him?" Rissa asked.

"Could you have stopped yourself from loving my dad?"

Surprisingly, Rissa laughed. "Not in a million years."

A few more steps and they reached the slope at the edge of the pond, the air filled with several *plops* as frogs dived for cover to escape the human arrival. "Liam is so good with kids. You should have seen him with Riley. I don't understand how he can be that way, then turn around and shut himself down like that."

"I think the bigger question is what are you willing

to accept? Once Liam isn't reeling from Zane's death, what then? What do you want? Do you want to continue to foster?"

Indecision warred within her. "I knew it wouldn't be easy," Carly admitted. "But I never expected it to be this hard or...to hurt so much. I know the kids I keep are temporary. I *know* they'll leave within a few days."

"But you got attached anyway," Rissa said.

"Hook, line and sinker," Carly whispered. But so had Liam. She thought of his expression when he'd realized Riley wasn't with her. The pain had been visible and she'd watched it spread across Liam's face.

But what about her? Giving up Sierra had been hard. Yet she'd interacted with Riley, kept him longer. If it hurt this badly each and every time... "I don't know what I'm going to do."

"There's no rush, Carly. You have time."

"I know, but it doesn't feel that way."

"Answer me this. Do you want to be a mother? Even after tonight? Even though Liam says he doesn't want to be a father?"

Carly stared at the moon reflected on the pond's surface, the way the water rippled. Her heart breaking even more because if Liam didn't change his mind... "Yeah. Yeah, I do."

EVERY TIME CARLY made a move to be closer to Liam at the funeral on Saturday, someone or something held her back.

First it was Liam's brothers playing defense and glaring at her. Then even her father waylaid her, stating quietly that maybe Liam needed some time alone.

The McKenna brothers had refrained from burying

Zane as long as possible, attempting to contact Zane's daughter in California so she could attend. Apparently several messages had been left, but the woman hadn't responded to either the written or verbal notices.

So the funeral had taken place without her, nearly the entire town turning out to pay their respects to a man who would be missed very much.

Lost in her thoughts, Carly looked up and spotted her chance to speak with Liam. Ignoring everyone else, she focused only on him. "Liam?"

She hurried to catch up with him, the thick grass around the well-kept McKenna burial plot dragging her heels. If she didn't talk to Liam before he disappeared into the throng of people going to the ranch house, she knew she wouldn't be able to speak to him alone.

When she'd dropped off a pan of lasagna and a home-made apple pie earlier, the kitchen had been filled with food, some of the local ranchers' wives pitching in to prepare for the post-funeral gathering. *"Liam."*

He turned and pierced her with a stare and in an instant her mind went blank, the speech she'd been rehearsing flying out of her head as fast as Liam had left her house. "I—I'm so sorry. For your loss."

A huff of sound left his chest. "Me, too."

"Liam?"

He stopped once more but this time he didn't turn. She was aware that those folks who lagged behind stared at her and Liam but she didn't care. "Can I talk to you privately?"

"Not now."

Not ever was what he meant. She heard it in his tone. "Do you like being alone?"

"This isn't the time or the place, Caroline."

Up close she saw how bad he looked. Dark circles stained the hollows beneath his eyes and he seemed thinner. "No, it isn't. But since you won't return my calls or talk to me, it has to be." She stepped close and lowered her voice. "Liam, you're a good, strong, *loving* man. You might not want to be but you are. You might not want to care for Zane or your brothers or me, but I know you do. Are you really going to let Zane's death scare you away from people?"

"What I do or don't do is none of your business."

"Dad said you tried to *resign,* that you're talking about leaving town once the will is read."

Saying the words aloud made her hurt so badly she felt ill. Her heart had broken when Liam had walked out but now it shattered because of his expression.

Because it was *true.* Liam was so afraid, he was about to run, to shove everyone away and cut ties. How could she help him conquer his fear of being abandoned, when none of it was in her control? He was the one ready to abandon his family.

"It's my life," he said, walking away.

"But you hold *my* heart," she countered, raising her voice to be heard. "I'll give you time, Liam, but I'm not going to let you give it back."

CHAPTER TWENTY-SIX

SINCE ZANE HAD suspected his biological daughter may not return for his funeral, he'd left instructions for the will to be read regardless of her attendance. To not delay further, the brothers had agreed for the document to be read after all the guests left.

After Liam had made the walk from the family's private cemetery to the ranch house, he had forced himself to meander room-to-room, shaking hands and nodding his thanks whenever someone offered their condolences. Finally the crowd thinned and Zane's attorney began to round up those mentioned in the will, asking them to linger awhile longer.

Liam and his brothers entered the living room to find Ernie seated behind the room's old desk, the bluebacked document in his aged hands.

As everyone settled onto couches and seats—Brad stood by the window as though longing to jump out and escape the proceedings because of what they might reveal—Zane's attorney cleared his throat to gather everyone's attention.

"I know this has been a difficult day for everyone and I hate that I have to make it longer, but I thought it best to read the will now, since...we're all gathered. Zane loved this big old house of his, and I can't help but think he'd rather have his last words read here instead of my office in town."

Just get it over with already. Liam wished he'd chosen to stand so he could at least pace instead of being forced to sit still.

"Let's begin," the attorney said, placing his glasses low on his nose and unfolding the document. "'I, Zane Gabriel McKenna, solemnly swear this is my last will and testament.'" The attorney looked up and zeroed in on Delmer. "'To Delmer Frank, I leave my Browning Citori. You've always admired the shotgun and I know it will have a good home with you. Enjoy it, my friend.'"

Delmer smiled at the gift, eyes sad and humbled. "That I will."

"'To Charles Mason, I leave the full use of the two-bedroom cabin located along the ridge road until your death. Charlie, it's time to put down roots and be the man you say you want to be. Make it right, Charlie. It's time.'"

Sitting across the table from Liam, Charlie kept his head down while the attorney read, his hands clasped in front of him. Charlie made eye contact with Liam and before the older man looked away, Liam saw a lifetime of regret in his gaze.

Liam was reminded of their conversation on the way to town that day, the one where Charlie had admitted to wanting to right the wrongs he'd done.

On one hand Liam was shocked by Zane's generosity but on the other, he wasn't at all surprised. Like it or not, Charlie and Zane had been friends for a few years now. And despite his own misgivings, Liam knew Zane had worried about the broken-down cowboy. By bequeathing Charlie the cabin, Zane had seen to his friend's elder years. Charlie would be warm and dry, and Zane knew Liam and his brothers would keep an eye on the man because that was the kind of thing neighbors did for one another.

Ernie continued to read the list of names and items, cash amounts donated to the church, as well as the boys' home where Liam, Chance and Brad had spent so many of their growing years between foster homes. Zane had planned ahead, and the donations were more than generous. Again, not surprising.

"'And last but not least, my children.'"

Like it or not, Liam's heart picked up speed. This was the question circling around in all their minds, the one none of them dared give voice to. He and his brothers were adopted. McKenna by name, but not by blood. What would happen now? The next minute or so would impact the rest of their lives.

"'Boys, you gave me life when I thought mine was over. Not a day went by when I wasn't proud to call you my sons. That's why I hope you'll honor my decision and have patience and forgiveness with what I've done.'

"'To each of my three sons, I leave a portion of the Circle M, allotted according to the map. With Brad running things, Chance minding the store and Liam pitching in where he's needed, I hope your grandchildren will inherit the Circle M one day and carry on the McKenna name.'" Ernie tapped the papers he held with one finger, and a glance at the sheet revealed it to be the map in question. "'And finally to my Ella.'"

Ernie stopped and lifted his gaze above his glasses to address the crowd. "I realize she's not here, but at Zane's request, I'm to read the will in full," he said, returning to the page. "'And finally to my Ella,'" Ernie repeated. "'I would have liked to know you better, which is why—'" Ernie paused to tug at his tie "'—I've given you my favorite tract of land—'"

"What?" The question burst out of Brad. He straightened from his position at the window, going ghost-white beneath his tan in five seconds flat.

Ernie tugged at his damn tie again.

Liam didn't dare breathe. He didn't think any of them did, as they waited for an explanation.

"'—in the hopes you will take the time to love the Circle M as much as I did. Brad, Liam and Chance, you will receive your portion of land immediately. Ella, you have an option. I know you love your life in Los Angeles and living close to your mother. And if you choose to remain there, your portion of the land can be sold only to the McKenna boys for a sum of $100,000. However, if you consent to stay and live in the ranch house for three consecutive months, you will receive full rights to your allotment, which holds an estimated value of... one million dollars.'"

Brad, the stable, usually levelheaded, mannerly one of the brothers, walked out of the room. He didn't utter a curse, not a word of goodbye. He simply left, his boot heels thudding through the house with every hard, heavy step he took toward the door. No one spoke. Not until the screen door at the front of the large house slammed in the wake of Brad's exit.

Liam sat there, his mind struggling to understand the sudden turn of events.

Sweat ran down Ernie's red face and he flashed Liam and Chance a pained glance.

Unbelievable. Once Gabriella knew there was money involved, Liam didn't doubt she'd come running, ready to cash in as soon as she got the message that she had inherited a small—or large—fortune, depending upon her decision.

No one said a word. No one moved.

Ernie sweated as though he sat in a sauna but it was because he knew the significance of what he'd read. They all did. Zane's favorite piece of the ranch held the waterfall and lake that fed water to the entire ranch. The *water rights* to the ranch. If those rights were taken away...

"'At that point in time,'" Ernie continued, "'the land is yours to do with as you please. But note it is my hope and desire that the land and my daughter remain a part of the Circle M. I want my family to be a family, all of you together.'"

Liam swore long and low as he stood and stalked across the room to the spot Brad had vacated. With his fist on the seal, Liam watched as Brad entered the barn, no doubt going to saddle up and ride until he burned off his fury.

"I'm sorry, boys," Ernie said. "Zane knew you would be upset, but this was the way he wanted things done."

And so they would be. Even though *Ella* couldn't be bothered to show up for her daddy's funeral.

The terms of the will sank in and total silence descended on the room. Not even the normally gregarious Chance had anything to say.

They didn't have a hundred grand lying around. But with some finagling they might be able to scrounge it up. Doing so could leave the ranch struggling because everyone knew ranchers were acre-rich and cash-poor. The money was tied up in equipment, cattle, the many ranch hands who kept the operation going.

If Zane's daughter showed up and decided to stay, decided to sell it for the million it was worth—what then? They definitely didn't have that kind of money.

Zane had done the unthinkable—and the daughter who hadn't given a rat's ass over Zane's welfare now held all the cards in her hands.

THAT EVENING, LIAM sat at a table in the corner of the Wild Honey, listening while Brad muttered to himself and scribbled on a piece of paper thinking of ways to come up with cash.

Everybody had known blood was thicker than water, and talk abounded about how fast the ranch would go under, considering Gabriella now held the most valued section of land for the entire ranch and even those ranches bordering the Circle M who paid fees—thereby supporting the Circle M another way—for access to that water.

Chance swore and hit the controller in front of him. He played an arcade game located with several others by the billiard tables, his mind obviously not on the game because he kept crashing. Thank God the volume was turned down.

Liam fiddled with the shredded napkin in front of him, his thoughts dark.

He should take off, leave town. But he couldn't do that to Chance and Brad. He had to tough it out and pitch in until Brad was in control once more. Then he'd leave the ranch and Carly behind. Go find some place else to settle, or maybe change gears and become a U.S. Marshal. Whatever it took.

He'd heard Carly's words when he'd walked away from her at the ranch's small graveyard. Four generations of McKenna's were buried there, but it was the ghosts of his past that had haunted him when he heard her make that comment about him possessing her heart. That he couldn't give it back.

But he had to give it back. Every time he thought about the ball and glove still on the floorboard of his truck, he got angry all over again. She'd said herself that any man who couldn't handle her decision to foster wasn't the man for her and God knew he couldn't handle it. The loss of Zane's death had hit them all hard but losing Riley, too?

Carly had told the sheriff fostering wasn't so much for the kids as for herself. Maybe it was her calling, the way being a cop was for him. He couldn't imagine doing anything else, and he was fairly sure Carly now felt the same way about being a mother. To end things now was…merciful. For both of them.

Even if by some miracle he changed his mind about love and parenting and the crap-load of emotions that came with it, he couldn't go to her empty-handed and, unless he and his brothers came up with a hundred grand to keep Ella in California, they faced a long road with only one end as they fought to save their home and lost it bit by bit.

Surely Gabriella wouldn't want to stay? Three months was a long time.

Charlie entered the bar, looking old and worn down. Something about him looking as sad and mournful as he did grated on Liam's last nerve and when Charlie asked to join them, Liam agreed—only because he needed answers.

Once Charlie had ordered a drink and the waitress left, Liam sat forward in his chair. "What was it?" he demanded. "What did Zane mean when he told you to make it right? Make what right?"

Chance looked over, the snowboarder on the video-game screen taking a nosedive off a cliff.

Liam glanced at his brothers, catching them in the act of exchanging a peculiar look. "What?" he asked them. "Don't you want to know what it is?"

"I need a drink," Chance said.

"God knows I do, too," Brad moaned, grabbing his paper and stuffing it into his pocket.

Both avoided eye contact and left like kids spying a candy bowl across the room.

What the hell? "Why are they clearing out? Don't tell me it doesn't have something to do with you." He glared at Charlie, his instincts going haywire because of his brothers' weird behavior.

Charlie lowered his head and stared at his hands.

"Spill it, old man. What did Zane mean and why are my brothers looking at us like we're a nest of rattlers?"

Charlie rubbed his hands together, the rasping sound of his chapped skin audible over the jukebox on the other side of the room.

"There's no good way of explaining."

"Try anyway."

"You already know part of it. I told you I made a lot of mistakes when I was young."

Liam barely managed to bite back a curse, not in the mood for a trip down memory lane. He had enough mistake-made memories filing through his head to last a lifetime. He didn't need to add somebody else's.

Zane was wrong. *Worthy* wasn't a term that applied to Liam. He'd caused Zane nothing but trouble and heartache in his younger years, biting the very hand determined to feed him, hell-bent on revenging his past even though Zane had been the only one looking forward to Liam's future.

"I got a girl pregnant, didn't marry her. I took off soon after."

"Not exactly original," Liam said. "That's one story almost every drifter can tell. How's it involve Zane?"

"Zane…he's been trying to get me to talk to my son for years, make amends."

That was something Zane would do. He'd spent his life talking about his daughter, Gabriella, even though Ella didn't acknowledge Zane at all. "Zane want me to help you track the guy down?"

"I tried to fix things back then but by the time I wised up and got around to it, it was too late."

Too little, too late. Liam knew that sentiment well. "What happened?"

"The girl got messed up with drugs, worse losers than me. Last I heard, she'd plowed into a tree she was so high. Killed her instantly."

"What about your son?"

Charlie was watching him closely and Liam shifted beneath the man's gaze, uncomfortable but not sure why. His gaze was dark with truth and pain and sorrow. Full of regrets. "He had a rough life from what I heard—until a man came along and adopted him and became the father I never was."

The blood pulsing through his ears drowned out the noise of the busy honky-tonk as Charlie's story replayed in Liam's head.

He shot up out of his chair, knocking it backward. "Son of a— Are you saying I'm—" The fact that his mother was dead meant little to him. She hadn't been a mother and Liam felt nothing but contempt for a person willing to torture a kid the way she'd hurt him, stoned, drunk or bitterly sober.

Liam wiped a shaking hand over his face, not doing a real good job of smothering his curses. He had to get out of there.

"Liam, wait. Son—"

"I am not your son."

"You are. You might not like it or want to be but… you are."

Liam swung around and headed toward the door as though a stampede chased him, aware that Charlie tried to follow but wound up bumping into a mountain of a man Liam had cut off as the guy made his way to the pool tables.

More curses abounded as something crashed to the floor. Liam turned to see the man's shattered mug at his feet.

"Watch where you're goin', old man." The warning was followed by a shove that sent Charlie flying onto a crowded table. The table shifted beneath Charlie's weight and sent him barreling onto the floor.

Liam told himself to keep walking but when the guy followed Charlie and yanked him up to punch him again, Liam grabbed the guy's arm. "He's twice your age and half your size. Leave him alone."

The guy's buddies jumped to his defense and Liam found himself getting held by the friends while mountain man punched him in the gut. Liam doubled over, staring at Chance and Brad's boots when they stepped into the fray.

It was a good old-fashioned free-for-all for all of five minutes. Until they all ran out of anger and strength—and the sheriff arrived.

CHAPTER TWENTY-SEVEN

LIAM SAT NEAR Charlie on the wooden-plank porch of the Wild Honey, their legs dangling over the edge. Both held ice packs to their faces and if he lived to be a hundred Liam knew he'd never forget the irony.

"That's some right hook," Charlie praised, his words muffled by the ice.

"Yours isn't so bad, either. You sure you shouldn't go get checked out?" Liam felt as though he'd been sat on by a one-ton bull. He could only imagine how Charlie felt.

"I'm fine. Busted lip and cut jaw is all. You boys got the brunt of it. Brad's eye is swollen near shut." Charlie lowered the ice. "You going to be okay with the sheriff?"

Jonas wasn't happy to discover one of his off-duty deputies in a bar brawl but witnesses had backed Liam's claim that he'd stepped in to protect Charlie.

As to why he'd done it…he still wasn't sure. "Zane knew?"

The abrupt change in topic didn't seem to faze the old man. Charlie spit and wiped his mouth.

"Yeah. Don't know how, but he knew. I'd hired on hoping to get to see you, meet you if I could. Your mama… She told me what she'd done about signing the adoption papers. I caught a lucky break during one rodeo and hired a man to find you. Zane corralled me within the first hour on the property. Turned out he'd done a little checking of his own, I guess."

"Why did you bother coming to find me?" Liam couldn't keep the bitterness from his voice. Why hadn't Charlie come back when his mother was putting out cigarettes on his skin? Why had he left in the first place?

"I wasn't good for you. Or your mother. I had big dreams but no cash. Your mama liked the idea of being with a rodeo star but I wasn't near that. She wanted a winner, not a loser. You weren't quite two when I came through town to see her and she told me not to come back unless I had a championship buckle and a pocketful of cash. Back then, I was following the circuit and didn't have two nickels to rub together. I knew things were rough, but I figured you were better off with her."

A low laugh rumbled out of Liam's chest. *Better off?*

"I know I was wrong now. But at the time I was ten years younger than you are now and maturity and stupidity part ways when the woman you love says she doesn't want you. I thought if I went off and won a big one, I could fix everything." Charlie lowered his head. "But I never won, and in the end I wound up under the hooves of a bull named Devil's Fire. Couldn't compete for almost a year. By the time I scrounged up enough money to come back this way, she'd married another man and given you a father."

"A stepfather." A man who had hated the sight of Liam, who had ordered his mother to get rid of him on a regular basis.

He closed his eyes briefly, failing to shut out the past, unable to bear any more as he ducked under the waist-high railing and slid off the porch to walk out into the night.

By the time he returned to the porch of the Wild Honey, Jonas was waiting. But with one world-weary glare, the sheriff ordered Liam to go home.

Half an hour later, he let himself into the cabin and headed straight to the bedroom. He stripped off his clothes, then showered. When the water turned cold he got out, intending to drop into bed and will himself to sleep.

But the light from the bathroom cast enough brightness for him to see the envelope Zane's attorney had given Liam after the will had been read.

Liam hadn't been able to bring himself to read the letter but now he picked it up, stared at it a long time and finally slid his finger beneath the seal. He needed answers and maybe… Maybe this would have them.

Legs weak, he sank onto the edge of the mattress.

Inside was a letter folded into rectangles. It smelled of Zane's favorite cigars. Liam opened it and something fluttered to the floor at his feet but he didn't pick it up. It could wait. If he was going to do this, it had to be now.

Liam, if you're reading this I'm gone. I'm not sure what to say about that, except every man has to face the day eventually. I was prepared for it. And I hope when the time comes, you and the other boys are prepared, too, so I can see you again.

I'm proud of you, son. You were a hard nut to crack, the hardest of your brothers to accept the Circle M and us as family. I hope even though I'm gone, you'll stick close to your brothers and realize how much a part of this family you really are, how much you've always been a part of things. We love you, Liam. Might not have said it often enough, but you know how that goes.

One of the first things I ever learned about you was that you had to protect yourself from an early age. Over the years, you've kept your distance and guarded your heart, ever since that day I caught you joyriding on my tractor. I understand why. But I also know the Bible says God puts the lonely in families, and a lonelier boy I've never met.

I know you probably think I'm an old man blowing smoke and that doesn't apply to you. But I know lonely when I see it, because He gave me you boys to keep me from being consumed by it myself. The day I found you boys, I stopped focusing on me and looked outside myself, and I want to say now that nothing you ever did made me regret taking you in. Nothing.

Liam, stop trying so hard to make up for past mistakes. They're done and over and you're not the boy you were. You've got nothing to prove. Not to me, not to anyone. Find a good woman. Be happy. Don't spend your life alone because of the past. You're a good man, and you deserve all of life's joys.

If Charlie hasn't already, sit him down and make him tell you his story. Every old cowboy has one. Charlie's a good man, Liam. I wouldn't have let him stick around year after year if he wasn't. Listen to him, give him a chance. Be the man I know you to be, the son I raised.

Let the past rest once and for all. That is my last request of you, and I hope you'll see it through. I love you, Liam. You will always be my son.

Zane

Liam folded the letter, only then reaching down to find whatever had fallen out. He grabbed the glossy paper and held it so he could see, choking on a smothered curse when he recognized it.

The edges of the photo were brown and burnt, but he knew exactly what it had looked like when it was perfect. It was the only picture he'd had of his father. One he'd burned in a fit of drunken teenage rage that left Zane's barn razed. The barn had been full to the rafters of hay and feed. And because of his stupid behavior, it had been a damn lean winter, the first winter he'd spent as one of Zane's sons.

Zane had questioned them all about the barn burning but he hadn't called Liam out, not even with the proof he now held in his hand. Zane had known all along but he hadn't condemned Liam for it.

I'm sorry. I'm so sorry.

Staring at the photo, Liam wiped his hand over his face. No wonder Zane had known who Charlie was.

Charlie looked twenty years older than his age due to the life he'd led, but the resemblance was there. And it was like looking at a picture of himself. The same dark hair, the same eyes. Why hadn't he ever noticed that? How many people had noticed?

Brad? Chance? No wonder they'd bailed at the bar when Charlie appeared.

Liam dropped the letter and photo on the bed and walked to the bathroom sink, splashing his face and looking at himself in the mirror.

Zane's request was that Liam let the past be.

But how was that possible, when all he saw was the past staring back at him?

CARLY BARELY GOT through the days following Riley's removal from her home and Zane's death.

Despite giving Liam time, he still hadn't called, and with every day that passed since he had walked away from her after the burial—five days and counting—her heart shattered even more. She dragged herself through work, came home and sat on her back porch and stared at the fence lining her small yard instead of tending to her flowers out front. To do that, she risked facing people and gossip and…she wasn't in the mood to play nice.

On top of her heartache for Liam and his loss, her father was still furious at her for going ahead with the fostering program in a way he considered to be behind his back. At the moment, her life felt like one big mess of emotions.

Sometimes keeping to oneself was the best option available.

Sighing, she hugged the pillow to her waist and gently dug her toes into Buster's fur where he lay on the floor of the deck, giving herself a soft nudge to set the porch swing in motion. Buster didn't even lift his drowsy-eyed head and probably considered the toe-push a mini massage.

"Hey," Mandy said as she rounded the corner of the house, two glasses of tea in her hand. "How are you doing today?" she asked as she let herself into the screened porch.

Buster greeted Mandy with a wag of his tail but didn't get up from his contented and obviously comfortable position.

Carly accepted the drink with a shrug, scooting over for Mandy to sit beside her. "Liam hasn't called if that's what you're asking."

"I'm sorry."

"Me, too. I can't believe what's happened, you know? I was so dead set against dating a cop in the beginning but... Look at me now," she said.

"So no more concern about Liam's job? You're truly okay with it?" Mandy asked before taking a sip of her tea.

Carly thought that over and came to the same decision as before. "Yes, I am. I mean, I'll never love it and I'll always worry but look at what has happened to Zane. There's danger everywhere so...yeah, I'm sure."

"Good. Because *I'm* sure he'll come around. You're going to have to have the patience of a saint while he gets it into his thick, stubborn head that he can't go through life without you."

Carly leaned her head on the tall back of the wood swing, surprised when Mandy did the same. Their shoulders touched as they swung in a slow, barely there, back-and-forth motion.

"Want some ice cream?"

Carly smiled. "No. The tea's good, thanks."

"Extra sweet—the way you always liked it. Carly... I know my timing sucks with everything going on but I thought maybe you would need to hear how thankful I am to you for helping Elysee. I never knew how much impact my words had until I had to live it through my baby girl. And...well, I'll be here if you need to talk. And it *won't* be like before, either. In case that thought has crossed your mind."

Mandy turned her head to look at Carly and with a twist of her lips and a nod, Carly confirmed Mandy's words. "Once bitten, twice shy, I'll admit."

"Yeah. Totally understandable. It's taken me a long time to grow up but I mean every word. I'm truly, truly sorry for hurting you."

Carly held her glass up for a toast. "To age bringing wisdom."

Mandy clinked her glass to Carly's. "And friendship."

"And friendship," Carly repeated.

They each took a drink, the swing still rocking at a snail's pace.

"You know," Carly said, "Skylar is never going to believe this. That we're friends again."

Mandy burst out laughing, so hard that she nearly spilled her tea. "Oh, you've got that right. Your stepsister *hates* me. With good reason."

"Of course."

"But still..." Mandy said, grinning. "Is she coming to visit soon?"

"Not that I know of. Why?"

Mandy laughed again, a decidedly ornery sparkle in her eyes. "Just imagining Skylar's face when she finds out. Don't tell her until she's here for a visit, okay? If at all possible, I want to see her reaction when you break the news to her."

LIAM WENT BACK TO WORK six days after Zane's burial even though Jonas wouldn't let him do anything but sit behind a desk doing paperwork or make drop-in visits on the shut-ins the station checked on regularly.

That gave Liam plenty of time to stew about the will. He would be okay. He could find another place to live if needed, especially since he could be a cop anywhere. But Brad...Brad lived and breathed the Circle M, not only residing there but putting sweat and blood into the mix.

As for Chance... Given a guilt-free opportunity to roam, they might never see him again if they couldn't work out a compromise that kept the ranch running and the family Zane had made together.

It was funny how Liam had always considered the ranch a roof and walls and employment after Zane had adopted him. But Liam had never considered it home until now, until the realization that he and his brothers could lose it and be right back where they started from, more or less.

It didn't sit well. It wasn't about the money or the business of ranching for him. It was about how much it meant to him. He didn't want to leave the only home he'd ever really known.

Liam was on his way back from checking on Martha Ingles when he heard a request for backup on a domestic-violence call. He was two minutes away and reported as such. Because he was so close, Jonas gave him the go-ahead to respond.

He arrived after another deputy and an officer from the Montana Highway Patrol had secured the scene. The man's body was being photographed in the yard, the woman in an ambulance where EMTs gave up attempts to revive her.

"Gonna be a double," the deputy said as Liam walked up to him. "She was a pretty thing, too."

They all were, in their own way. Domestic calls were always the hardest for him to stomach. "What do you need me to do?" he asked, taking in the yard strewn with toys. "You called Children's Services yet?"

"Why?"

Liam indicated the yard. "Those toys belong to someone."

The rookie stared at the toys, his cheeks darkening.

Liam's heart stopped cold. "You didn't look for a kid?" He could see the guilt on the guy's face. "You check out here. I'll check inside."

Liam hurried to the front door.

The inside of the trailer had been trashed. Tables had been overturned, lamps broken, books scattered. The fight had been a bad one. Most likely the abuser had chased the woman through the house, taunting her, scaring her, but never letting her get too far away. "Hello? Anyone in here?"

Glass crunched beneath his feet. Liam checked the kitchen, looked beneath the cabinets and inside the washer-dryer closet, the bedrooms. Behind the shower curtain. The house appeared to be well kept except for the damage done during the dispute.

Liam found no sign of a child, and he hoped the kid was safe at a relative's or friend's house.

Liam walked through the house again and was about to leave when he heard a slight thump sound from the kitchen. Quietly, he returned to the area and waited, hearing another soft thump.

He opened the laundry closet and scanned the tiny space. Nothing except... "If someone's in there you need to come out. It's okay now. Everything is fine, it's over. I'm a policeman. I'm here to help you."

Nothing.

"I'm going to open the door, okay?" He pulled the dryer door open and froze. Inside the tiny space, two big green eyes stared out, surrounded by a mop of curly hair, a blue cast on a too-thin arm. "Riley?"

The boy's face was covered in tears. Riley surged out of the dryer and threw himself against Liam's chest. "It's okay. I've got you. It's okay."

Riley trembled, his arms locked around Liam's neck. The boy smelled of fear and soap and that unidentifiable boy smell, one of dirt and sweat and candy. "Can you tell me what happened? Come on, buddy, talk to me. What happened, huh?"

"D-dad hurt her."

Dad? Dear God.

"Deanna made me promise to b-be quiet. She put me in the d-dryer and said not to come out and said— She said I wasn't here."

And probably saved the boy's life in the process. "Who's Deanna?"

"My aunt."

"Do you know what they were arguing about?"

Riley struggled for breath. "Me. Dad didn't want me

to live here. He said my mom took me away from him and now Deanna w-was and he was sick of it."

Staring into Riley's green eyes, Liam realized how lucky he was to have found Zane—or rather that Zane had found him and his adopted brothers. Liam remembered what he'd said to Carly regarding her choice to foster. He also knew if people like Carly didn't answer their calling, if they didn't care, kids like Riley would be lost forever. The way Liam would have been if Zane hadn't ignored the crap Liam spouted and cared for him regardless.

"You found him. Good," the patrolman said from the doorway. "Children's Services are on the way. Said they have a caseworker in the area. She'll be here in fifteen."

"I'll stay with him in here while you finish up outside," Liam stated, his gaze pointed. He didn't want Riley to see the bloody body of his father lying on the grass. No kid needed that.

When they were alone, Riley reached out and traced a finger over Liam's badge.

"Carly said I'm not s'posed to be afraid."

Liam's heart tripped in his chest. Out of the mouths of babes. Maybe it was time. Time to stop obsessing over the past, to put it behind him and build the life he'd dreamed of having as a kid before he'd shut down and turned cynical.

A life similar to the one Caroline envisioned with a home and kids and laughter, not pain.

But where did he start? How could he set aside his past, when it was such a part of him? "She did, huh?" he asked, his voice husky. "What else did she say?"

CHAPTER TWENTY-EIGHT

CARLY HAD JUST SETTLED into the hot tub when her doorbell rang. Given her mood, she ignored it and slid deeper into the bubbling water.

Moments later, the sound of her fence gate slamming closed on the spring latch had her eyes open again. She blinked the blurry sting of chlorine fizzes away and focused. Liam?

She sat up so fast she slipped off the seat and went under.

Scrambling, she resurfaced with her hair plastered to her head and a black smear of mascara and eyeliner on her fingertips after she wiped her eyes.

"Need some help?"

A towel pressed gently against her cheek. She accepted it without comment. "What are you doing here?"

Liam crossed his arms over the top of the hot tub and gave her a slow, lopsided smile, the one that always made her feel like kissing the scar on his lip and jumping his bones.

"You said I couldn't give it back."

"Give what back?"

"Your heart."

Did that mean he was going to try?

"I want you by my side, Caroline. I want you in my

bed. I want your hand in mine whenever things get rough and I get…scared."

If she lived to be a hundred, she knew she'd never forget Liam's words, the expression on his face. She melted then and there.

Liam bent and gave her a lingering kiss. One that left her heart thumping so fast in her chest she pressed a hand to the spot so it wouldn't jump out.

"The night I picked you up from the side of the highway seems like years ago because I'm not the same man I was then. You changed that, and you changed it for the better."

"What does that…mean?" she whispered, afraid to ask and yet she had to be sure.

"It means I love you," he said for the first time. "It means I'm here and I'm staying, if you'll have me."

"I'd love to."

"So that means yes?"

She smiled. "You haven't asked me a question."

Liam actually looked embarrassed by the reminder. Embarrassed and nervous and so very sexy because he wasn't perfect, he was simply a man terrified of what he was feeling but braving it anyway the way all heroes did.

"Will you be a parent with me?" he asked softly.

The wording wasn't lost on Carly. "Oh, Liam. I'd *love* to be a parent with you."

"Good. We can start right now."

She blinked, the hum of the hot-tub motor clicking off and leaving the back deck strangely quiet as the last of the air bubbles popped to the water's surface. "You mean…*now?*"

It was a little soon to get pregnant and he hadn't

asked one really important question. But when Liam straightened and held up the towel for her to get out, she stood without hesitation.

His gaze heated. "We are going to play this scene out again later tonight."

"Why wait?" she asked, moving close to wrap her arms around his neck and raising her face for a kiss.

Liam swallowed audibly. "I'm on duty."

"Yeah, but I'm the sheriff's daughter."

He smiled at her boast. "I love you, sweetheart, but that doesn't hold any rank."

"I don't know," Caroline drawled, playing with the buttons of his shirt. "I can talk a good game."

Sweat beaded Liam's forehead—clearly debating giving in to the temptation she dangled in front of him. "We can't."

"Why not?"

"You have company. Out front."

"I do? Who?"

Liam dropped his head and kissed her, lingering over the contact. "Caroline, will you marry me?" he asked, his voice rough with need and no small measure of fear. "I want this—you. I never knew how much until now. Marry me."

The first had been a question, then a plea, the last an order. She liked them all. "Yes. Yes, of course I'll marry you," she said, kissing him. "Go get rid of whoever it is."

"I can't."

"Why?"

"Because one day soon I hope he's our son. He needs us. Almost as much as we need him. Riley doesn't have anyone else."

Carly struggled to breathe. *Our son. Riley?*

She kissed Liam once more, long and sweet, cherishing the moment because right here and right now Liam transformed completely from frog to genuine prince. He carried his warts with him in the way of cigarette burns from his past but those things didn't matter. Together, they would teach Riley that the scars he carried didn't matter. Love did.

Ending the kiss, she smiled, happier than she ever thought possible. Determined to rock Liam's world the moment they were alone. "Let's go get our boy."

EPILOGUE

Two years later

LIAM TRIED TO HIDE his anxiety when Carly's nails dug into his hands as she bore down. Hard.

"That's it. That's it," the doctor encouraged. "Perfect. Once more."

Behind Carly in the large bed, Liam held her steady and pressed forward, holding his breath and willing it to be over, for his wife and baby to be fine.

"Perfect!"

Carly collapsed into his arms, gasping for air.

"Is she okay? Why isn't she crying?"

Carly's questions sent a shaft of fear through Liam.

"Stop worrying." The doctor laughed softly. "I'm cleaning the nose and *he* is fine. Looks like there was a bit of a misread on your last ultrasound. This little guy is most definitely a boy."

Still bearing Carly's weight, Liam collapsed onto the softness of the bed behind him, burying his face in her hair and neck to hide the tears of relief as the baby's cries filled the room, loud and strong. The tears really came then, too many to hide.

"Oh, *Liam,*" Carly said softly, her tears of happiness mingling with his.

He tried to speak but couldn't, too choked up from the emotions bombarding him from all sides.

Carly had told him once she'd rather be sorry than safe. What she'd meant was that she'd rather love with all her heart than hold back. He understood that now, because this feeling, this overwhelming, completely humiliating behavior was him loving that much.

He'd never felt so rich in his life and he didn't know how to respond. He wanted to shout from the rooftops. Cry like his newborn son.

For a cop with no family, it never ceased to amaze him how large his had grown in the months since Zane's death. With his marriage to Carly, he'd gained all of her family, and with Riley's adoption, Liam had gained a six-year-old who surprisingly reminded him so much of Zane sometimes, Liam wondered if Riley was somehow channeling the grandfather he'd never met.

Now the waiting room was filled with their combined family, anticipating the news.

"What's his name?" the doctor asked as he placed the baby in their arms.

Liam ducked his head and wiped his eyes on Carly's hospital gown before exchanging a look with his wife. They'd been so focused on girl names, they hadn't picked out a boy's.

"Zane," Carly whispered, a knowing, tender gleam in her eyes.

"And Jonas to be fair." He winked at her, adrenaline pumping through his veins, making him weak. "He's not only my father-in-law but also my boss," he teased, ignoring the emotional huskiness of his voice.

He was…full. Happy. Complete in a way he'd never thought possible.

"But we can't leave out Charlie."

No, they couldn't leave out Charlie. It had taken time but he and Charlie were slowly mending fences, one rail at a time.

"How about Zane Jonas Charles McKenna?" Carly whispered.

"Mighty long name for a little boy."

"I like it. I think it's perfect."

Liam pressed his lips to her cheek, tasting the salt of her tears and his. When he picked up Carly that night along the road, he had never dreamed this would be possible. Now he wondered how he had ever lived without Carly in his life.

She had dragged him kicking and screaming into the world, out in the open with a bull's-eye on his back, out where he couldn't hide anymore, where life hurt—but not in a bad way.

He stroked his thumb over his son's head, breathed in the scent of Carly's hair. "So do I. Want me to get Riley and the others?"

"You better. Rissa is probably sitting on my dad to keep him under control." Carly smiled. "Liam?"

He paused in the act of trying to get himself out of the delivery bed without jostling them too much. "What?"

"I love you."

Eyes burning, the lump reappearing in his throat, he gave her a slow, sweet kiss. "I love you, too, Caroline."

* * * * *

Harlequin Super Romance

COMING NEXT MONTH

Available October 11, 2011

You can find more information on upcoming
Harlequin® titles, free excerpts and more at
www.HarlequinInsideRomance.com.

REQUEST YOUR FREE BOOKS!
2 FREE NOVELS PLUS 2 FREE GIFTS!

Harlequin

Super Romance®

Exciting, emotional, unexpected!

YES! Please send me 2 FREE Harlequin® Superromance® novels and my 2 FREE gifts (gifts are worth about $10). After receiving them, if I don't wish to receive any more books, I can return the shipping statement marked "cancel." If I don't cancel, I will receive 6 brand-new novels every month and be billed just $4.69 per book in the U.S. or $5.24 per book in Canada. That's a saving of at least 15% off the cover price! It's quite a bargain! Shipping and handling is just 50¢ per book in the U.S. and 75¢ per book in Canada.* I understand that accepting the 2 free books and gifts places me under no obligation to buy anything. I can always return a shipment and cancel at any time. Even if I never buy another book, the two free books and gifts are mine to keep forever.

135/336 HDN FC6T

Name _____ (PLEASE PRINT)

Address _____ Apt. #

City _____ State/Prov. _____ Zip/Postal Code

Signature (if under 18, a parent or guardian must sign)

Mail to the Reader Service:
IN U.S.A.: P.O. Box 1867, Buffalo, NY 14240-1867
IN CANADA: P.O. Box 609, Fort Erie, Ontario L2A 5X3

Not valid for current subscribers to Harlequin Superromance books.

Are you a current subscriber to Harlequin Superromance books and want to receive the larger-print edition?
Call 1-800-873-8635 or visit www.ReaderService.com.

* Terms and prices subject to change without notice. Prices do not include applicable taxes. Sales tax applicable in N.Y. Canadian residents will be charged applicable taxes. Offer not valid in Quebec. This offer is limited to one order per household. All orders subject to credit approval. Credit or debit balances in a customer's account(s) may be offset by any other outstanding balance owed by or to the customer. Please allow 4 to 6 weeks for delivery. Offer available while quantities last.

Your Privacy—The Reader Service is committed to protecting your privacy. Our Privacy Policy is available online at www.ReaderService.com or upon request from the Reader Service.

We make a portion of our mailing list available to reputable third parties that offer products we believe may interest you. If you prefer that we not exchange your name with third parties, or if you wish to clarify or modify your communication preferences, please visit us at www.ReaderService.com/consumerschoice or write to us at Reader Service Preference Service, P.O. Box 9062, Buffalo, NY 14269. Include your complete name and address.

HSR11

*Harlequin Romantic Suspense presents the latest book
in the scorching new* KELLEY LEGACY *miniseries
from best-loved veteran series author Carla Cassidy*

*Scandal is the name of the game as the Kelley family fights
to preserve their legacy, their hearts...and their lives.*

Read on for an excerpt from the fourth title
RANCHER UNDER COVER

*Available October 2011
from Harlequin Romantic Suspense*

"**W**ould you like a drink?" Caitlin asked as she walked to the minibar in the corner of the room. She felt as if she needed to chug a beer or two for courage.

"No, thanks. I'm not much of a drinking man," he replied.

She raised an eyebrow and looked at him curiously as she poured herself a glass of wine. "A ranch hand who doesn't enjoy a drink? I think maybe that's a first."

He smiled easily. "There was a six-month period in my life when I drank too much. I pulled myself out of the bottom of a bottle a little over seven years ago and I've never looked back."

"That's admirable, to know you have a problem and then fix it."

Those broad shoulders of his moved up and down in an easy shrug. "I don't know how admirable it was, all I knew at the time was that I had a choice to make between living and dying and I decided living was definitely more appealing."

She wanted to ask him what had happened preceding that six-month period that had plunged him into the bottom of the bottle, but she didn't want to know too much about him. Personal information might produce a false sense of intimacy that she didn't need, didn't want in her life.

"Please, sit down," she said, and gestured him to the table. She had never felt so on edge, so awkward in her life.

"After you," he replied.

She was aware of his gaze intensely focused on her as she rounded the table and sat in the chair, and she wanted to tell him to stop looking at her as if she were a delectable dessert he intended to savor later.

Watch Caitlin and Rhett's sensual saga unfold amidst the shocking, ripped-from-the-headlines drama of the Kelley Legacy miniseries in

RANCHER UNDER COVER

Available October 2011 only from Harlequin Romantic Suspense, wherever books are sold.

Harlequin

SPECIAL EDITION

Life, Love and Family

Look for
NEW YORK TIMES AND *USA TODAY*
BESTSELLING AUTHOR

KATHLEEN EAGLE

in October!

Recently released and wounded war vet
Cal Cougar is determined to start his recovery—
inside and out. There's no better place than the
Double D Ranch to begin the journey.
Cal discovers firsthand how extraordinary the
ranch really is when he meets a struggling single
mom and her very special child.

ONE BRAVE COWBOY,
available September 27 wherever books are sold!

www.Harlequin.com

SE656257KE